MY HUSBAND'S SIN

By

Mary T. Bradford

Tirgearr Publishing

Published by Tirgearr Publishing
Ireland
www.tirgearrpublishing.com

ISBN 978-1-910234-18-1

A CIP catalogue record for this book is
available from the British Library.

10 9 8 7 6 5 4 3 2 1

DEDICATION

For Colin, and our children, Liam, Lisa, Audrey, and Stephen, with much love.

ACKNOWLEDGEMENTS

I would like to thank all in Tirgearr Publishing for their encouragement and support and in particular my editor Christine and her wonderful help, thank you. There are so many friends and writing friends who encouraged and supported me, shared laughs and rejections, especially my best buddies in my local library whose staff are wonderful, thank you.

Finally to all of my family, thank you for your support and belief in me.

CHAPTER ONE

JULY

Lacey fled the Sherman and Jones Solicitors' office in turmoil, only pausing to catch her breath before descending the cold solid steps. The appalling words kept ringing in her ears. How the bloody hell could a mother do this to her child? A bitch, that's what she was. Lacey should have trusted her instinct all through the years.

The pleasant July day was lost on her. Without thinking further, she sought solace in the bar further down the street. In the dimly-lit pub she was the only woman.

Lacey Taylor didn't drink alcohol this early, but placed in front of her now was a double vodka with bitter lemon. Taking the glass in her trembling hand, she drank swiftly. The sour liquid made her shake her head. God, it was unpleasant. In one corner, two elderly men were sipping their stouts. Another up at the bar was reading the day's paper.

The barman came over to where she sat and smiled. "A tough morning so far then?" He wiped down the glass-topped table and replaced some beer mats with fresh un-tattered ones.

Lacey didn't reply. She couldn't. The shock of this morning's events was still gripping her tight. Christ, her life had been turned upside down in the stroke of a pen. Her hands still shook.

Looking the barman up and down, she acknowledged he was kind of cute. If times were different, she might even flirt with him; his tight black t-shirt groaned across his chest, but she didn't have time to daydream. Reality had her gripped in its cold heartless hand.

1

"Can I have another?" Lacey called out to the bar attendant as he moved on to wiping down other tables. He nodded and went to the bar to get her fresh drink.

Her mind was swimming with horrible thoughts of her mother. Dear Lord, she mustn't think like that any more. She was Lillian, not Mother. Where do you start to pick up the pieces of your life after something like that? Her mobile phone rang: it was Sally. Lacey snapped at it, turning it off in one quick touch. Bloody family. Her bloody family!

The fresh glass was placed in front of her. He seemed to linger for a moment, waiting for Lacey to make eye contact. She really did not want his company but he wasn't going anywhere, judging by his stance before her. She looked up at him. Yep, definitely cute.

"You could try talking. This will only lead to a headache and misery." The guy smiled encouragingly, but all she did was stare back at him, confusion and anger in her eyes. Throwing a twenty on the table, she stood up and paused.

"Maybe misery is what I deserve."

Her taupe Guess handbag and caramel jacket hung on the chair. She shoved the bag onto her shoulder, took her jacket, and walked out. Kind, attractive barmen were not what she wanted. She desired space and freedom to take in and assimilate the horrible rotten words that she'd heard today. Who would believe it? Who would have thought when she'd wakened this morning at seven, that five hours later her life would have crashed down around her? With her mind troubled, she wandered without direction through the busy streets.

Lacey's world had stopped, yet around her cars passed by beeping their irritation with the slow traffic, people pushed and chatted without a concern for the young woman in their midst. She strolled along, not fully noticing life around her. Those words, those poisonous words, kept swirling in her mind. The look of horror on her siblings' faces would be etched on her memory forever. She couldn't face them right now. What must they think of her?

"Watch it." The woman grunted at Lacey.

"Sorry." Lacey didn't know what she was apologising for, but it startled her into realising she needed to get home. It would be safe there.

Closing the apartment door behind her, the silence was welcome. Standing in her hallway, she stared in the silver-edged mirror. She looked no different. Peering harder at her image, she tried to see what was different, but nothing came back at her. On the outside, she was the same Lacey Taylor who had walked out her door this morning, but it was undoubtedly a different woman who had returned.

Wrapping her arms around herself in a hug, the tears came easily. Her phone showed numerous missed calls; the red light on her answering machine flashed, showing more messages awaiting her. She ignored them all and decided to go to bed. It didn't matter to her it was only lunchtime. Like a little girl scolded for being bold, she wanted the warmth of her duvet, the comfort of blocking out the world. Why? Why did it have to be her? Damn her parents. Damn the whole blasted lot of them.

Before the reading of her mother's will, she had only been worried about what to wear and how long the process would take. In the end, she had gone with a caramel pant suit with cream camisole, complementing her auburn hair. She emitted a slight laugh as she remembered her older sister, Willow, advising her not to wear the sexy red party dress. Her sister. Lacey wondered if she had the right to call her that any more, not forgetting her other siblings, Robert and Sally.

To think, she had sat innocently in the solicitor's office, letting her thoughts drift as she noticed how the stifling room was kept cool by a small discreet fan. A large potted fern in the corner had swayed a little when the fan swirled in its direction. On the wall above the plant, Mr. Sherman's credentials were neatly framed on the wall. The clock placed above the doorway had ticked away the minutes as they waited.

Lacey buried herself deeper beneath the soft duvet. She was cocooned now, only wisps of her hair peeking out. From her safety net, she recalled the morning's meeting.

As she hadn't been present for the reading of her late father's will, the reading of her mother's was a new experience for Lacey. She had noticed how the brown leather chair dwarfed Mr. Sherman when he sat. He had a head of thick snow white hair and, together with the light colouring of his suit, he appeared very pale. But it didn't reduce the impact his voice made. It came across like a judge passing sentence as he read from Lillian's will.

There were no surprised gasps when, as expected, Willow and Sally were left their mother's jewellery collection. They knew it was stored at the local branch of their bank in a safety deposit box. Robert's bequest of his father's art collection again provided little surprise. However, when Sally's name was revealed as the new owner of the family home, the siblings wondered about Lacey.

Willow being the one to pose the question. "Excuse me, but what about Lacey? Mum seems to have overlooked our baby sister."

Now curled up in bed, she closed her eyes tight and stuck her fingers in her ears to drown out those dreadful words filling her mind as the solicitor's deep voice resounded in her head. She had hoped that the sanctuary of her bedroom would make her feel safe, make the nasty experience of today disappear. That she would have shelter within her own four walls. But no such luck. Did he have to say those words, those nasty life-changing words?

It was no good. Hiding beneath her duvet did not stop the horror that was rising in her chest. Instead of comfort, it became claustrophobic. Lacey threw back the coverings and snatched her dressing-gown. The fluffy material rubbed against her and she tied it tight while she headed for the sitting room. Peeping out of her handbag was the evidence that this morning had really happened.

She stared at the envelope with disdain. Her name was written clearly across it; there was no mistaking who it was for. This was the reason their pre-arranged family dinner tonight had been cancelled. Would this be the sign of things to come, her siblings cancelling any future family get-togethers?

Tears fell as those fatal words Mr. Sherman had struggled to say rang in her ear, and she could no longer ignore them.

CHAPTER TWO

Talk about a calamity. What had his mother been thinking? Robert Taylor hated the formalities that death brought to life at the best of times – the removals, wakes and funerals, and will readings. He sat in his navy Mercedes and tried to clear his head. Earlier, going up in the lift to the solicitor's office, he'd had no idea of what lay ahead. His mood dark, he'd looked at his watch, hoping it wouldn't take too long. It should only be a matter of procedure.

Willow and he had chatted last night and there were no surprises expected. All going well, Robert should be back in his own office within an hour, give or take. Well, how wrong he'd been.

As Rob watched Mr. Sherman collect the formal papers and rearrange them on the large desk, he'd wondered how long would it take to read the will.

"I offer my deep sympathy to each of you at this difficult time right now."

Ah, Rob thought, at last we have a start.

Philip Sherman shook hands with each one of them before he sat down. The solicitor was mindful of his manners and asked the grieving family if they would require any refreshments. Robert remembered smiling discreetly when the others declined. From the strained looks on his sisters' faces, he reckoned they too wanted out of there as soon as possible.

"I, Lillian Taylor, being of sound mind and body…" the elderly gentleman began reading. Robert's heart had given a little jump when he heard his mother's name. She was a strong woman,

5

a mother who looked out for her children. He missed her. He sniffed back the tears that were edging their escape. He didn't want to cry there; he could do that in the privacy of his own home. Even with Aoife, he didn't feel comfortable to release his sadness. Their relationship was still in its early stages, even though they'd been friends for years before finally dating.

In his car now, he was close enough to the seclusion he yearned and the tears fell silently. He wiped his cheeks with the back of his hand and caught his reflection in the rear-view mirror. All he could recall was Lacey smiling over at him in the solicitor's office. The poor mite, he had thought then, all babies need their mum no matter what their age. Smiling back, he had hoped it reassured her.

All the morning's proceedings were running through his mind. How he'd nodded his head appropriately when it was revealed he would be getting his father's art collection. The house was to be Sally's; fair enough. But what about Lacey? Robert had been about to ask but Willow got in before him. He shook his head at the memory. Worse was then to come.

He saw it all again, how they were all sitting forward in their seats, shock covering them in an icy blanket. Had Robert heard the old man right? Willow was grabbing her chest in pain and Lacey was staring at an envelope in her hand.

"Lacey, wait, please wait," he had shouted after his sister, the awful words of his mother's will ringing in his ears.

Grabbing his seat-belt, he fastened it and started up the car. He would go straight home. He would seek his sisters out later, but right now Robert was overwhelmed. A hug from Aoife would help; he would ask her to come over and share dinner.

* * *

She didn't like offices; Sally was the outdoors type. She really hadn't wanted to go to the will reading. Willow and Robert had told her that it would be okay, that it was straightforward and shouldn't take long. She'd only returned to Dublin six months ago from her latest travels, but felt relieved she had been living at home when Lillian died.

Now Sally walked along the busy streets, having given up searching for Lacey. A nearby bench caught her eye and she went over to sit down. Her normally calm mind was in turmoil. She couldn't imagine being able to sleep soundly another night after the disastrous morning they had all just gone through.

Flashes of that disaster sparked in her mind. In the office, she'd kept a firm grip of Willow's hand for support. Sally hadn't been able to contain her tears flowing down her face, she had wiped at them with a crumpled tissue held in her fist. The large office was stuffy with so many of them gathered there, the air struggling to remain fresh.

Sally had admired the strength her older sister Willow had shown. She looked tired but hadn't flinched when Mr. Sherman mentioned their mother's name. Sally had struggled to take in what was being said; her grief gripping her in a haze of confusion. Forcing her concentration to listen, Sally recalled hearing Willow ask Mr. Sherman a question.

His reply had struck the Taylors like a cold slap in the face. Then Lacey was running from the office clutching an envelope.

The breeze chilled her a little as Sally rocked back and forth on the timber bench, not knowing what to do next. What would this revelation lead to? she thought. What would happen to them all now?

* * *

Alone in a side room, the offices of Sherman and Jones in Merrion Square, Dublin, were not strange for Willow. She recalled being here at the reading of her father's will some years before, but how different a day that had been.

She sipped the hot sweet tea the young receptionist had brought her. Sweet tea was supposed to be the answer to all of life's problems, including shock. Boy, what a shock! Her mother had played an ace; if she had wished for a surprise at the will reading, then Lillian Taylor had got her wish.

Willow missed her mother greatly. They had shared so much in life, it was strange not hearing her voice each morning. It was their little ritual, one of many that they had shared. Every morning her mother would ring at nine o'clock to see what was planned for the day. Willow's days always included some contact with Lillian, be it lunch, shopping, or just popping over for coffee. That had all changed since she died. As head of the family, Willow would expect to be the one her siblings would turn to. Would that still be the case now?

No matter how angry she should be with her mother for destroying the family unit, she couldn't help but have sympathy for her. What a burden Lillian had lived with.

Willow knew it was hard on Lacey to lose two parents in a relatively short space of time. Now thinking back over it, Willow shivered. How would she have reacted if it had been her? Willow sat up straight. She needed to regain her composure. After all, the Taylor name carried weight in the community. She placed her trembling hand on her chest but the pounding of her heart had quietened.

Trying to get a grip on what had actually happened, she shook her head, hoping to recall with clarity what had been said. She remembered that her little sister had been omitted from the will, and that was strange. Not wanting Lacey to be upset, she had seen it as her duty to remind Mr. Sherman about Lacey. Why did she open her mouth? It rattled in her weary mind now how she had asked, "Excuse me, but what about Lacey? Mum seems to have overlooked our baby sister."

Willow had been rather embarrassed to be enquiring, but she was now officially head of the family. Oh, the memory was upsetting all over again as she recalled what happened.

The solicitor's voice had been clear and soft as he replied. "I shall be getting to that, Mrs. Shaw, if you permit me to continue." Glancing over at Sherman, she had seen him hand Lacey a sealed envelope.

"Finally, to Lacey Taylor, daughter of Joe Taylor, I give you a letter. I did my best and at last I am free of you – my husband's sin."

That was when Willow had felt faint, the office walls closing in around her. Had she heard right?

CHAPTER THREE

Lacey lounged in her comfy pyjamas thinking, with Milly curled up beside her, purring gently. She was indeed Joe Taylor's daughter but not Lillian's! It was a revelation she had not been expecting, but yet it explained a lot when she thought how her life had been until Lillian's death.

Robert, her loving brother, was only her half brother; her two sisters were now half sisters. Mr. Sherman had expressed his sympathy at revealing the awful truth, but he was only carrying out his duties. They had all left the office dazed and speechless, the family dinner planned for that evening quickly cancelled.

It was now four days since the will reading with all its revelations, and almost two weeks since they'd buried their mother.

In that time Lacey's world had turned upside down and where she had once belonged, she was now adrift. The letter had told everything, spilling the beans of – how had Lillian put it? *My Husband's Sin!* She had been nothing more than a thorn in Lillian's side.

The others had all been in shock, and no-one could offer any word after the revelations. Lacey had little recollection of how she had reacted in the solicitor's office. She knew she'd refused Robert's offer to drive her home, before running from the building upset. She remembered the gasp from Willow and the deep moan that followed.

But Lacey needed space and time. She needed to go over the events on her own, in her own time and in privacy. The solicitor had refused to comment on what was in the letter Lillian had left her, saying he had a confidential oath to honour and that only

Lacey was allowed to open it. He did, however, explain that Lillian was not Lacey's mother. So calm and cool, clearly it was nothing new for him to witness families' lives upturned in minutes at the reading of a will.

Lacey had not opened the poisoned letter until she arrived safely into her own sitting room, having promised the others she would phone them later.

She'd switched off her mobile and put her landline to answering machine; her door closed to the outside world. Her sisters and brother – no, correction, her half sisters and half brother – would have to wait. The time for sharing its contents would be her decision alone; it wasn't their identity that had been shattered.

Lacey couldn't get her head around the whole horrible revelation. In parts it made sense, in others it was unbelievable, a nasty joke. She didn't find it one bit funny.

They, her siblings, had buried their mother nearly two weeks ago but Lacey now knew she had not. They could grieve for the woman they called Mum, but Lacey could not. The only spark, the only grain of goodness to come from all this horrible mess, was that Lacey now had an answer to a lifelong puzzle. She understood at last why Lillian had been cold, unloving and indifferent towards her. Lacey no longer felt bad about the dreadful thoughts she had entertained by the graveside.

As she stood at her apartment window, she remembered watching the coffin being lowered into the ground had scared her. It was horrible to think of what was to come, cold heavy soil thrown on and the darkness. Everything decaying, rotting into dust, *"ashes to ashes, dust to dust"*. She had shivered at the words. Then, that woman deserved to rot! Oh God, what had she thought? This was her mum. That was evil, wrong on all levels. She recalled wishing it was over and she could go home and forget about the day. As each minute passed by at the large open grave, she had felt more and more detached from the events at the cemetery.

Turning away from the window, it was there. The letter, that awful letter, so neatly penned, was lying on the coffee table. Her name so clearly written in blue ink by her mother, oh damn! Not her mother! She was Lillian. How was she supposed to think after reading it? How was Lacey ever to pick up her life and continue? Life lay in smithereens around her, cracked and broken like smashed egg shells, never to be put together again.

Robert and Willow had phoned her a dozen times and each time left messages. They begged her to contact them, to pick up the phone, to at least let them know she was alright. *ALRIGHT?*

How could she be alright? She was furious, she was miserable, she was confused – all at the same time. And that was on a good day. What were they expecting of her? That she could shrug off all that had been made known and still be the girl that she was before.

Sally had phoned on a few occasions, but also called to the apartment twice. She was the only one who had made a physical effort to call over. On both occasions, Lacey had refused to open the door to the incessant knocking and the loud doorbell. Having received no welcome or reply, Sally slipped a note underneath the apartment door that simply read,

Hey, Sis, I'm here if you need me at any time, Sally x.

The note lay beside the shocking letter. How different the contents were – one a simple note offering a hand of support, the other letter spilling venom with a slap in the face. More like a stab in the back.

Lacey felt bitter not just towards Lillian, but also to her father. Why had he not told her, or left something to explain this messy saga? Had he not thought it important that she should know her true birth details? What lousy parents they were.

She opened the fridge door and searched for something to eat. She had eaten all the cereal and now hoped there was something lying forgotten in the fridge. The yogurts were out of date, the cheese had mould, and the carrots were soft. She tried the freezer. A pizza would be nice, or a scoop or two of chocolate ice-cream, but no, nothing except meat that needed defrosting and roasting. Lacey didn't feel like going out. She could order a takeaway, but then discovered there weren't any teabags or milk either. Well, that decided things.

Pulling on her navy tracksuit bottoms and top, and slipping on her sneakers, she grabbed a grey hoody top and put it on. She didn't bother combing her auburn hair or checking her appearance. This Lacey Taylor didn't care what people thought of her at the corner shop. It was so unlike her, but who had she to answer to?

The cool fresh air of the outside rushed in as she pushed open the doors of the apartment block. It was welcome after the staleness of her home. Lacey stood still for a moment.

It felt strange to be a part of the world again. Traffic going by, people on mobile phones, and roadworks being carried out, it had all continued while Lacey had hidden away in her home being miserable with her cat, Milly. *"Laugh and the world laughs with you, cry and you cry alone."* How bloody true it was, she thought.

Grabbing a shopping basket at the entrance to the small Shop Express, Lacey picked up readymade dinners and some fruit, cereal and milk, and a couple of bottles of white wine. The shop assistant paid no heed to her at the checkout, being more interested in checking out the new guy in the fruit and vegetable aisle. Another sign of dismissal in this world of anonymity, Lacey thought resentfully. Did anyone count in this world any more? Could this woman serving her not see that Lacey was not her usual smart, neat self? For goodness sake, she popped in here every second day for the evening paper and her favourite gossip magazine.

Here she was with no make-up; red-eyed from lack of sleep and crying; hair in a mess, clothes not matching. Yet no-one even cared or noticed. She would have thrown a tantrum if she was two years old. Instead, she stamped her foot in frustration. The cashier looked at her and dismissed her just as quickly. Lacey was nothing but an intrusion in the young woman's day.

Lacey Taylor's whole life had been a lie, and insignificant – the world kept turning with or without her.

Hostility sneaked into her heart. The cold dead hand of Lillian had twisted all that was good in Lacey's life and ripped it apart. Her world now lay ruined and who really cared? No-one! That's who! *Feck them all, I don't need any of them*, she thought, and realised she was crying as she walked back down the street.

Opening her apartment door, she wiped the tears away. She would fight Lillian, even if she was in a grave, and make her life mean something; Lacey Taylor may be down, but she was definitely not out!

CHAPTER FOUR

Earlier in the morning, she had phoned work and asked for two weeks' unpaid leave. Working for a government department, her clerical job was enjoyable and she was allowed the time off without hassle; her workmates were supportive and understanding. They knew the grief of losing a loved one, but little did they know the bombshell that had dropped on Lacey after Lillian's death.

Her boss granted her leave and agreed for her to take some extra holidays due to her, if she wanted them. Lacey took the kind offer, so she was not due back for another three weeks. Surely she would have her head around this ugly mess by then.

Next she had to contact her half siblings and face the fallout.

"Hello, Sally. It's me, Lacey, I want–"

"Lacey! Oh, Lacey, thank goodness you're alright! I've tried to contact you, I even called around."

"I know, Sally, I'm sorry. I needed space, just some time to let it sink in."

"And well, has it? I mean, Christ, Lacey, I don't even know what to think, so you must be going through hell!" The genuine concern in her voice was obvious. "Can we meet up soon?" she added, when Lacey remained silent.

"I need to phone Willow and Robert, and maybe we can all meet at my place? Next Tuesday? Around eight, maybe order in, would that suit you?" she asked Sally. Lacey's tired, feeble voice couldn't disguise the hurt inside.

"Sure, Sis. I'll be there." Even if Lacey was unsure, it seemed Sally still considered her the same little sister she'd always been! Sally, Lacey knew, was a real gentle soul.

14

Their conversation gave her some confidence to contact the others. After some deep breaths and a strong cup of coffee, Lacey set about phoning Robert and Willow. Willow was polite on the phone with her; it was an awkwardness that embarrassed them both. Lacey wanted to tell her how much she loved her, how the love and affection from Willow during the years of growing up had been a lifeline to her. She needed that love and support more than ever, yet now there was no warmth in Willow's voice, nor did she encourage the conversation with Lacey to linger. Where were her big sister's soothing reassuring words?

Willow remained quiet and courteous and said just enough to confirm her attendance on Tuesday evening at 8pm. Both women had been dealt a blow by Lillian's revelations, each dealing with it in their own very different ways. That was how Lacey reasoned with herself over Willow's stiff and abrupt conversation.

Robert's phone went straight to answering machine, which usually meant he was away at a conference or in a meeting. Lacey knew her brother almost never turned his cellphone off unless it was really important. She hesitated before speaking; it felt strained and uneasy leaving the message, especially after the cold conversation she and Willow had just shared.

"Hey, big brother. I know I've not been in touch and I'm sorry, but I was thinking of us all meeting next Tuesday at 8pm here, and maybe a takeaway? Willow and Sally are coming, hope you can make it."

Lacey decided she would try him again maybe on Monday, just to confirm. Knowing Robert, he would be worried about his younger sister and would probably phone over the weekend anyway.

She was drained by her actions of the day. Sitting curled up on her sofa with Milly sleeping contentedly, she relaxed. Between the broken and sleepless nights, and the relief of having taken the first difficult steps to contact her family, she was now exhausted. She dozed off into the first decent sleep since the reading of the will.

* * *

Following Lacey's phone call, Willow headed straight to her rich walnut drinks cabinet. It may only be eleven-thirty in the morning, but she needed some vodka. Pouring the clear drink into the crystal glass, she tried to steady her hand. My God, she was shaking! Adding some ice to the tumbler, Willow felt ashamed of herself.

She took her glass into the pristine white kitchen and sat at the light oak table. What was she doing? She'd barely been able to converse with Lacey. It was her little sister, for goodness sake; it wasn't like she had spoken to a great axe murderer! But life had changed and there was no going back. She knew this deep inside her broken heart. She had loved her mum so.

The bitter vodka felt good as it hit the back of her throat. It settled her, made her sit up and take notice. Willow really needed to gain control of her emotions. It was Lacey who had been dealt the severest of blows; it was her world that had been turned upside down. But was it just Lacey's, though? She, too, felt hurt. Her mother had lived with a terrible secret and her father had lived with a lie. Willow, as the eldest child, felt the betrayal most.

The shaking in her hand stopped; she felt more composed. Glancing at the kitchen clock, she realised it was time to start preparing lunch for her and Derek. Even though people said there was no smell from vodka, Willow decided to brush her teeth anyway. Unwrapping the plastic covering from a new toothbrush, she proceeded with the task.

"Ouch," she spat. The brush was hard in her mouth. "Like a bloody yard brush," she said, with a mouth full of frothy toothpaste. She stared into the mirror and continued with no mercy shown to her gums. There was no point having Derek asking unwanted questions.

* * *

Robert listened to the message over and over again. Lacey sounded fragile and worn out. Next Tuesday they would all meet up at hers – and what? What indeed! If someone had told him that his life was going to be brought almost to a standstill over two weeks ago, he would have laughed. Now he constantly wondered what the next hour would reveal. Never would he take things at face value again.

Robert Taylor – six foot two, successful businessman, Mercedes owner, with a wicked sexy smile that all the ladies adored – was angry and confused. What had his father been truly like? Robert had loved the man without question, and Joe Taylor's death had been a real arrow through his heart. He'd never considered for a single moment that his dad was capable of deceit, especially deceit concerning his own flesh and blood.

And his mother, what had she gone through? Why had she gone along with the lies? He had always believed his parents to be a strong, united, loving couple. They had seemed to have the type of old-fashioned marriage where couples suffered bad times only to rejoice in the good. But living and hiding lies; how could they? Now at 30 years of age, he came to the bitter conclusion that every time he looked at Lacey, he would be reminded of everything that had been wrong in his parents' lives.

What would Aoife make of it? Of him?

CHAPTER FIVE

Nerves took over, making Lacey pace the apartment all that weekend. On a number of occasions she was tempted to phone the others and cancel Tuesday evening. When she'd try to sit and watch some TV, she would find herself wondering, what if? What if they were hostile towards her? What if they blamed her for their mother's death? Oh my God, she hadn't really thought about that until now. Maybe Lillian had suffered her heart attack because of the horrible secret she'd carried all those years.

Lacey's palms became sticky, her hair damp, and her armpits felt moist and uncomfortable; a cold sweat made her shiver. That's it! How had she been so foolish as to not realise it before? She had killed her mother! Well, her stepmother technically, but those small issues didn't matter. The point was Lacey Taylor had caused her mother to have a heart attack! She ran to the bathroom where she threw up, that horrible thought circling her mind.

Lillian had carried her husband's infidelity to her grave. She could have told Lacey before now, especially after her father's death. Why had she not done so? Why did Lillian wait until after her own passing to reveal all? Having to act the part of mother dearest all those years must have been a strain, so why did she not tell Lacey then? Did it give Lillian more pleasure knowing the young girl would feel an outcast or unwanted by revealing everything after her death?

Wiping her mouth, she washed her hands, her mind full of dark thoughts. No, Lacey hoped Lillian hadn't hated her that much. After all, she did protect Joe Taylor even after *his* death. So what was it? What was the reasoning behind this confused and horrible scenario that Lacey found herself living in?

She had not been an outcast or unwanted, surely? That was a thought she really didn't want to entertain. Her father had been there for her and so had Lillian – to a certain extent – even if it was against the woman's will. Lacey strolled back to her sitting room, unsure of so much.

Stretching out with Milly on the cream suede sofa where she seemed to have lodged for the past month, she didn't believe she had been unloved by her father. Where did that leave her real mother? The letter that revealed her true origins gave little away about her birth mother. It just gave Lillian's view of things, which had been nasty at that! There had to be something else out there, some documentation that told her the real story and not just a one-sided view.

Oh, why did her father die so suddenly and not leave her a letter? Did he not see the whole thing as being a huge deal in Lacey's life? Surely he had wanted to explain, even defend why he did what he did. Maybe he hadn't cared at all. Maybe, having reared Lacey with his other children, he felt his part was done. Why rock the boat? Had he believed there wasn't any reason that everything should be revealed? It looked as though she would never know what he'd thought.

She ran her fingers through her rich long hair and wanted to scream.

"Why not?" she spoke out loud. "I can do as I please, and right now I want to scream." So she did. She let out an earth-shattering scream that came from the depths of her belly. She felt the anger, confusion, frustration and helplessness of her whole self come tumbling out, filling the sitting room. Milly ran for cover beneath the coffee table and screeched along with her mistress.

Lacey stopped. Her throat ached with rawness and tears washed down over her cheeks, staining all in their path. But damn it, she felt better. It was better than thumping a pillow.

Suddenly there was a knocking on her door. Still in the throes of confusing questions and not really thinking at all, Lacy automatically went to open it.

19

"Hey, Mrs O'Shea, how are you?" Lacey said, when she saw her neighbour standing before her.

"Lacey, I heard terrible screams. Are you okay"? The older woman's eyes took in her young neighbour's red eyes and blotchy face, and tried to look over Lacey's shoulder to get a good view into the apartment.

"Sorry, Mrs O'Shea, it was me. I have a sore throat and one of the girls at work told me to scream out loud. Apparently, it helps clear the throat and aid healing." She hoped the blush in her face would be mistaken for a high temperature.

The woman at the door, still unsure, subtly tried to manoeuvre inside but Lacey put her arm up and rested her hand on the handle. Mrs. O'Shea took the hint.

"Well, why don't you just go to the doctor, or gargle with some lemon and hot water like the rest of us?"

"You're so right, Mrs O'Shea, but I just thought I'd try it. Sorry for disturbing you. I didn't realise how bad the soundproofing is in these apartments."

Lacey flashed a fake smile at the woman, hoping she wouldn't decide to chat for any longer. She certainly wasn't asking her in for a tea or coffee.

"You'd be surprised what you can hear through the walls. Not that I'd be listening or such." The older woman backed off.

"Sorry again for disturbing you," Lacey simpered with as much false sympathy as she could rustle up towards the nosy cow before her. Then, rather than waiting for an answer, she closed the door and, smiling, headed to the kitchen to make a cuppa for herself.

Perhaps there was more of her father in her than she realised. After all, she had found the lies for Mrs O'Shea from somewhere. They'd come quite easily to her, like they must have for him when he had deceived both Lillian and the family! Oh, Joe Taylor, will we ever know the real you?

* * *

Robert wasn't looking forward to Tuesday evening with his sisters. Things were hectic at work and he really wanted to go home and chill out with a beer, instead of hearing how his father had cheated on his mother. Lillian's face flashed before him. How he missed her! She had never let a week go by without inviting him for dinner. He often brought her a box of her favourite hand-made chocolates and she would lovingly scold him that he was trying to fatten her up.

Lillian Taylor had always kept her appearance in tip-top condition, never seen without her hair styled and her lipstick applied. But she had been a warm woman; a good mother, he remembered. How difficult it must have been for her harbouring his father's adultery.

She had often bailed Robert out after he moved from home and his finances were tight. She would slip him a €50 here and there and say, "Treat yourself, pet." Those €50s often meant the difference between having petrol in his car or not. But now that he was successful, he liked to pay her back with little presents – a trip to her favourite spa hotel, or a meal in a top restaurant.

At least he had introduced Aoife to her. His mother had approved, too. She liked that Aoife joined them for lunch sometimes, and always called her Mrs. Taylor. It showed the girl had manners. "She respects her elders," his mother had confided in Robert.

But now his mother was gone. No more time to spend chatting together over a pot of tea, discussing the politics of the day, or trying to finish a crossword. Lillian had loved her crosswords.

If Tuesday's meeting took a turn for the worst – although it shouldn't – Robert just didn't know how he would cope.

CHAPTER SIX

Willow put the phone down to Sally. Her sister was looking forward to the evening ahead, with the family all together for the first time since the solicitor's office. Willow didn't share her enthusiasm, but agreed that it would be good to sort out the sorry mess. And she was desperately keen to know what was in her mother's letter.

Luckily, Derek would be staying over in Cork tonight, so Willow didn't have to serve up dinner before she went to Lacey's apartment. What she needed now was a nice warm bath, with candles lit, and her favourite CD of Phil Coulter playing while she tried to relax before joining the others.

Her home was everything to Willow. She had put great thought into each and every detail of the expensive décor. Every surface gleamed and every piece of furniture was spotless and luxurious. Yet she often wondered if she would trade it all for a few sticky fingermarks on the patio doors or coloured crayon scribbles on the walls. It didn't occur to her how Derek would feel about children, nor did she want to know. Now climbing those dark timbered stairs, she felt the loneliness of her home. There were no family photos dotted about, only cold impersonal artwork that spelt wealth rather than warmth. Since her mother's death, Willow had been left with more time to spend in the big silent house.

She had loved her chats and shopping with Lillian. They would travel to auctions and soak up the atmosphere of the auction houses. Twice they had been bold enough to place bids. Once, on a beautiful walnut writing desk, and later, on a Queen Anne chair that was upholstered in deep pink velvet. Back home they had celebrated with a bottle of sparkling white wine and giggled like schoolgirls as the drink made them tipsy. Derek used to be amused to come home and find his wife and his mother-in-law singing along to the kitchen radio, an empty wine bottle on the table.

"Why, Mum? Why did you have to go?" Sobbing, Willow ran the warm water and added some herbal mix bubble bath, which promised to soothe and de-stress a troubled mind. Sinking into the inviting bath, her tears continued to fall. Her mother's death had unleashed a whirlwind of emotions within her and Willow was not happy. How could she be? Not just the loss of her mother, but maybe a sister, too. Here she was, rattling around in an empty house, alone with the pain of not able to phone her mum.

Willow had been shopping at the Blanchardstown Centre the day her mother died. She and Derek were due to attend a business dinner later that night and she had needed a silk scarf to finish the soft caramel outfit she intended to wear. Willow loved the west Dublin shopping haven – Blanch, as it was fondly referred to. There was a homely feel to it, Willow felt. The Dundrum Town Centre was delightful, but full of designer posers who flashed their labels while dashing around with their skinny lattes.

As she'd finished paying for a light blue scarf, her mobile had rung. The shop assistant had been so helpful when Willow burst into tears, offering her glasses of water and getting her a seat. She'd sat there unable to take it in – her mother, Lillian Taylor, was dead. The mother she'd lunched with every Thursday, sharing life stories and gossip, always laughing and hugging each other goodbye, knowing they would be on the phone chatting in a few hours time, was gone. Derek had come to the shopping centre to collect her; Willow's world was shattered.

Who would mourn her when she died? There were her sisters, and Robert and, of course, Derek. But was that it? Who would shed tears day in day out, not accepting her death, feeling the need to hear her voice and her laughter each day as a child does for their parent? As she did now for Lillian?

Eventually, the bubbles in the bath went flat and the water

began to cool. Sighing, Willow climbed out and got on with her day. She would dress later. The softness of her dressing gown was comforting like a hug. She relished the closeness of it around her sad self.

Tonight she could ask the others how they were coping since the revelation of Lacey's true parentage. Did they have the jungle of mixed emotions to struggle through each morning? She decided she would have to ask; she needed to know that they, too, were suffering.

* * *

Sally felt strange to be back living in the family home again. She walked around the house looking at the many photographs her mother had placed here and there. Family group photos were displayed alongside individual portraits of the children as they were growing up. Lillian had been very proud of her children, but did that include Lacey? Sally had never looked at the photos properly before, never really studied them. Everyone seemed happy enough in most of them. Could you tell from a photo, though, what was really happening behind the scenes? What was the old saying? Ah yes, the camera never lies! Well, let's put it to the test, thought Sally.

The kitchen table would be the place to examine them – plenty of room there, and she could make a cup of tea while she played detective. Her mother had kept a clean and tidy house but it was beginning to show the signs of no longer having her capable hands polishing and dusting. When Sally picked up some photos from the mantelpiece, the dust marks remained on the wood. It was the same with the side table and also on the shelves.

A normal domestic routine of playing housekeeper would never appeal to Sally; travelling was the real way to live. Picking up bar work, fruit picking, even writing travel pieces for different newspapers and magazines, had all paid her way. Of course, she would have to tackle the dusting and cleaning eventually, but not just yet. God, how monotonous her mother's life must have been, each day the same, each morning getting up to start the routine of almost fifty odd years! But times had changed. Women were no longer tied to the kitchen sink unless it was their choice. And it certainly wasn't Sally's.

With her sun-kissed skin and auburn hair, she loved the freedom of being on the road. The cultures and the people of far distant places lived in her heart and flowed in her blood. She adapted easily, whether it was China or Australia, North America or South America; she soaked it all up like an eager, willing student.

Though Lillian had been houseproud, the children were always encouraged to play as long as they tidied up after they finished. Funny, though, Sally couldn't recall any times when Lacey had played in the sitting room with her dolls scattered around her, or with the jigsaws their dad always bought them. But then, Sally had been young when Lacey was a little girl, so she wouldn't have been interested in how her sister's social skills were developing.

Determined to unravel this mystery, she gave it more thought. She recalled Lacey playing in her bedroom by herself, and sitting quietly reading on their dad's favourite armchair. Surely this hadn't been a sign of a lack of affection or love on Lillian's behalf, had it? Was it punishment? But Lacey was an innocent child in their parents' mess.

Sally let out a heavy sigh. Looking at the photos gathered together on the table before her, she gasped out loud as it dawned on her. From the outside, they were like any other family photos. But on closer inspection, Sally noted there was not one single photo which showed both Lillian and Lacey.

The clicking of the boiling kettle startled her out of her discovery. Distracted, she hastily threw a teabag in a cup and added the smallest drop of milk. She placed the hot tea on the table beside the photos and sat back down. What a discovery! It had to mean something.

"How did Mum achieve that?" Sally spoke out loud to herself. If Lillian was in a photograph, then Lacey wasn't; if Lacey was in a photograph, their dad, Joe was, but not Lillian. It was as though Lillian would only be photographed with *her* three children.

"Oh God, tonight will indeed be a good one," Sally whispered, and sank back in the kitchen chair, sipping her drink in disbelief. Should she share her revelations with the others, or would it be better not to? Did it really mean that much in the order of things? She mused, her fingers tapping nervously on the kitchen table.

* * *

Lacey cleaned up her apartment that afternoon, polishing tables and shelves with such gusto that her arms ached. She washed the floors that already gleamed, and placed candles in what she thought were strategic places for best effect. She rushed out to the Shop Express and bought their deluxe bouquet of fresh flowers. The colourful blooms certainly helped to brighten her day, as her mood was far from light. It was important to her that tonight went well. She needed her half-siblings to understand that she loved them, that their presence in her crazy life was important, and had not changed. She hoped they would feel the same way.

She hadn't heard from any of them since she'd contacted them to inform them about tonight, even Robert. And that surprised her. It was unlike him not to check if she wanted to meet up for coffee at the weekends. She hoped he would be the first to arrive; he always knew the right thing to say and do. She missed seeing him, and their long chats about anything and everything. He was the best big brother anyone could ask for; she had so many happy memories of times shared with Robert. But now that Aoife was more involved in his life, it was only natural that he would have less time for Lacey.

Of course, Willow was always kind, too. She adored her baby sister and loved being the grown-up of the four children. She had always organised games and stuff to do when they were on family holidays as kids. Maybe, being the eldest, she would have answers for Lacey; for all of them. Maybe she could shed light on this awful darkness that had totally clouded their lives. She hoped their awkward conversation on the phone had only been a one-off. After all, they had both been in shock. Those awful lines Mr. Sherman read out had caused such ripples through their lives.

After a hot soapy shower, Lacey wrapped herself up in a soft cream towel and stood in front of the mirror. She stared hard at her reflection and scrutinised each detail on her face. Did she have her real mother's eyes? Her nose? Hair colouring? She was auburn, but then so was Sally; that must be Dad's side. Robert and Willow had freckles – just a few – but she didn't. Lacey couldn't recall if Sally had. Actually it would be quite difficult to tell with Sally, on account of her permanent tan from her overseas travels.

Lacey definitely had her dad's nose, the way it went at a nice slant downwards with a slight tilt upwards at the end. So what part of her was her real mother, then? Was it physical or personality? Did she share her real mother's talents? If so, what were they? Was it her love of animals? She adored Milly, who had been a rescue kitten. Passing the local vet's practice one day, Lacey had seen the poster looking for homes for some kittens. It was the poster photo that did it to her. It melted her heart; the cute black and white face with big blue eyes. Without thinking further, she'd found herself inside the practice declaring she wanted a cat.

Neither Milly nor the mirror before Lacey was forthcoming with answers.

Her frustration built up again and she wanted to scream, but that had brought nosy Mrs.O'Shea to her door the last time. Instead, this time she strode into her bedroom and pounded her pillows like her life depended on her knocking the stuffing out of them. Once she felt better, she started to get dressed.

CHAPTER SEVEN

Lacey,

What do I say? Where do I start? Yes, you are your father's daughter but I am not your mother. I tried my best for you, at times it was unbearable and I would just walk away. Your father was adamant that you did not find out about your birth mother unless there was a true need for it. While he lived, I agreed. But after his death, I decided to write this letter. You are the result of an affair and, because of other circumstances that surrounded our marriage at the time, your father and I came to an understanding that we would stay together. These reasons were between me and your father, it is of no benefit to anyone what they were or why.

Your mother didn't want to raise you as a single mother and happily left you in our care. I was angry, hurt, and totally against such a thing, but in the end it was agreed. Your father named you Lacey and truly did love you. I could not.

At times when I looked at you, it seemed you were destined to be a thorn in my side, so embedded in my flesh that I could not be relieved of you.

Life is cruel and I do not write this to damage you further, but only to clear the air between us. You must on occasions have felt the anger and contempt I held you in. Well, now you know why. My only regret is that my darling three children will probably be dragged into this horrible secret. There is no point in seeking answers or asking questions. Accept this and get on with your life.

I did. So can you,
Lillian.

Lacey read the letter out to them, then passed it around to each one. No-one offered a word as they allowed the whole truth to sink in. In the pristine sitting room, tension and awkwardness filled the air. No amount of scattered scented candles could hide the discomfort that surrounded the Taylors.

"Anyone like something to drink?" It was Lacey who shattered the fragile bubble they'd found themselves trapped in since they'd arrived at the apartment. Doing something physical, something practical, might calm the charged atmosphere encircling them.

"Have you vodka?" Willow seemed totally taken back by the letter. She held the sheet of paper in her hand and looked at it with distaste; she looked stunned. Perhaps a drink might go some way toward clearing her thoughts.

"I'm fine. Nothing for me, thanks." The normally strong voice of her brother seemed shaken, and his appearance visibly pale.

"Want ice in the vodka?" Lacey asked from the kitchen, as she fixed the drink for Willow. They hadn't jumped to any conclusions against their parents so far. In fact, the silence was torture. It was murderous to sit there with them, each one feeling numb and in disbelief.

Willow joined her sister in the kitchen.

"If you have ice, fine. If not, no worries." The older woman held up the glass of vodka to check it. "Add another bit, would you? I'll drink it straight." She gestured with the glass towards Lacey.

"Are you sure?"

"After what I've read tonight, I need a drink. And anyway, I didn't know you were counting." The clipped tone was a slap to Lacey. The sharp words stung her with surprise.

"So, ladies, what's the verdict?" It was Robert who threw down the gauntlet. He got up and paced around the room.

"A bastard, that's what I think. He was a complete bastard." Willow sat down and knocked back the clear drink in her glass.

Sally remained quiet. She was well known for thinking things through before speaking. Not reacting to the mutterings of Willow, she curled up in the armchair and wrapped herself in a red check throw then silently re-read the letter.

Lacey could almost imagine what was going through Sally's mind. Why had their mother felt obliged to turn Lacey's life upside down? Why discredit their father so much? He'd had an affair; that wasn't earth-shattering, surely? A lot of men and women have affairs. Why didn't she just leave him? Why not abandon him and let him raise the child by himself? So many questions, so much unanswered. Sally sighed and placed the letter back on the coffee table.

Robert reached for it again. "Where do we even start? I mean, Dad had an affair, Mum and he agreed to stay together, all that I can comprehend. But what did she mean by…" he searched for the sentence he needed and continued, "…'because of other circumstances that surrounded our marriage? Anyone got any ideas or thoughts on that?"

He looked around at his sisters. Lacey recognised that he was keen to treat this like an everyday problem he could solve in the boardroom. Staying detached and focussing on the words to be clarified might allow him to keep his calm appearance in place. Perhaps letting it get more personal would be too difficult for him to handle. He sat back down on the sofa.

So far, Lacey had been out of the firing line, their thoughts were all aimed at their parents.

"How dare he upset Mum with some young floozy." Willow was angry. The eldest Taylor sat upright to take command of the room, making sure her feelings would be heard.

"Probably some young one who saw dollar signs and filled Daddy's head with nonsense. A mid-life crisis, definitely, I'm sure of it! Poor Mum." She handed her empty glass to Lacey and indicated a refill.

"Are you sure?" her youngest sister asked.

"Of course I'm sure, all men go through these mid-life crises – they think it's great to be able to hop on some cheap young one and feel they are eighteen all over again. Disgusting, that's what!"

"Actually, I meant another drink," Lacey sighed. She had never seen this side of Willow before. Usually she was always so calm, so together, so...sensible; that's the word she was looking for. Not this ranting drunk going on about old men's sex lives!

"Look, Lacey, if you are going to start keeping check on what each of us is drinking, then I'll happily bring over a bottle to you another day to replace tonight's one, okay? Now be a good girl and just fill it up." Lacey was dismissed to the kitchen.

Robert threw an angry look at Willow, who was well past tipsy, then turned to try and catch Sally's eye. She remained silent, her expression giving nothing away. Wrapped in the throw, her legs tucked under her, she appeared indifferent to the carry-on around her.

Lacey returned from the kitchen with her sister's glass and the bottle of vodka. She plonked them both in front of Willow then sat next to Robert on the sofa. She was so unsettled by the earlier comments that she wished her eldest sister would go home.

With some kind of order restored, Robert spoke again.

"Lacey," he turned towards her, "how do you feel, or what do you think about the letter? I mean, it's your life that has collapsed, and I know Willow..." he shot a sharp look over at her and continued, "well, all our lives have been hit hard. But you talk, Lacey. Tell us, what did you make of it?"

He ran his hand through his hair, despair in his eyes, the corners of his mouth down-turned and his jaw muscles tense. Robert Taylor looked completely at a loss.

Lacey shook off her shoes, pulled her feet up, and sat hugging her legs to her chest. She stared at the floor and shook her head. No voice would come. She opened her mouth and tried to say what was going through her mind but remained silent. Sensing the distress and difficulty his sister was suffering, Robert put his hand gently on her shoulder. "It's okay."

Lacey knew what her feelings were, but it was Willow's reaction to the letter that frightened her most. Willow had intimidated her tonight, so she felt it better to remain silent in her eldest sister's presence for now.

CHAPTER EIGHT

It was nine am. Sally had not slept well. She had wakened a few times with a sudden start, drenched in sweat. Her duvet and sheets, all in a tangle, revealed how much she had tossed and turned in her sleep.

Pulling on her baby pink dressing gown, Sally went to the bathroom. Staring into the mirror, she wondered who she most resembled, her father or her mother. Right now, she didn't want to be reminded of either of them. Last night had been too much for her to get her head around. Her happy childhood now had a dark cloud hanging over it. A question mark hovered accusingly over every memory she held. Damn her parents! Damn, damn, damn! Now her whole life was filled with doubt, and Sally knew her only way of regaining control was to face her demons.

She was relieved that she had not added to last night's events. Willow had really gone for it – just stopping short of insulting Lacey – and some of her comments had hit rather close to the bone. It wasn't like Willow to be sharp and biting to her family. Obviously their mother's death was playing on her mind a lot. She wondered if she shared her thoughts with her husband; maybe it would help Willow to talk more.

* * *

It was ten-thirty, and Robert rubbed his face wearily. He had been glad of the brandy he'd drunk last night after arriving home, but now his head was filled with a dull ache. Some peppermint tea would soothe the body but not get rid of the mess his parents had heaped on them. Peppermint tea in his cupboards was Aoife's touch. He liked that their relationship was moving forwards. From the day she had started work in his company, they had clicked. But he'd never thought that they would end up together.

Christ, wasn't life meant to get easier as you got older? He couldn't face the office today; his mind was racing with daft thoughts and he was in no mood to deal with trivial issues at work. Blast his parents. He was angry with them; he hated wasted days.

This whole bloody thing with Lacey was huge. Sinking back on his pillows, he rubbed the stubble on his chin. Did he actually believe that issues from work were trivial? Issues that involved multi-million Euro deals, other peoples' futures and livelihood – all unimportant now because of his father's great bloody love affair? Why couldn't the bastard have kept his pants on? It was a sham; his whole relationship with Joe Taylor was tainted. "Honesty", that's what he had preached to his son. The mighty Joe Taylor had so often sung about it being the best policy, yet he'd gone to his grave withholding a secret so damning that it undermined everything he used to stand for.

How had he got his wife to agree? That was the big question for Robert. It would take all the skill of a shrewd businessman, and then some, to get your wife not only to forgive an affair, but to agree to raise the love child it produced! Oh God, he felt he was going to be sick, and rushed to the bathroom.

Standing at the sink a few minutes later, he rinsed his mouth. He refused to look in the mirror, afraid that he would see his father looking back at him. So many times he had been told that his father couldn't deny him, they were so alike. Robert recalled all the deals in business he had clenched by fast talking and reeling in the clients, letting them believe that they were part of some major decision and that without their input, the deal was worthless.

Is that what Joe had done with Lillian, reeled her in with some false promise for the future? She already had two daughters, so it wasn't the desire for a daughter that did it. Money? No, Joe Taylor had always provided a better than average lifestyle for his family. There was something, though, there had to have been, something that meant so much to Lillian that she'd agreed to raise Lacey.

Robert was determined to find out what it was. He would not rest until he got his answers.

* * *

It was eleven am. Lacey was acting on auto-pilot. She had so much going on in her life that she hadn't even noticed that Milly was not around, until she locked up last night. Normally the cat would be purring contentedly in her bed while Lacey went about securing the doors and windows.

In robot mode, she showered and dressed and then reached for the kettle. A cup of tea was what was required. After all, it was an Irish miracle cure for all things surprising; the one thing guaranteed to right the world's wrongs.

"Here, Milly! Come on, lazy bones, it's breakfast time," she called out, opening the balcony doors to look for her wandering pet.

"Milly, where are you?" Lacey searched outside and then inside the apartment. Usually the smell of food in the bowl was enough to bring the little cat running. That's strange, she thought, but when had she actually last seen her pet? She couldn't remember. Was it last night, or the day before? Her life was so messed up even her furry friend had been ignored lately. This had to stop. Lacey needed to restore order to her life again. Her heart sank further.

Maybe the cat was hurt, or maybe she was visiting a feline friend elsewhere. But Milly was always around for breakfast. In fact, Milly normally came home every night.

Lacey left the patio door open; the fresh air was uplifting. Sitting at the breakfast counter with her hot drink, she leaned back into the soft red cushions on the high chrome chair. The only signs of a life in turmoil were the empty wine bottle and glasses on the coffee table. The vodka bottle, half emptied by Willow, joined them. Now she could add her missing Milly to the list. As her globetrotting sister often quoted, "Life's a bitch."

So, where to and what next with her miserable life? If only Lacey could flip a switch and change everything back to before Lillian's death. She wondered if her siblings hated her for creating this debacle. Hundreds of questions raced through her mind, but who to ask? How do you go about unravelling a puzzle that started twenty-three years ago, and two of the main characters are dead? This was stuff you read about in novels, not something you had to deal with in your everyday life!

There was only one person who could help, one person who knew why the Taylor marriage survived and Lacey had been left with her father. There was one person who owed Lacey the answers to all of her questions, and that was her birth mother. Find her birth mother, and maybe order could be restored to her life.

Feeling new energy and life seep into her body now that a sense of direction had been achieved, Lacey headed towards the counter tops to tidy up. Putting empty cartons into the rubbish bin and food into the fridge, her kitchen took on a clean, well-organized look. Soon her life, too, would be back in order. She had a purpose once more. It felt good to have something positive to focus on. Finding her mother would solve it all.

Maybe Robert would come on board, or Sally. She had been quiet last night, and Lacey worried about what her sister was feeling. Maybe they could investigate together! It might help restore the family unit and seal the cracks that were threatening to demolish the remaining Taylor dynasty.

She hadn't included Willow in all her thoughts. Willow seemed to have hit a self-destruct button and Lacey wondered if it was all to do with their father's affair. Pushing thoughts of Willow to one side would be best; Lacey had more than enough to contend with at present, and the others would surely keep an eye on their disturbed sister.

She would put it to Robert and Sally, and then maybe all would be right with the world again. She buzzed with the joy of having a solution; she so desperately wanted her world to be normal again. She better search again for Milly, too.

* * *

It was noon. Willow was still suffering with a hangover; mixing the grape and the grain was never a good idea. How did alcoholics do it? Did they have a permanent hangover, or did they just

35

readjust their life to misery mode? Derek wouldn't be home until the evening so she had ample time to tidy up and prepare dinner.

What a nightmare last night had been. Her parents' marriage a sham, their father a no-good – oh, what was the word she was looking for? a no-good scoundrel, or a no-good failure maybe, or a plain damn crook? None of them. Bastard was better.

Looking at the silver-framed photo she kept on her side table, all she saw were two people smiling back at her. Two people, who had loved her, had held her within their hearts and had always been there for her. How did Joe and Lillian battle through living with secrets for all those years? Is that what true love is about? Surely not, love is meant to be happy and...and...what? What was true love and marriage all about? Did anyone really know?

She thought about her own marriage. Derek was easy-going. The issue of children raised its head now and then, but he never really pushed it. Then, of course, she never pushed it either, because deep down having a family wasn't part of her plan for life at this stage. Image was more important. So her marriage ambled along. Truth be known, Derek was often pushed to one side; everything she shared, she had shared with her mum.

Willow fixed herself a cup of strong coffee. She would have to apologise to Lacey for her rudeness. She had been rather sharp with her. She wondered what it felt like to have your mother taken from you twice over; once in death and again in a letter. How damaging a piece of paper could be. Just ink on paper, yet the power those words wielded was mighty. It was true, the pen is mightier than the sword.

Willow was numb when it came to her feelings at the moment. Leaving her coffee to go cold, she wandered through her house in the soft cream dressing gown with her initials embroidered in gold on the lapel. WTS. She rubbed her thumb over the raised stitching, remembering the morning her mum had presented her with the gown. It had been her 35th birthday and they'd gone for lunch and then on to an evening show, enjoying a few post-theatre drinks. They'd giggled and whispered like the close friends they were.

Willow plonked herself into the recliner in the conservatory. It was placed so she had full view of the garden, yet shielded from any nosy neighbours. She valued privacy. Looking out, she noticed the garden had become neglected. Debris was gathering and weeds were poking their heads up. The grass verges were tatty and the lawns appeared as if they were having a bad hair day. She knew unless it was she who put on the gardening gloves and outdoor shoes, those weeds would remain.

Derek had no interest in gardening. He saw golf as the way to relax. When she had broached the subject of having a gardener in to maintain it just once a week, the answer had been a resounding "NO". It was fresh air and exercise for her, he said. He reminded her she was always telling anyone who would listen at those boring business parties, how she loved her garden.

Willow had been upset. Derek rarely raised his voice, but when he said no it meant no, and don't ask again; so unlike the usual easy Derek. Other issues niggled their way into her thoughts. Like her married name; it wasn't aristocratic enough, just plain old Shaw. How many Shaws were out there? When she had checked the phone book, her disappointment had only deepened. That was why Mum had *WTS* sewn on her dressing gown. *Willow Taylor-Shaw* sounded more upmarket, more important, and more significant.

Willow was still in a nostalgic mood. She needed to grieve for her mother, yet everything was in a mess with this Lacey business. Mum could have stayed quiet and left the past in the past. Why did she have to throw open this can of worms? Didn't her mother know how it would impact on all of them? On her, Willow?

How could she have been so selfish in revealing it all? Willow wasn't good at coping with difficult issues, her mother knew that. Lillian, not Derek, had always been her shoulder to lean on. She understood Willow's yearning for an upmarket niche in society, to be someone of standing – even minor importance – amongst her upper-class friends. It was the little touches, like making her name double-barrelled, going to the theatre, attending readings by poets and authors who came during the Arts Festival. It was the little things that meant a lot, but also made a difference to their social life.

But now her life would change. Derek wouldn't accompany her to those outings. He saw enough people at work and had no desire to mingle for the sake of appearance; golf and a quiet pint in their local was enough for him.

She recalled the bright hot summer's day they buried her mother. The people gathered at the graveside had queued to shake her hand and offer their sympathy. How many times did she hear "sorry for your troubles"? She and the others had stood there, going through the rituals, the murmuring of prayers, the sea of black clothing, so dull and dreary on such a beautiful July day. The memories of lowering Mum's coffin were a foggy recollection because of her tears that fell non-stop that day. It was like looking at everything through a mist.

Now she was on her own. Willow faced the horrible truth – without her mum, Willow Taylor-Shaw would be lonely. It was Joe's and Lacey's fault, her dear mother having to carry that burden each day alone. What a horrible ordeal it must have been. If her father had been man enough and told Lacey himself, if he'd owned up to his mistake, her mother might still be alive. Anger stirred inside her. It would be hard to forgive her father this awful revelation. Having Lacey to remind her would not dampen her spirits any less.

She needed a drink, something to steady her thoughts. Just a small glass of wine would be soothing. By now it was no more than two-thirty, it could be her lunch-time drink, like the times she and Lillian had often enjoyed a glass with their lunch.

The rich red berries of her claret came through as she inhaled deeply, so comforting in her now miserable world. Tears fell unchecked and Willow poured another drink. Time slipped by in silence without her noticing or caring that it had. Her life was a sea of tears.

* * *

"Hi, sweetheart, where are you?" Derek called out as he hung up his jacket. Taking his tie off felt good, those after-lunch meetings could be tough. Better to have them in the mornings when everyone was mentally alert and present. Some of the older employees were a bit slack in their lunch time-keeping and often returned late, messing up the day even more.

Strange he couldn't smell any dinner; usually the aroma of a nice roast or casserole would greet him as he came in. The kitchen radio was off. Usually *Drivetime* on Radio One echoed around the kitchen, filling it with chatter.

"Willow, honey, where are you?" Heading for the conservatory, Derek heard glass shattering.

"Christ Almighty, Willow, are you okay? What on earth happened?" He helped his wife up from the cool tiled floor. Glass splinters and shards scattered around her.

"Well, well, you're home then?" Her words came out slurred and awkward.

Holding his wife steady, he guided her towards the hall. She didn't seem to have cut herself with the broken glass but she was clearly drunk, and he spied the empty red wine bottle rolling on the floor by the shattered wine glass.

"You're drunk, woman. Let's get you to bed." Holding her, he steered his wife upstairs. Leaving on the dressing gown, he settled her on the bed and pulled the duvet around her.

He saw a pattern emerging with Willow's behaviour lately and he was fed up and angry by her selfish attitude. They had all been dealt a blow, but she was the only one who seemed to be entertaining it each day and letting it fester. Tomorrow they would talk. He could not ignore things any more. Maybe she needed a bereavement counsellor. The situation needed to be broached and he would have to insist if she refused. Drinking was not the answer.

CHAPTER NINE

"Hey, Robert, are you free to chat or would you prefer to talk later?"

"Now is good. How are you, Sal?" He breathed a sigh of relief that it was Sally. Slumping back in the leather chair, his shoulders sagged with the freedom of it not being Lacey. He couldn't handle his youngest sister now. And as for Willow! Well, she seemed to be away on planet Mars, and that was something he definitely didn't have the energy to entertain.

"Just wondering how you are, Rob? I'm still trying to get a grip on the whole Dad thing. Each time I think about it, I end up with more questions than answers. It's eating me up. Any chance we could meet for a chat?"

"Sure, I know what you mean. Aoife is at some exercise class with her mates, so I'm free tonight actually. How about six at Mum's; I mean, at your place?" His voice shook and betrayed the loss of his mother and how much she had meant to him. He had always been her little boy.

"Six it is, I'll fix some supper for us. See you then. Oh, and Rob, thanks."

* * *

Sally had been feeling powerless and not in control, which angered her more than her dad's affair. Travelling around the world had instilled in her a self-confidence that she could handle almost any situation. Now that solid self-belief was threatened, and she felt totally lost.

But as she replaced the phone, Sally felt a little lighter. She was looking forward to seeing Robert; her strong brother, who had been reduced to a pale sad man when he'd come to tell her of Lillian's death.

That July day, Sally had been mountain climbing at a new indoor centre for outdoor activities. Her phone had been turned off while she negotiated the climbing wall, pulling on harnesses and safety ropes that were clipped onto her. It was Robert who'd eventually found her, having remembered her mentioning the place when they'd last met up for a drink.

When Sally had noticed her brother striding across the hall towards her, she'd gone cold; it was his appearance, the pale grey colour of his face, and the sadness in his eyes.

"It's Mum," he'd said gently, "she's gone."

They'd stood together in silence until Sally had summoned the strength to move, and thrown herself into Robert's arms. He'd held her tightly as the sobbing shook her slim, athletic body, and then he'd placed his arm around her as they walked outside. He had been remarkably calm, Sally remembered, very much in control – until they parked in their mother's driveway.

Then she had watched his body tremble and heard his breathing become heavy. Robert had panicked, his hands gripping the steering wheel, his knuckles white, afraid to let go, afraid to leave the safety of his vehicle. Sitting in the car with Sally, he'd admitted he didn't think he had the energy to walk. But Sally had quickly and quietly reminded him that Lacey was inside, and that she needed them. Their little sister was the one who had found their mother collapsed in the sitting room.

Shaking herself from her thoughts, Sally put on her jacket and headed for the local shops to buy something nice for supper. It was such a lovely summer's day. The children in the neighbourhood were playing on the green; happy, carefree and laughing, with their return to school in September still a number of weeks away.

Sally smiled as the playground scene reminded her of her own happy childhood, the many times she and Willow had played dress-up, sneaking into Lillian's bedroom to take her make-up and shoes. How Willow loved the high heels. Then they would go out to the back garden and bring their tea sets, and pretend they were all grown-up. An upturned brown cardboard box was their table, and they would kneel on a cushion each. How simple, but what joy! Willow had always claimed the best roles as hers. But Sally didn't mind. They'd been happy playing together having fun.

If their mother cared about her make-up being ruined, she had never said. Lipsticks got broken and eye-shadows splattered with bits of grass and dust. The only time Lillian raised her voice and banned them from her bedroom was because of the pearl episode.

What a hullabaloo that was! The atmosphere in the Taylor household had been icier than the North Pole. Robert had been involved, too. The children had watched a film on TV about life on the high seas and how pirates robbed the ships that sailed their way.

Lacey wasn't even born then, so they must have been quite young, Sally recalled as she strolled along. Robert had wanted to play pirates and Willow agreed, as long as she was queen of the ships that had the treasure. Sally, of course, had been the sole crew member on her sister's ship. They'd dug out scarves and Robert's toy swords, but realised they needed treasure. It was Willow who had the brainwave of using their mother's pearls. Snatching the nail scissors from the dressing table, in seconds they had the pearls loose in their tiny fists.

Then they'd scattered the gems in the flower beds so that it would be a real treasure hunt. It had been a great game and lasted for hours until they were called for dinner. Seated around the kitchen table, they had chatted and eaten heartily; they were a family full of noise and laughter, sharing their day over a meal. When their dad had asked what they'd been playing, Robert filled him in on the wonderful pirate game with real treasure everywhere in the garden.

"Real treasure?" Joe Taylor had laughed. "Can I see the real treasure? Or must I join your ship and help search, too?" Ruffling his young son's hair, Joe had chuckled happily, as though recalling his own innocent youth.

"There is, Dad, really. Willow told us so and she was right. Look!" The young boy had handed him six or seven pearls, with a triumphant smile on his face so big it lit the room.

"Where did you get these?" their father had asked quietly, his eyes sliding warily towards Lillian.

"Willow got them, and they're hidden in the garden under the flowers and in the wheelbarrow and…" Robert had grinned broadly. "Come and play, Dad."

Lillian's scream had lifted the children out of their seats in shock.

"*MY PEARLS!* What have you done? My gorgeous, beautiful pearls!" Her shoulders had shaken with angry sobs and the children knew they had committed some terrible act.

Their father had sent them to their bedrooms, and the frightened children watched as he put an arm around their weeping mother. She had never screamed like that before. They had never seen her cry before, either. What had they done?

Sally smiled nostalgically. Did children play like that any more, using their imagination and pretending? she wondered. Or was it all computers now? All around her in shops, on buses or trains, children seemed to be armed with hand-held devices. Where were the colouring books or sketch pads? Indeed, where were the novels? She couldn't recall the last time she had seen a child reading; even books were on computer devices now. Browsing in second-hand book shops in different countries had always been one of her favourite past-times. Many a time she had found a secret treasure among the many shelves.

Approaching the large supermarket, Sally returned to the events in hand. Walking into Supervalu, she grabbed a shopping basket and wandered the well-stocked aisles. She was happy now that she had phoned Robert. It would be good to talk, even take a small trip down nostalgia lane. Thinking again about the pirate episode, Sally grinned, and decided on a salmon salad for supper, with baby potatoes.

* * *

The office was hectic with staff rushing about, trying to reach the latest deadline. Robert was manager of the overseas business dealings but, due to his absence for his mother's funeral, business had been put aside until his return.

Sipping on a strong black coffee, he re-read the files before him. No matter how many times he left instructions for the others on how to handle their clients, there was always a large bundle of invoices and orders awaiting his approval when he returned.

He was glad he was meeting up with Sally. He didn't want to face his quiet house and be alone with his troubled thoughts. They were seriously interfering with his sleep. But now he had a deadline to motivate him, he would work through lunch and then knock off at about five-thirty and head to Sally's.

He switched the office phone to answering machine, and then pressed his intercom.

"Aoife, honey, I'm not taking any calls for the rest of the day, okay? Sally was just on to me, so could you maybe bring me some coffee every now and then? When you have a moment, I mean. I'm going to try and tackle the backlog, so I don't want to be distracted, if possible."

"Sure, Robert, is everything okay with Sally?"

"Long story, I'm heading over to her's at six, so I want to get some work done first."

Robert really liked where his life was going with his personal assistant. Aoife had worked with him now for four years, and was the epitome of discretion. They'd started out as good friends, and a deep trust had developed between them. Then, after last year's Christmas party, dating had seemed like the next logical step for them both. That night he had been messing and laughing with some of the lads, when they'd dared him to see how many kisses he would get with some mistletoe. Searching the pub where all the revelry was going on, he had realised there was only one woman he wanted to share the mistletoe with – and that was Aoife.

Armed with the small sprig of flower, he'd slid an arm around her waist and asked for a kiss. He recalled her blushing and smiling demurely as she'd leaned into him. That kiss had been filled with all the magic of Christmas and they'd reluctantly broken apart when their workmates began applauding and cheering. Sighing now, he thanked God he had her in his life.

Ploughing through the pile of paperwork before him, Robert made steady progress and only stopped briefly to eat a couple of sandwiches at his desk.

With Aoife screening all incoming calls, Robert relaxed a little. But then his mobile started to ring; damn, he should have put it on silent. Glancing at the screen, he saw Lacey's name. He hesitated. Should he, or shouldn't he? Too late now – it had gone to voicemail. Waiting a few minutes, he checked his messages.

"Hey, big bro, just me," said the voice. "I was wondering could we meet, maybe without the others? Well, without Willow, anyway. Just for now, I mean, don't get me wrong. But I want to run an idea by you. You must be in a meeting, so give me a buzz when you can. Okay, that's it, chat later so. And say hi to Aoife for me." Her voice sounded lost and innocent, a slight plea in the final words.

"Lacey, oh Lacey," he muttered to himself.

Throwing his pen on the table, he sank back into his chair. Rubbing his forehead, he felt the tension rise once more within him. Bloody hell, what was he to do now? Ring her back and invite her to Sally's? Wait until tomorrow to contact her? This was bloody awkward.

"You okay, Robert?" Aoife came in to refresh his coffee.

"What? Oh sorry, just family stuff. Ever want to take a week away somewhere where no-one can contact you – just you, sun, and a pitcher of beer?"

"Only a week? Rob, you haven't met all my family yet. I'd love a month. A week would be too short! Sun, yes, but also a tall dark handsome guy to massage my weary shoulders," she teased him.

He knew Aoife had been a little anxious about him since he returned to work. She knew his mother's death had hit him hard, had noticed the extra frown lines on his forehead and the tiredness in his deep brown eyes.

"Why don't you forget about Sally's and take tonight off from all things family? Tell them Dr. Aoife said so." Hearing the concern in her voice, he stopped writing and looked at her. She was so good to him – and pretty, too. She leaned in and kissed him softly.

He knew he would be lost without her, not only here in the office but in his life. Maybe he should confide in her, tell her his worries about Lacey and his parents' revelations, but it was all still too raw.

"If only. What time do you finish your class tonight? Hey, we haven't been out for lunch this week. You got some new guy that's keeping you away from me?" He loved teasing with her at work, although they kept their behaviour professional when outside his office door.

"Nine-thirty, I'll send you a text before I go to bed, sweetheart. Say hello to Sally when you see her." She turned for the door and left him to his work.

Sneaking a peek at Aoife, his gaze lingered on her gorgeous long legs, the navy pencil skirt showing off her elegant calves and slim ankles. When she coughed softly, Robert looked up and a slight blush sneaked along his cheeks.

"Liking and admiring what I see, that's all," he smiled seductively. It was her turn to blush as she walked out of the office.

Watching her leave, Robert knew she was the right girl for him. Maybe it was time to take a risk. His mother's sudden death had made him realise that life was short, so why not grab it and live while you can?

CHAPTER TEN

Finding her birth mother would take a lot of time and effort, and Lacey knew the others might not be on board with her idea. But that would be for them to deal with. She had every right to seek answers; she was suffering the most and she needed to pursue this.

She decided to contact the family solicitors and start her enquiries there. Maybe her father had left documentation regarding her "adoption" in their care. She'd need to get a copy of her birth certificate, too, but she expected Lillian would be named as her mother. When Robert called her back, she would fill him in. She might even have some news for him by then.

Now, if only Milly the rascal would come home, her day would look much brighter.

A quick phone call saw her arrange an eleven am appointment with Mr. Sherman in two days' time. Ever the stickler for discretion, he would not discuss over the phone whether her dad had left any documents in his care. But it was only a slight hitch; Lacey was sure she would find out more at their meeting.

She was feeling much more upbeat – being pro-active was the right way to handle things; the feeling sorry for herself stage was over. Heading out to the local park for a walk, she left a small window open in case Milly returned. Her apartment was three floors up, so who would break in? And, if they did, it wouldn't be anything harder to deal with than what she was already going through. The fresh air would boost her mood. Where *was* that silly cat?

* * *

Willow gave in to the deep sorrow that overwhelmed her, staying at home and refusing any offers of lunch from the golf club wives' committee. Even the women from the flower club had invited her on their annual outing, which was planned for September, even though she rarely socialised with them. She enjoyed the gardening and flower arranging, but not all of the group were to her taste. Willow was a snob.

Anyway, getting dressed up and having to make small talk did not appeal to her at the moment. Derek was concerned at her refusal to leave the house. He'd offered to take her away on a mini-break. "To recharge the batteries," he said. But she knew he was just offering because he felt he should. Once there, Derek would be uptight and fidgety for the few days, finding it hard to unwind; it was always the same on holidays.

As a couple, they were chalk and cheese. He loved to visit his local pub, to be part of his community and mix with neighbours. Willow liked to socialise, but she was a lot fussier about who with. She made the effort with the golf club set, as in her head she felt they were of a tad higher standing. But the flower club, anyone could join. There were no large fees to be paid like at the golf club and, although the women were gracious and inviting, she felt they were a little too friendly. It was important to keep some distance. It wouldn't do to go telling the gardening women her troubles.

Yet, as Derek pointed out, the floral wreath which the flower club had sent to her mother's funeral had been huge and beautifully created. The card had read: *To our dearest friend and colleague, on the sad death of your mother.* She couldn't recall seeing a wreath from the other committees she was involved in.

Willow knew she was a snob and that cutting herself off from those hands of friendship was wrong. Yet she felt she couldn't change her ways now; too much water under the bridge. Too much time invested in making the right connections.

The house was silent; polished but silent, nothing out of place, all exactly the same as always. Derek was away for the next few days, over in England. The office was expanding and it was his job to interview candidates for the new positions. He had been helpful but cool when he had found her drunk. Losing your mother wasn't easy, she'd reminded him. It was still early days and grieving was a long process, she'd pointed out. His invitation to go away was ridiculous, she reckoned. Imagine going away as if her world hadn't crumbled but had just hit a hiccup. Silly man.

Willow's troubles were not all about grief for her mother, or what Lacey's existence represented to her, but the silence of her own house. It was only bricks and mortar, nothing more. Not a home. It would be a home if it was full of the laughter and mess of children, she believed. That would be a sign of it being lived in.

Tests had revealed that both she and Derek were healthy, and there was no reason why they couldn't have a family. Yet it hadn't happened. They'd both followed diets and tips that Willow had researched in order to enhance their chances, but so far having children had eluded them. Yet another hurdle in life for her to jump; why was there always some obstacle for her to conquer?

Their family doctor told them to relax, that nature would take its course. Derek had agreed with this and, as the years went by, he seemed to accept more than Willow that having children may not be on the agenda of life for them.

There was always the option of IVF, but she kept putting it off. If the truth were to be revealed, she liked her freedom and independence of coming and going a little too much. Over the years she had realised this more, and the tiny seed of selfishness had flourished as time passed. Sure, a child would be a blessing, but deep down she knew her need for a child was not top of her "most wanted list".

The selfish spot in her heart was a little larger than she would admit, but only Willow knew this. Sharing it with her husband would cause hassle and arguments. She didn't want Derek poking his nose in any further. As it was, he watched her every move. She knew he definitely had something on his mind, but now was not the time to discuss it. She needed to grieve, to adjust to her life without her mother, and to accept Lacey's new position within the Taylor family.

* * *

"Thanks for supper, Sal. It's always tastier when someone else does the cooking, as Mum always said."

"It's strange being here without her, Rob. I keep expecting her to turn up and give out about the mess I've made." Smiling sadly, Sally cleared the plates to the drainer. She lifted her cup of coffee and sipped.

"Let's bring the coffee out to the garden. There are some biscuits in the top cupboard on the left."

The evenings had become cooler but it was still pleasant enough to sit outside.

"So out with it, Sis, what do you think of our little predicament?" He looked over towards Sally as he stretched his legs out and relaxed.

"Did you say little?" she bantered. "I don't know. Honestly, I just don't know what to say, what to think. I just don't know." The exasperation was clear in her tone.

"I know what you mean, it's like we're drifting out aimlessly to sea," he sighed wearily. Then, catching his sister's amused expression, they both laughed out loud at his attempt at being poetic. Their rich laughter sparkled in the evening silence in the garden.

"Oh, Rob, that was good. I needed that laugh, I do know that!" Sally grabbed her tummy as the ache inside her spread. It was a good type of ache, though.

"This is what I mean, Sal. When did we last have a laugh? Why should we feel guilty for laughing because we buried our mother recently? Sure, I miss Mum, but damnit, life goes on, doesn't it? Or is it different for women?"

Tossing the contents of the coffee cup onto the grass, Sally only shrugged. They didn't have the answers, only questions. And each day seemed to bring more.

"Let's break this mess up, Rob."

"What do you mean?"

"It's what I've always done when I've been abroad and my troubles seemed greater than my cashflow," she smiled. "The way

I see it, we have three issues to deal with."

Robert nodded. It felt good to have someone else lead the way; his sister taking charge was good.

"First, there is Mum dying, so we have to grieve and deal with all that brings emotionally. Second, we have Lacey – our little sister, whose life has become such a saga that no-one would believe it. Then third, we have Dad and his affair. Now there's a revelation we didn't expect!"

Slapping her hands down on her thighs, she moved on the timber deckchair then got up and paced the garden. This discussion and thinking out loud was finally giving some shape to their situation.

Robert had never seen his sister in this role before. He had always seen her as the happy hippy type, heading off out into the world and letting nature take over. How wrong he'd been. She was a capable and courageous woman who would be brilliant in the business world.

It crossed his mind that he should talk to her about joining the board in one of their offices overseas, but that was for another day. Thinking of business allowed Aoife to slip into his mind, and he wandered off in a daydream. He was glad his mother had approved of her. Lillian could be hard to conquer, but her regular invitation for the two of them to come over for dinner had been a sign of acceptance.

"Are you with me so far?" Sally asked her brother. "What? You think I'm wrong?" she asked, resting her hands on her hips, her auburn hair framing the determined look on her face.

"No, I'm just admiring my sensible sister who I always thought was a bit of a hippy and a little loopy." His smile was warm and he gestured for her to continue, as though he was chairing an important business meeting.

"How does Aoife put up with you? Okay. Grieving for Mum, that's done and dusted. Nature will take its course and we'll have our sad moments, but we'll pull through." Robert nodded in agreement.

"Lacey. Okay, we need to be there with support. Let her know that she is still our sister, full stop! Nothing has changed between us at all. This is still her home, too, and...and...and whatever."

She looked towards her brother. His head was nodding in agreement again, but something in his eyes suggested otherwise.

"Okay, you have an issue with that. Spit it out," Sally challenged him. She was good at reading people. She'd told him once that it had stood her in good stead on her travels, knowing who to trust or when decisions needed to be made regarding living arrangements. She'd learned to think on her feet and trust her intuition a lot. That gut feeling was the difference between being safe and placing yourself in danger.

"Lacey will always be our sister, I agree," said Robert, "but it *has* changed. I mean it's like a bone with a hairline fracture that is so fine you can't pick it up with the naked eye; it's there; it's the same, but damaged." His eyes were filled with sadness, and Sally sat beside him once more and held his hand.

"Yeah, I know exactly what you mean, Rob, but I think if we sort out the next issue, then it will help all the mixed-up stuff that's linked to Lacey."

* * *

As they sat together in the garden, allowing the brightness and birdsong of the late summer evening to comfort them, Robert couldn't help thinking that he still hadn't returned Lacey's phone call. He really didn't want to; not tonight anyway.

This time he was sharing with Sally was good. It eased his troubled thoughts and any guilt about their baby sister was disappearing, for tonight at least. He knew he was avoiding Lacey only because he did not know what to say to her. What if she asked too many questions? Spoke ill of his parents? Was he in a position to hear his family being torn apart?

Tonight it could wait. Tonight was his.

CHAPTER ELEVEN

It had been an age since Lacey had been to the cinema, but she was determined not to sit on her own at home again. Her walk to the park had made her realise that life needed to be taken on and challenged, so she headed out for the evening with renewed determination for living.

The darkness of the cinema was rather comforting. Lacey was relieved to see that she wasn't the only person here on their own, and the light romantic comedy suited her needs. When her thoughts wandered off at times, it was simple enough to pick up the plotline again.

Crunching on the warm buttered popcorn, she relaxed and allowed the people on the screen to entertain her and occupy her mind. It was easy to drown with longing in the company of the gorgeous Colin Firth. If only she knew a real life Colin Firth hero who would sort her out with the right words and hold her tight in a loving embrace.

* * *

When it got too cool to sit in the garden, Sally and Robert moved inside and settled in the living room. He decided he would stay over so that they could continue their talk. Lillian had always kept a room for Robert. It would be there for as long as their home remained, she'd said.

"I was looking at the photographs here, Robert, and I found something very interesting. Actually, it's a bit freaky, I suppose. But, anyway." She handed him two photos that were on top of the now dusty walnut sideboard.

They were two photos of a happy Taylor family, one taken at Dublin Zoo. They had always been great days out. Robert smiled as he remembered the time they had gone there with their dad. Instead of looking at the wild animals, they had chased a mouse as it ran from the monkey cage into the nearby bushes.

The other photo had been taken at a Christmas school play, with Willow as the chief angel in charge of minding the baby Jesus. No minor role for Willow; even back then she had been capable of being centre stage. In the photo, Lillian held hands with Robert and Sally, while Willow, in her white costume complete with halo, stood near her brother.

"They were good times, Sally. Innocent, carefree times."

"Yeah, sure were. But come here and look at some of these."

Striding across the room, he stood beside Sally.

"Wow, so many memories here." He replaced the two photos he had been holding.

"You would never make a detective, Rob. Look and see if anything catches your eye."

He studied the items in front of him. There were about eight or nine framed photographs to admire. Everyone was smiling; happy families, or so it seemed to him. The quizzical look on Sally's face told Robert that he should be picking up on something.

"You really don't notice anything?" She looked at her brother in amazement.

"No, all I see are happy family outings and lots of dust you seem to have ignored, Sally Taylor," he teased.

"You really are blind, Rob."

"Well, tell me then, Miss Marple, what should I have noticed?"

"Any photos that Lacey is in, Mum isn't, and vice versa."

"But some were taken before Lacey was born."

"I know that, and those are the only ones that both Mum and Dad are in, apart from the odd one here and there, of course."

He searched once more. This was impossible, surely. Their own mother had run the Taylor home with military precision, right down to who was in the photos that were taken.

Robert sat back down, stunned. So his mother had taken Lacey in, yet managed to avoid her while raising her. This was really complicated.

"Sure was one hell of an actress our mum, wasn't she?" he commented, while Sally went for some fresh coffee.

* * *

Coming out of the cinema, Lacey glanced at her watch: ten-thirty. Pulling out her phone, she switched it back on and felt disappointed not to see any missed calls or messages from Robert. The pleasant evening, though, had soothed her, and Lacey strolled slowly back to her apartment. While hanging her coat in the hall, she hesitated for a couple of seconds only before grabbing her keys again and out to her car. She didn't know where she was going, but she would let the night take her where it wanted.

The pubs had their tables and chairs outside, and here and there people sat sipping their drinks, laughing and sharing stories. She drove through crossroads and down side streets, the traffic lights seldom against her. When she saw the high wall looming up out of the darkness, she realised where she was. She had pulled up outside the cemetery. The place where both her father and Lillian lay, side by side, united once more in death.

The tall grey gates were locked at this late hour, the flower sellers' stalls closed. Getting out of her car, she walked towards the cemetery. Lacey stood by the soaring ornate iron gates, clutched the cold metal bars and stared into the other world – headstones of all styles; and flowers – some fresh, some withered, and others plastic. The tall dark green cypress and yew trees stood to attention in a world of silence and peace.

Her heart ached with emptiness. Yet deep in a corner of her soul lay anger towards her dad and Lillian. How many more secrets were buried in this sacred place? How many families had been pulled apart after losing a loved one? Had other families' lives fallen apart like theirs?

Beyond the gates, it looked so serene and composed. It was here outside the gates that chaos reigned. Turning, she walked away; the silence followed her like a shadow. Easing herself into the car, her whole body sagged with exhaustion.

Maybe being drawn here was a message. Did her dad and Lillian want her to leave well enough alone? Perhaps they wanted her to forget going after her birth mother and just get on with her life, as Lillian had told her in the letter. The now familiar tiredness washed over her as she started up the car to drive back home.

Passing by The Long Mile pub, Lacey realised she was close to the family home, and thought maybe she should call in to Sally for a quick hello. Turning right at the next set of lights, she drove towards the house. Glancing at the clock, it was eleven-thirty. Was it too late for a social call?

Pulling up outside, Lacey noticed the upstairs lights on. It looked as though Sally was getting ready for bed. Deciding to leave, Lacey checked her mirrors to drive off when something caught her attention. Robert's car was parked in the far corner of the driveway, tucked from sight of any passing traffic.

So he was here with Sally. And judging by the lights on upstairs, he was spending the night. Yet he hadn't returned Lacey's call. Instead, he was here with their sister, probably discussing her and the mess her existence had created in their life. Her bloody big brother was avoiding her.

The anger and hurt bubbled up inside her and she slammed the car into gear and drove off, fighting back tears. She would search for her real mother without their input. Let the Taylors have each other; she would not be a source of pity for them. It would be a cold day in hell before she would let that lot know what her plan of action was!

* * *

Lying in his old bed, Robert's head was filled with memories. His room was immaculate now, very different from when he was growing up with posters of his favourite football team, pictures of racing cars, and his clothes strewn around the floor. He remembered his mum saying he had the largest odd-sock collection ever. It was good to be here. Chatting with Sally had been consoling for both of them, he reckoned. It had brought some sort of comfort to them, knowing they shared similar feelings.

Tomorrow he would phone Lacey and ask her to lunch. He was in a better frame of mind now to help her. Turning out the bedroom light, he heard a car rev up as it drove off, probably one of the neighbours. He had forgotten how close to a busy road the house was, but it wouldn't disturb him. He knew he would sleep well tonight.

* * *

Milly hadn't returned again. Fine, thought Lacey stubbornly. If the lousy cat wasn't going to come home, then she could stay out all night. She slammed shut the small window and went to bed. She was frustrated and angry with herself for thinking things wouldn't change within the family. Lying in the silent room, she held her tummy tightly. Hurt and abandonment mixed with crushing disappointment churned inside her.

Clutching her stomach tight, she thought she could manage to squeeze away the pain. As a child, when her tummy ached she would press hard on it and pretend the nasty feelings were banished forever.

Lacey didn't want to cry; she wouldn't cry. Tossing and turning, she knew sleep was not going to happen tonight. She wrestled with the soft green duvet as she tried to settle both mind and body, but failed miserably. Why wasn't Milly here to curl up with? What was with that cat? Damn the Taylors! Damn Robert for ignoring her!

* * *

Mr. Sherman ordered some coffee for them both. Even after all these years, he still enjoyed his job, the feeling of being on the inside, knowing how many people's lives were never as they appeared in public. But he was the soul of discretion. He prided himself on never even discussing with his wife the more explosive and seedy details of some high publicity clients' court cases.

He knew that others in his profession discussed juicy bits of gossip with their partners or spouses. His wife would return from her lunch with her friends and excitedly share the latest rumour that had come straight from the horse's mouth. Nine out of ten times, the details were wrong and exaggerated. Without interrupting her, he would smile, never offering a word to dispel or encourage her breaking news.

Looking down at the blue folder, he shook his head. The file on his desk was a complicated case, fraught with difficult emotions, and he was uncomfortable with the task ahead of him. Lacey looked fragile and Mr. Sherman so wanted to help her, but how much he could was a different story. If she was expecting answers or revelations about her parents' marriage, then she would be disappointed.

He knew some details, but all the answers didn't lie in the folder of documents that sat between them today. He could only advise her, maybe direct her to the proper support systems.

The young woman was pale, dark lines around her eyes, her hair scraped back in a tight ponytail. She looked lonely to him. Mr. Sherman had questions of his own. He was curious why the girl was here by herself this morning. The others had been so adamant that she be included in the will not so long ago. Yet here she was sitting in front of him, all alone and vulnerable. Had the others abandoned her so soon?

CHAPTER TWELVE

Willow was so surprised to see Sally at her front door, she stood blocking the doorway and didn't think of inviting her sister in. Sally stared at her.

"Are you going to let me in?"

"Sure I am. Sorry, I wasn't expecting anyone and I was going to head out actually," Willow stammered a little.

Sally wasn't convinced her sister was telling the truth, as she had her slippers on and no make-up. No-one saw Willow Taylor-Shaw without make-up.

"Oh right, anywhere special? Maybe I could join you?"

"No, no, it can wait. Come in, Sally. I can leave it till the afternoon." Willow turned and walked away, leaving Sally to close the front door behind her.

Walking through the house, Sally felt the heavy stillness that seemed to reach out from every corner. How did Willow stick it? The house screamed of emptiness. Approaching the kitchen, Sally was relieved to hear the radio on. At least there was some evidence of life in here.

The worktop was covered with food and delph not yet stacked away. The sun cast its warmth on the table where Willow indicated for Sally to sit, but the black leather and chrome chair was uncomfortable. Designed to look good only, but not for sitting on for too long.

"The heat is lovely when the sun comes in, Willow," Sally tried to make conversation. "I love that you put the table and chairs here."

"Yeah, it's a good spot to have a cup of tea and read the papers or have a chat."

Sally guessed Willow didn't have too many friends stopping by for chats, even the chairs discouraged it. The politeness between the two women was strained and awkward, which seemed ridiculous. They were sisters and should be comfortable together.

"So what brings you here?" Willow flipped the switch on the kettle as she busied herself getting out cups and putting some ginger cake onto plates. The crockery matched perfectly. No chipped plates or ugly heavy mugs in this smart kitchen.

"I haven't seen you in a while and took a chance on calling to see how you are doing."

"Oh right, do you take sugar and milk?" Keeping her back to her sister, Willow dealt with the two steaming cups of tea before her.

"Just milk, thanks. So, how are you?"

Willow grabbed a spoon and then placed it back down. Her shoulders drooped with weariness. They needed to be honest with each other but neither approached the true answer of how they were feeling. Turning to join Sally at the table, she smiled and offered her sister some cake. "Any sign of Robert? I've not heard from him lately, but I guess he is busy."

"I was chatting to him in the last few days. I rang him for a quick chat to see what he was up to." Sally had noticed the change of subject, but didn't comment.

She didn't tell Willow that their brother had come for supper and stayed over. Somehow, she was sure Willow would feel left out. Damn it! Here she was acting like she had a secret fan, and it was only Robert, for Christ's sake, *their* brother. What had become of them all lately? The secrets and lies seemed to come too easily to her; she didn't like this change in herself at all. Her sister's sharp voice broke in to her thinking.

"No fear of him, Sally. The big businessman will be fine. He has his work and his girlfriend to occupy him and he won't be giving us a single thought, I can tell you." The bitterness in Willow's voice filled the kitchen with an air of hostility. She sounded jealous of her brother having his work and Aoife to fill his days.

"Ah no, Willow. I'm sure he is confused and has questions, just like the rest of us."

"Why, what did he say?" Willow sounded as though she wanted to hear Robert was suffering.

"Nothing, I mean nothing dramatic. He felt let down by Mum and Dad and why they never told us, that's all." Sally wondered why she felt the need to defend her brother. Was their trust in each other gone forever? Looking at Willow, she wondered why her sister seemed so resentful, were they all not experiencing change?

Fiddling with a spoon, Willow squirmed as Sally stared at her across the kitchen table. "More tea?" She stood and busied herself with the kettle, filling it up again.

"Willow, what's up? I mean, I know we all have stuff to get our heads around, but is something else bothering you?"

* * *

Sally's question caught Willow off-guard and she closed her eyes tightly. Silence seemed to stretch between them. It was the splashing of water as the kettle overflowed into the sink that caused both women to act.

Willow dropped the kettle with a loud bang and leant in over the sink as she started to cry. Jumping to her sister's side, Sally took control.

"It's okay, I've got it." She turned off the tap and carefully guided her sister to a chair. Pulling out the nearest seat, she watched Willow sink down on it.

"Hey, hey, come on. It's me, Sis, tell me what's wrong?"

But the crying continued with great heavy sobs. The relief to finally let go was immense, and Willow sat with Sally's arms wrapped around her. The hug was so comforting. As the eldest, Willow had always led the way for her siblings. Now it was Sally who seemed to be the glue holding the family together in the face of the latest revelations. Willow felt a failure yet again. The sobbing eventually subsided, as she pulled herself a little together.

"Right, wash your face, put on some lippy and let's head to the shops. I feel some serious retail therapy is required."

"Oh, Sal, you're a Godsend. I so needed that cry and yes, a bit of shopping and spending Derek's money sounds good to me,"

Willow said between sniffles, with a weak attempt at smiling. She wiped her nose with some kitchen paper that Sally handed to her.

It felt like old times for Willow. Out shopping with her sister, instead of her dear mum, she was determined to stop feeling sorry for herself and to enjoy their trip. The hustle and bustle of the shopping centre was the perfect remedy to the lousy start to her day, and it was a treat to share it with Sally. Giggling at some of the clothes on the rails proved the perfect antidote to the misery they had both been feeling since the reading of Lillian's will.

"Hey, Sal, what do you think?" Willow held up a purple Lurex boob-tube.

"Wait! I saw the perfect mini to match," Sally said, and the two burst into laughter.

"What about this?" she held up a scarlet bra with a fur trim, and pretended to model it.

"Oh my God! My dear sister, if I were to get that, my Derek would collapse with a heart attack! Can you imagine his face? It would be a picture." Willow laughed and rolled her eyes heavenward.

"So you and Derek are still active then?" Sally teased, as she placed the bra back on the rails.

Willow pretended to be shocked with her sister, but couldn't help smiling.

"We're not that old, I'll remind you."

"Well at least you're getting some. It's been so long for me, I'm rusty!" She pulled a silly face.

"Sally Taylor, are you turning into a nun on me?"

"Lord, no! I just haven't met anyone in the last year that I'd jump into bed with. Actually, the last time for me was in a tent, the night sky our blanket, and a campfire outside casting a warm glow over us." Willow stopped searching the rail of clothes and looked at her sister, disbelief on her face.

"Sal, are you serious?"

"No, dear Willow, not at all. I was just dreaming. The last time was in a rickety single bed and it was over in two minutes!"

"Oh that's terrible." The two women giggled again and left the shop arm-in-arm.

They wandered happily around the shopping mall, treating themselves to new make-up and delicious handmade chocolates. Not once was their mother's death or the nasty business with Lacey mentioned. This was a day of chatter and giggles, and both women felt more content with life as they strolled through the crowded stores amidst ringing mobile phones and children's excited voices.

"Let's finish the day with a trip to the cinema," Sally suggested, as she checked her watch.

"Why not? Let me ring Derek and let him know I won't be home for dinner."

Her husband, back from his overseas trip, sounded relieved to hear Willow in such happy form. No doubt he hoped Sally would work her magic on Willow and remind her how to live life and have fun. He assured her he would grab a takeaway on his way home from the office.

The sisters dropped off their purchases to the boot of the car, and headed to the cinema, grabbing some popcorn and drinks in the foyer.

CHAPTER THIRTEEN

"How are you keeping?" Mr. Sherman enquired, as he gently plucked a speck of fluff from his trousers. This meeting was going to be awkward. When he had noticed on his list of appointments that Lacey Taylor wished to speak with him, he had cleared extra time in his schedule for her. This young girl, whose life had been turned upside down, wasn't much older than his youngest daughter and he felt obliged not to rush her. In truth, he felt sorry for Lacey and really did want to help her if he could.

Friends from way back, Philip Sherman had been surprised all those years ago when Joe Taylor had approached him about handling a delicate matter. At first the solicitor thought a business deal had gone wrong and Joe had lost some money, or maybe he had an associate that needed advice. His friend had never struck him as the wandering type, and he'd barely disguised his surprise when Joe told him he had fathered a daughter with another woman and wanted to raise her with his wife, Lillian. The paperwork and arrangements involved had provided a few headaches and late nights for Philip, he recalled.

Lacey sighed. "I'm doing better than I thought I'd be," she answered honestly, her slight frame made smaller by the large desk.

"And the others? I've not heard from them, I presume they are doing as well as can be expected?"

"Well yes, I suppose they are," she hesitated a little.

He sensed uneasiness in her voice, something lying beneath the surface that she wasn't telling him. Her hands fidgeted with the fringes of her mustard scarf, as though she was uncomfortable talking about the others. Should he push the issue or leave matters alone? The anxiety on her young face prompted him to ask.

"Is everything with the family okay, Miss Taylor?" His tone was soft, almost fatherly.

"Call me Lacey, please. It's okay. Well, it is and it isn't." She stared up at the ceiling, anywhere but at Mr. Sherman.

"I see, and what is it you need me to do for you today? Had you anything specific in mind?" He needed to be careful how he approached the task. Lacey was fragile, even if she wasn't aware of it herself.

She cleared her throat and straightened her shoulders.

"Don't get me wrong, my brother and sisters are all fine, I'm sure," she said. "I mean, we are all fine."

Somehow, her words came across as faltering and unconvincing.

"Lacey, are you okay? You've gone pale, do you need some water?"

"Sorry, Mr. Sherman, it's all been so overwhelming, I need direction. That's why I'm here. I need you to give me advice and direction...please."

Although she felt abandoned by her siblings, she lay back into the chair and relaxed a little more. Philip sensed it had taken a lot of effort and heart-searching to reach this stage.

"Well, what exactly do you mean by direction? Did the letter not explain the special circumstances surrounding your, er, place in the Taylor family?" Now he felt a little awkward. Dear Lord, was he blushing? He could feel colour sweep his cheeks as he coughed to clear his throat.

"Explain? Listen, all that letter did was tell me that the woman I called Mum all my life was not my mother, and how she always despised me and I was nothing to her. Her only concern was how her three precious children would be affected by the disclosure."

Her anger filled his office, her voice strong and her wide eyes staring him down. He was shocked at the turn of events and the outburst from the young woman. This was not what he had expected to hear. Should he buzz for some tea? Would it calm the situation?

"I'm sure Mrs. Taylor didn't mean it to sound that way. No

doubt emotions are running high after the funeral and perhaps you misinterpreted the letter, Lacey."

Rummaging in her handbag she pulled out a sheet of well crumpled paper. She threw Lillian's letter on his desk and pointed at it, her hands shaking as if she had handled poison.

"You are joking, aren't you, Mr. Sherman? You have no idea the life I had with Lillian Taylor. I may have called her Mum, but she was as warm towards me as an iceberg. Oh, she meant all that she said. She always made sure I was on the edge of the Taylor family." She pointed at the piece of paper and indicated for him to read it.

After reading the damning letter, Mr. Sherman was struggling for words.

"But your father, Lacey, surely he handled situations differently?"

"My father, he...He loved me, I know he did. He tucked me in at night when he was at home in the evenings. He would hug me, and twirl my hair between his fingers, and said I was his special little girl and how he loved me." She gulped as though the kind memories were flashing before her.

Lacey's tears poured out and all the fight and anger of earlier melted and disappeared. She was like a lost little girl, longing for one of her father's hugs. Unconsciously, she wrapped her arms around herself for comfort. The old solicitor got up and went around to where she sat.

He handed her some tissues and placed his hand tenderly on her shoulder.

"Yes, your father did love you, Lacey. He loved you from the moment he knew you were on the way, so to speak. He was adamant from the start that you would be in his life, a part of his family. I'm sorry that Lillian didn't feel likewise, but these were unusual circumstances. Life was different, society was different. It would have been difficult. But I thought through the years that she had accepted the situation. I'm sure your father felt that, too." He scratched his head and did not know what else to say, so he walked back around the table.

Lacey stood up. Her eyes held brightness; a new spark had

ignited behind them as she leaned in towards him. She rested both hands on the desk and peered down at him like a schoolmistress addressing her class of children, her stance defiant in its position.

"You knew my father well? I mean, you knew him outside of this office? You were friends, weren't you? Tell me what you know please, everything, anything. I want to know it all. I want to know my real mother, I want to find her." The words gushed out full of strength and determination.

Hope was written all over her face. She glanced at the name block on his desk: *Mr. P C Sherman*.

"What does the C stand for Mr. Sherman?" she asked.

"Clarke. Philip Clarke Sherman," he sighed. Why did he feel he had been found out? He hadn't seen his role in the adoption as anything other than work, but it meant everything to the girl in front of him. How could he help her? He didn't have all the answers she sought, but he guessed she wouldn't leave things be until he told her all he did know.

Philip Sherman sensed a difficult afternoon lay ahead, and a headache that would throb and bother him until late into the evening.

CHAPTER FOURTEEN

AUGUST

Robert kept thinking back to the night when he and Sally had chatted. It had been strange sitting in the family home without either of his parents walking in or making a noise somewhere else in the house. But it had been a defining moment of sorts. It had brought home to him that both his parents were now indeed gone, no longer there to share a laugh with him, or solve a problem, or to simply have a cup of coffee with. The next generation was moving up; possibly he would be the parent next.

Sally surprised him with her resilience. She was an amazing person and he felt he had never really known that before. While he was growing up and finishing school, she had already been away on her journeys around the world. All he knew of her trips were the postcards she sent home and the short unannounced visits when she surprised the family, before striking off again on another expedition.

Robert had never considered travelling the world. He had inherited Lillian's drive and ambition to do well. His father had been a success in the business world, but Robert wanted more and he had worked hard since leaving university.

Now he acknowledged that if the family was to stay united, it would be Sally who would hold them. She would be the one who would whip them into shape without any of them even realising it. Not Willow; she wouldn't even come close to it, he acknowledged.

This morning when he came to the office, he had brought with him a photograph he'd got from Sally's – a lovely picture of his three sisters linking arms and laughing. Aoife had been impressed when she saw it, although she'd teased him a little that most men put a wife or girlfriend on their desk, not a photo of their sisters! The snap had been taken on a summer evening, but he couldn't remember when and for what occasion. Placing it on his desk stirred up happy memories and reminded him that, despite the shock of Lacey's true parentage, she was still his sister and he loved her. The realisation spurred him into action. He would take her out to a meal tonight and they could talk and catch up. He still felt lousy about not returning her call last week.

He would clear the paperwork on his desk this morning and then make arrangements with Lacey. Yes, he thought, life was beginning to return to normal. With a feeling of satisfaction, he tackled his workload, humming quietly as he signed off on contracts, tidied up loose ends, and arranged meetings overseas.

Aoife brought him in coffee. It was only when she offered to get some lunch that Robert realised how quickly the time had slipped by. She was a life-saver; if it wasn't for Aoife, he would often go without eating during the working day. She was more than a good personal assistant, more than a good friend. He enjoyed her company, looked forward to their times together out of the office. Was it love? Could she really be the one?

By six-thirty, Robert had completed a great day's work, and felt better than he had in ages. Now he had time for Lacey.

"Hey, Sis, how's it going? What you up to?"

"Oh Rob, how are things? I'm not doing anything, what about you? Any news?"

"Nope, just got a shitload of work done. I meant to ring you back. Sorry about that."

"So have you seen the others lately?" she asked.

"Ah, not seen Willow, but I was speaking to Sally briefly a while back." He thought it better not to tell her he'd been for supper and stayed overnight. She might not understand.

"Anyway, what about we meet for a catch-up? Are you free tonight?" she suggested, expecting him to back out.

"Sure. That would be good."

"Perfect. How about eight-thirty, at O'Reilly's?"

* * *

Grabbing a quick shower, Lacey got ready. She picked out her favourite red top with the pussy bow collar, and her white jeans. She applied a little mascara and some lippy, then closed the door behind her. She felt and looked good. Meeting at O'Reilly's suited her, as it was near enough for her to walk.

It was difficult for her to stay bitter towards Robert. Hearing his voice had melted the anger and suspicion she had harboured earlier. She had missed their chats, and she felt silly about being cross with him. Sally was his sister, too, so why shouldn't he visit her? Maybe Sally had needed his wise words as much as Lacey did.

Determined to leave all daft thoughts at home, she was looking forward to telling her brother all her news. Mr. Sherman had been really welcoming. They had agreed to meet up again so that she could update him on her progress, but outside the office next time. It would shift the focus of what they chatted about onto a more friendly level; his office was too stiff and formal.

The solicitor had seemed keen to help Lacey. He told her he and Joe Taylor had looked out for each other, and he would be happy to help Joe's daughter to the best of his ability.

As she approached the pub, Lacey smiled happily. Robert would never abandon her, no matter who her mother was. Was life going her way at last?

Glancing around the pub, she realised she was first there and settled in a corner where they wouldn't be disturbed by the comings and goings of the other customers. The room was dark and the lighting dim but, once seated and settled, it was easier on the eyes.

She had loads to share with Robert; maybe he would help her in her task. Sipping her iced water, she looked at her watch. It was eight-twenty but she knew parking around the pub could be difficult.

The tables and seating were all dark wood. A single candle on each table was the only adornment; no tablecloths or napkins until the customers ordered food. Simple was the way they worked at O'Reilly's.

It was the rich laughter that caught her attention. The couple walking in together looked so at ease with each other, engrossed in each other's company. But Lacey's smile quickly disappeared when she realised that half of the perfect couple was Robert. What the hell was he playing at bringing Aoife? Surely he knew she needed to talk to him alone.

* * *

Closing up the office, Rob had been surprised to see Aoife still at her desk.

"Are you not going home?" he asked, as he shoved his arms into his black jacket.

"In a second or so. I'm finishing off some orders so they will be ready for your signature in the morning." She smiled up at him and shuffled some papers, then switched the phone to answer and grabbed her bag. She was almost ready to head home.

"Come on, grab your coat, you can join Lacey and me for a bite to eat." Rob was still in a positive mood. Getting through so much work had given him a real boost, and he held up his hand to ward off any protests that she might offer.

He and Aoife were sharing a story about one of their colleagues as they entered the dimly-lit pub. Adjusting his eyes to his surroundings, he caught sight of his sister sitting alone at a table tucked away in one corner.

"Hey, Lacey, sorry we're late. Had to park miles away." He leaned in to hug her.

"Hi, it's okay," she stuttered, as Robert pulled out a chair for Aoife to sit down.

Lacey didn't look happy. She fiddled with the menu as though hiding her annoyance, her eyes averted from Robert's gaze.

"I hope you don't mind, Lacey, it was your brother's idea for me to tag along." Aoife looked at the young woman across from her, unsure whether she minded her being there.

"Sure, Aoife. Sorry, my manners are awful." Lacey managed to replace her smile, but she struggled to summon up any welcoming warmth in the voice.

"So tell me, Sis, what have you been busy with these days?" Robert asked, as he studied the menu, oblivious to the tension he'd stirred up by bringing Aoife along. "The fish here is brilliant, by the way," he added to Aoife.

"Oh, this and that. I've taken some unpaid leave from work to sort–"

"Really, for how long?" he interrupted her.

"Six months to start with. A mini career break, with a view to making it a year," she spat. Robert was annoying her now, and she pouted in the same way she had as a youngster when things didn't go her way. But Robert didn't notice.

"Jesus, Lacey, what for? I mean, surely after what we've been through...I would have thought you'd be better off being kept busy, not lounging at home. It's certainly working for me." He waved at a waiter who came over to the table. Aoife sat in silence, not daring to interrupt.

Lacey's mood was blackening by the second. Her brother was bugging her with his questioning and total lack of understanding. She decided to dismiss any chance to talk with him tonight about her plans for the future.

Her big brother was not her rock any more. Lillian's letter had changed things, whether the others realised it or not. Lacey knew she would have to stand on her own two feet and take responsibility for her decisions. The Taylor family would never be the same again.

CHAPTER FIFTEEN

After the success of their shopping trip, Willow and Sally agreed they would tackle cleaning out Lillian's clothes and belongings. They were both unsure about asking Lacey to join them; it was potentially both awkward and embarrassing, if not just extremely uncomfortable. In the end they hadn't – a decision Sally was still unsure about. But it was too late now to include their young sister.

Willow arrived at Sally's by ten-thirty that morning, armed with boxes and stickers for all the clearing and sorting required. As they put the stickers – *Recycle, Charity Shop* and *Rubbish* – on the boxes, Sally smelt alcohol off Willow; a slight whiff, that was all. It was only morning, but Sally reasoned that her sister had maybe had a few glasses too many of wine with Derek the night before.

Their mother had been a tidy woman. Everything in her wardrobe was arranged to colour and season. The girls were amazed at how organised the room was, but it felt strange to be going through her private belongings. It was like they were snooping and she might walk in any minute and ask them what the hell they were doing in her room.

As the bedroom door had been kept closed since her death, the scent of her perfume and lotions still lingered faintly in the air. Her trinket boxes were displayed on her dressing table, along with her brush and mirror set. The book she had been reading lay on her night-stand, the bookmark on page 119 indicating how much she had read. Her slippers – the cheery red tartan ones Willow had given her the previous Christmas – were placed by the end of the bed, and her dressing gown hung from a hook on the inside of the bedroom door. There was stillness in the room, which reinforced the sense of trespassing that the two sisters felt.

"Hey, Sally, look here. Do you remember these?" Willow was holding a pretty box inlaid with mother-of-pearl, and had taken off the lid. She was staring into the ornate box in her hand.

"What have you got?" Sally asked, as she crossed the room.

"Take a look. Do they remind you of anything?" Willow sat on the bed and waited for Sally to speak. Tears pricked at Willow's eyes.

"Oh my God, the pearls! Oh look, she kept them." Sally sat beside her sister, both silent, lost in their memories. In the box were twelve or thirteen cream pearls, the very ones they had used to play Treasure Island all those years ago.

"Dear God, Willow, what treasures. How did they not kill us for breaking the necklace and losing most of the pearls in the garden?"

"I know, I think I'd murder any little brats of mine if they did that to me," she whispered, as she closed the box and laid it on her lap. She ran her fingers gently over the box of memories.

"You keep them, Willow. After all, it was your idea to use them as the treasure!" Sally put her arm around the other woman and gently added, "It's not too late yet, you know."

The room was filled with sadness. They were surrounded by memories of so many happy days.

"Too late for what?" Willow asked, as she blew her nose.

"For those little brats you mentioned. You can still have them."

"No, Sally, not at this stage of our life. We had all the tests and there is no reason why Derek and I can't have children. We are both in perfect working order." Sighing, she placed the jewellery box back on the dressing table.

"So what are you saying? You chose not to? That's okay, too, you know."

Willow went to the window and opened it to ease the heaviness in the room.

"I'm saying that I didn't, really. I always thought I did, but when push came to shove, I couldn't bear it. I like my freedom, I like being a housewife with time on my hands. I loved my shopping days with Mum. Having children would have stopped all that. Yes, I was lonely at times, but who isn't? The grass is always greener and all that."

Sally got up and hugged her sister, but sensed Willow felt uncomfortable with her sympathy. "So long as you and Derek are happy, that's all that matters," Sally reassured her. "I'm sure the pair of you have discussed it at length, and it's for you two to decide, no-one else. Now let's get on, yeah?"

With renewed energy, they sorted through the closets and drawers, sharing laughter and more tears as memories came flooding back. Sally's bubbly personality rubbed off on her sister, and the time passed without further hitches.

Their task was almost over when they found a locked metal box underneath a pile of Lillian's sweaters on the top shelf of her wardrobe. Not very big – about the size of a large, man-size tissue-box – it had been pushed right back into a corner, out of sight. Neither of the girls had seen it before and there was no sign of keys anywhere in the room.

They decided to take a break and took the box downstairs with them, their curiosity aroused. The black metal box, with gold stencilling at each corner, lay on the coffee table.Both women sat in silence staring at it. What should they do next? Should they try opening it? Should they phone Robert and Lacey to tell them about their find? Maybe if they called the others and it turned out to be a simple keepsake box, there would have been a lot of hassle over nothing. After all, it couldn't be very important. Surely the solicitor had all the papers and documents that were specific to their parents' estate?

But what if the contents had value of a personal nature? The box remained a mystery.

"Okay, it's settled so, once we get all the other belongings sorted, we'll open this box," Sally asked, glancing at Willow for her agreement.

"Suits me. It's probably photos and bits from our childhood inside there. Remember, Mum loved our paintings and homemade cards. This is probably her memory box, that's all."

"I agree. How about we go and grab a bite to eat and finish the rest tomorrow?"

"Well, I have to cook for Derek, so why not join us tonight?" Willow was putting on her cream jacket and grabbing her red leather bag from the nearby chair.

"Give me an hour or so to shower and wash the dust from Mum's stuff out of my hair, and I'll call over then. Thanks, Willow," Sally replied, tiredness pulling at her words.

Taking the metal box upstairs, Sally put it inside her own wardrobe and pushed it towards the back of the closet. It would be safer there in case it got mixed up with Lilian's belongings that were being thrown out.

* * *

Opening a bottle of white wine while she prepared dinner, Willow was happy. She had enjoyed the day much more than she had expected. Tonight, Sally would help fill the silence that often lingered between her and Derek during mealtimes. The silences had become more common lately, and she'd noticed her husband had taken to eating out more regularly before he came home from work. She never complained, though; it suited her to have him around the house less. She knew he watched her in the evenings when she poured her nightcap, or two.

Tonight would be nice. She had phoned Derek on the way home to tell him that Sally was joining them for dinner, and he had sounded genuinely pleased. Her sister had done something with her life and had entertaining tales to tell about her many travels.

What had Willow done with her life? She shook off thoughts of her earlier conversation with Sally about children. Her sister assumed that Willow and Derek had discussed not starting a family; how wrong she was. She had no idea whether her husband agreed with her decision or not; she was too frightened to ask the question. But that would all take a back seat tonight, they had company for dinner. Willow raised her glass of wine in the air, toasting a hard day's work well done. The stuffed chicken breasts were in the oven and she would complete the sauce just before serving.

Sipping her wine and topping up her glass, she began to set the dining table. She would use her Denby crockery tonight and the lovely Tipperary crystal glasses. A crisp white linen tablecloth was the finishing touch. She had earned these few drinks. It had been hard work today amid the memories and heartache of clearing her mother's possessions. Derek wouldn't understand, of course, but to hell with him and his nagging!

* * *

"I'm home," Derek shouted, as he hung his jacket on the coat stand. The smell of home cooking wafted through to him and he inhaled deeply. Whatever faults his wife had, her cooking skills were excellent.

"Hi." She turned from setting the dining table. "Sally will be here shortly. How was your day?"

He hugged her and smiled warmly as she kissed his cheek. Derek desperately wanted his marriage to work, but the strain of being sole provider was getting to him at times. Willow liked to act the part of an upper class lady but she tended to spend more than he earned, leaving him with the headache of balancing the budget. Maybe if they had children things would be different, but he knew better than to broach that subject.

"Ah, fine. Dinner smells wonderful. I'll just go wash up and be ready in ten minutes."

"Open some wine, please, when you get a chance, that bottle is almost empty."

"Have you drunk all of this?" Derek was astonished that his wife could drink a full bottle of wine before dinner.

"No. Sally and I opened it earlier over at hers. We had a couple of glasses with our lunch and then I brought it home with me."

Willow turned away from her husband and started on the vegetables, but not before he'd noticed the blush on her cheeks. He sighed. At least they weren't facing another silent dinner for two.

CHAPTER SIXTEEN

The morning sun was warm on her face as Lacey sat by her apartment window and wrote a list of things she needed to do. The evening with Robert and Aoife had rattled her. Although they'd enjoyed a pleasant meal and the chat had been varied, it hadn't allowed her the chance to tell him about her plans and her conversation with Mr. Sherman. The urgency and excitement she'd felt about sharing her news had gone and she felt a bit deflated. She was still annoyed with her brother. It wasn't Aoife's fault she had been thrown into the meal by Rob; she couldn't have known about Lacey's plans.

Philip Sherman had said he would go through other files and find out whatever he could for her. She'd told him she was going to tell Robert of her plan to search for her birth mother, and that had been her intention. After last night, she had decided against it.

"My birth mother, my real mum," the words tingled on her tongue as she said them aloud, feeling warm and comforted. It was strange to think that her mother was out there, living a life Lacey knew nothing about. She could not entertain the thought of her real mum being dead; she needed to believe she was still alive, for she had a thousand questions she needed answered.

Did she look like her? Lacey knew she resembled her dad in some ways. But where did her love of animals come from, her mother maybe? Her stubbornness and her dislike for celery, were they from her mum's side? Silly small things suddenly seemed of great importance. Did her mother think about her at all? Was she hoping that Lacey would come looking for her? Maybe her parents had signed an agreement when she was born; was her mother happy about that? Did Joe Taylor send Lacey's mum photos of her at different ages? Did he keep in touch with her and not tell Lillian? Did her real parents love each other, or was it just a silly affair?

Lacey was so giddy with the potency of it all, she felt she could hardly breathe. Trying to calm herself, she stepped out onto the balcony. The rattan sheeting around the balcony rails was torn in parts; Milly's handiwork. She wondered what had happened to her cat. It was a couple of weeks now since she'd disappeared. The feeding and drinking bowls lay empty, a sign of another time, and Lacey's happiness dimmed a little.

Her cat had been her one constant companion but, like Lacey's sisters and brother, Milly had shied away from her. She, too, had disappeared from Lacey's life. Each week she went to the local vet's practice to see if Milly had been found. There were posters up in the local shops with a picture of the cat, yet there had been no sighting. She thought of Milly's cute black and white face, and hoped she was okay, that some kind person was looking after her and that she wasn't lying hurt, crying for help.

Going back indoors, she sat back down at the table and re-examined her list. She had phone calls to make. The one to her work was a priority. She had been mulling over resigning from work, convincing herself that a change of career would be the first step in her new life.

Her funds from her dad made her decision easier. She had never needed to dip into the savings before, something she was glad of now. She needed to concentrate on playing detective to find her birth mother, and didn't need the distraction of work getting in the way.

Mr. Sherman had only been able to tell her that her mother had been young; early twenties, he recalled, when her father and her mother met. Joe hadn't wanted her identity known, as he'd believed the less who knew their business the better. Mr. Sherman had never met or even seen a photograph of her, but – based on his conversations with Joe – he knew she was educated but, no, he didn't know where she came from, he told Lacey. Although he and Joe had chatted about different aspects of the situation, there were certain issues that her father had kept to himself. Everything had been handled properly, nothing underhand had taken place, Mr. Sherman had assured her. But to answer all of Lacey's questions, he would need to check the storerooms where all his files were kept. He promised that the next time they met he would have more information for her.

Each night Lacey dreamt of meeting her mother. In her dreams, they would agree to meet in a public place, and she would know her instantly. Through the crowds of shoppers, she would pick her mum out and run towards her. There would be a big smile on her mum's face and her arms would open wide, waiting to hug her long lost daughter. It was all running through the crowds and rose petals falling from the sky, people around them smiling and applauding the big reunion. Lacey would know a real mother's love at last. The years raised by Lillian would fade, and she would create new family memories. On several occasions, she had woken with tear stains on her face from her dreams.

Leaving work was a good idea, she had so much else to concentrate on in the coming weeks. The telephone rang, breaking into her thoughts. She was tempted to ignore it but then she felt guilty for no reason, and picked up the receiver.

"Hey, Lacey, thought you were out. I was just going to try your mobile. What are you up to this weekend?" Robert sounded happy that he'd caught his sister at home.

"Hi, Rob, I'm sort of free at the weekend, why?" She wasn't pushed about telling him what plans she may have yet.

"Well, I want to make it up to you. I know you weren't expecting Aoife the other night, but she and I had worked non-stop so I kind of owed her a meal. What about we meet at the Sea Horse on Saturday and we can talk properly? That sound alright for you?"

She sensed he was a little tense as he waited for her answer.

"Yeah sure, why not? What time are you thinking of?"

"Oh, six-thirtyish will be grand. I may ask the others, too, okay? It'd be good to all get together."

Lacey hesitated. Was he afraid to meet her on his own? Was she that much of an embarrassment to him? Her silence sparked a curiosity in her brother.

"Is there a problem?" Robert enquired cautiously.

"No, no, not at all. Okay, see you on Saturday evening."

Damn it, Lacey thought, as she cut off the call. She hadn't planned on that. Meeting her family did not appear on her agenda, but she guessed it only natural that the others would still be in touch with each other. What was she thinking? Of course they would be; she was the outsider, after all. These days she didn't see herself as part of that family any more. Her energies were focussed elsewhere and she planned to keep it that way. She hadn't stopped loving them, but she'd felt a distance develop and somehow it protected her.

Her life now ran on a different path to theirs. They were in mourning for their mother; she was living in limbo until she met her real mum. Dealing with her feelings about Lillian stayed very much in the back seat. Lacey was too preoccupied with what her future held than grieving for her past. This was all so damn exhausting. Maybe she could find an excuse to opt out of Saturday night? Hell, she could do what she wanted. She would leave it for now and see how she felt on the day.

CHAPTER SEVENTEEN

"This is so bloody inconvenient," Willow grumbled as she looked at the clock. Just after six and she should be heading to the restaurant for dinner. As usual, Derek had abandoned her for some silly club meeting. It was amazing how these events always cropped up on an evening when she needed his company. He had seemed surprised with her complaints about him not going. He had even challenged her about it, asking since when she needed him to go visit her brother and sisters. He had been more argumentative lately, she'd noticed.

Willow had been looking forward to relaxing with a few drinks this evening, but now she would have to drive.

"Why not get Lacey to collect you? She is passing by, after all," Derek had questioned his wife, still curious why Willow was being so insistent on his presence at the meal.

"Willow. I said, ask Lacey."

"No, no, it's okay. I'll get a taxi. She might be walking or...or maybe she's busy."

"Well, you won't know unless you ring her and find out. Do you want me to ask her?" Derek pulled his mobile phone out of his shirt pocket and began flicking through its menu.

"Stop, Derek!" she snapped impatiently. "Just leave it, will you, for God's sake!" He stepped back from the raised voice of his wife. "Go to your meeting, I'll sort myself," she said, in a more gentle tone.

She couldn't admit to him that she had not seen her little sister in weeks. In fact, she hadn't even given Lacey any thought lately. She had meant to phone her, of course, but life seemed to get in the way.

"Fine, I'll drop you to the Sea Horse and maybe one of the

others can give you a lift home." He ran his hand through his hair, looking weary from the hostile exchange.

Willow's mood was dour. Derek knew how to upset her. Obviously, he wasn't happy at the expense of getting a taxi; miserable sod. He really was so insensitive to her needs. Thinking of needs, she really could do with a quick gulp of vodka.

Rummaging in her deep handbag, she searched for the small bottle filled with her favourite tipple, the mixer already added. It was her emergency bottle, her safety net to relax her. Small enough to fit discreetly into her bag, the bottle of clear liquid would pass for water if she were ever challenged. Derek would never know.

* * *

Robert arrived at the restaurant by six-fifteen. He wanted to be there to greet his sisters. His tall, broad frame and melting chocolate eyes drew admirable glances from the women diners. The male diners ignored him, threatened by his good looks and strong presence. He was wearing his jeans and checked shirt. He liked to be smart but casual when out of the office.

He wasn't sure if the others had met up recently and didn't know exactly how relations lay between them. Lacey's attitude on the phone had left him questioning.

Sally arrived next and hugged her brother; Lacey joined them minutes later. She refrained from hugging and just sat down beside Sally, with Robert on her other side.

"Anyone heard from Willow and Derek?" Sally asked, as the waiter brought a jug of iced water to the table.

"Derek can't make it. He's got some meeting. Pity, I could do with another man to help me with three women. Anyway, he's dropping Willow off. I told him we might meet for a few drinks after our meal and his meeting." Robert's gaze wandered around the room. The place was not filling up like before, during the boom years.

"So, Sally, what have you been up to? Are you settled back home?" Lacey smiled at her sister. The older woman's understated flair made simple look elegant without effort. Her pale blue vintage-style top beautifully complimented her black trousers.

"Not much, it's strange living back there without Mum," her voice trailed off, a slight blush staining her cheeks as she mentioned her mother.

"Look, Sal, it's okay, she is your mother. I just think of her as Lillian so don't be embarrassed, please." Lacey laid a reassuring hand on Sally's arm.

"Of course, I'm being silly. Anyway, how are you? That's what is more important."

"Oh, I've been busy. I've taken unpaid leave from work and I've actually thought about resigning. I'm sure Rob's told you."

"No, he hasn't." Sally glanced sharply towards their brother but he was engrossed in what the menu offered for the evening.

"What am I being accused of now?" he replied, happy to have selected his meal.

"I was just telling Sally I'm off work. I thought you'd have told her." Lacey glared at Robert, his lazy casualness rankling her. He didn't seem to notice; his mind was clearly elsewhere.

"Sure, I've not seen Sal in ages," he replied without thinking, while looking at his watch.

"I thought you had both met recently. My mistake." Lacey's annoyance at the white lie was bubbling beneath her smile. The sense of disappointment in her brother and his indifference to see her hurting mingled within her, pushing Lacey's patience to the limit.

"Where the hell is Willow?" He was looking towards the door. He was hungry and didn't want to delay any longer.

"Let's order and she can look after herself when she arrives," Sally said, and signalled for the waiter. They chose lamb, fish, and a Thai chicken dish for their mains.

With their orders taken, the three siblings chatted about the politics of the day. People expected the new Government to make great changes to help them out of the dreadful recession that had gripped the country. Robert admitted business had been affected overseas, with investors being slower to think about Irish businesses as a good place to invest.

As they tucked into their starters, their appetites matched the lively conversation. It was as though they had made an unwritten agreement to talk about anything but family matters. But it was surprisingly pleasant. Lacey felt her irritation towards the others fade; it felt good to be with them again.

The restaurant was relatively quiet for a Saturday evening, with only a dozen other tables occupied. It was another sign of the recession. People were staying in and spending their money on the essentials.

It wasn't until they were waiting for their main courses that Willow made her appearance. She looked flushed and breathless, and Robert stood up to hold back the chair for her. Lillian had always insisted on her children having impeccable manners.

"Are you okay, Willow? Has something happened?" Sally's voice was full of concern.

"Sorry I'm late. Are you eating?" She looked around the table, not acknowledging anyone.

"Finished our starters. We're waiting on the main course. One sec and I'll get a waiter to take your order." Rob waved his hand and the waiter arrived.

Willow ordered a main course only, so not to delay the others. By the time the food arrived, she seemed more relaxed and settled, although she still hadn't explained her reason for being so late.

"Is it safe to ask what the delay was?" Sally ventured, between mouthfuls of fresh lemon sole.

"Don't ask! We got a flat tyre driving over here and Derek got grease on his shirt, so we had to return home so he could change. It was a nightmare." Willow sounded a little flustered again.

"So, Lacey, what have you being doing since we met last?" Willow asked.

"Trying to get my life back to normal, I suppose," she replied, taking a sip of water. She wasn't drinking tonight. She planned on keeping a clear head in case she missed any detail that might pass between the others. Dear God, she was being paranoid now, she realised, as she replaced the glass on the table.

"Normal. I know what you mean. It's been so hard since Mum

died. I've been all over the place emotionally. I miss her so much. Each day brings something different, another event that Mum and I would have shared. It's been so difficult. Poor Mum! I really miss her warmth and our chats," sighing, Willow put her cutlery down and a gloomy silence descended around them.

"Pour me another glass of red wine will you, Rob, please? I'm still trying to get over the journey here."

Willow was already on her second glass of wine and seemed to have no intention in slowing down. "Rob, what's work like? Are you busy, or have things gone slow a bit? Derek seems to be flat out these times." Willow spoke between mouthfuls while still eating, as though she didn't want any lulls in the conversation.

"It's picking up a bit. I was blessed to have Aoife help me get back into my stride since Mum died," her brother replied.

"She really is a lovely girl, Robert. How long have you two been dating now?" Sally spoke. Her soft voice suited her, Lacey thought.

"Oh, eighteen months or so. She's so easy to get on with, isn't she, Lacey?"

Lacey realised they were all looking at her.

"How would Lacey know? When did you meet her?" Willow directed the question at her, curiosity rising.

"I met her a few days ago with Robert. We had a lovely evening. Why ask such a question?" Lacey frowned at her oldest sister. She didn't like the dismissive way she was being spoken to by Willow.

"Well, after all the hullabaloo with Mum's death, you were so shocked and seemingly upset, I didn't think you'd be out socialising so soon, that's all." The older woman's sarcasm was notable in her voice.

Lacey looked at Willow in disbelief. Was this woman for real? "*Seemingly upset?* What are you on about? My life has come crashing down around my ears and you think I'm making it up? You have no idea what it's been like for me for the past few weeks. Lillian never loved me, and she admitted it. She made it clear she wished I had never existed." Lacey's voice rose with each breath.

"Can you honestly blame her?" The two women glared icily at

each other, youngest and eldest. "C'mon, Lacey, that secret must have weighed heavily on her shoulders all that time. I'm sure it contributed to her ill health at the end." Willow sniffed a little and picked up her napkin.

"Are you suggesting that *I'm* the cause of her dying? I don't believe this!" Lacey jumped to her feet, knocking over her chair. "How dare you! To think I looked up to you. My big sister! To think I wanted to be like you when I grew up. Well, I'm glad I'm not like you. You're just another Lillian, a selfish, cold cow." As she leaned over and pointed accusingly at her sister, she knocked over a wine glass.

"Oh, sit down and stop the dramatics," Willow hissed. "People are looking. Sally, grab that waiter's eye and get another bottle of red, will you?"

"You should apologise first, I think, before you drink any more." Sally glared at Willow, not hiding her disgust at her elder sister's behaviour.

"What is this, let's-all-love-Lacey-night? For goodness sake, what I said is true! Mum kept Dad's dirty little secret for him and look where it got her – an early grave." Willow pointed towards Lacey as she said the stinging words.

Lacey was shaking with rage. She had reached her limit and, without thinking, she leaned over and slapped Willow across her cheek. Diners nearby gasped at the stinging sound.

"How dare you call me a dirty secret, you selfish bitch!"

"Can't take the truth, can you?" Willow's face was reddening where Lacey had slapped her.

"Truth? What about Dad? He had an early grave, too." Lacey's throat tightened as she spat out each word.

"He got his just desserts. But my mum was innocent remember. MY mum, not yours, MINE!" Willow spluttered back, her hand held to her cheek.

Robert stood up before any more blows could be exchanged, and firmly gestured towards the exit at Lacey. "There's no need to hit anyone. Can't you see it's the drink talking? For goodness sake, Lacey, I thought you would have more restraint."

Lacey looked at him with incredulity. He was taking Willow's side in this? Her brother's actions just heaped insult upon insult. Hot tears stung her eyes, almost blinding her as she stumbled her way through the dining room, bumping into chairs as she headed outside.

This was a dream. A nightmare! It had to be. Did she really slap her sister in public? Yes, and she had so deserved it. Had Lacey over-reacted? No, she had been perfectly in the right.

Her face was wet, her eyes stung, and her chest ached. Lacey hailed a taxi to take her back to her apartment. Her legs were weak and shaking, she couldn't take a step if she wanted. Slamming the taxi door, she heard her name being called but she did not look back. She needed to get home, to get away from here, to get away from the Taylors.

"Lacey! Lacey. Wait, please!"

* * *

Sally saw the taxi take off as she rushed outside to check on her little sister. She was too late. The car was gone, and she was left standing outside the restaurant, dazed and shocked by what she had just witnessed.

She had never seen Lacey so angry; would never have believed that she would slap anyone. But she had certainly been provoked.

Sally could kill Willow. This was more than drink talking, no matter what Rob wanted to believe. Willow had been totally out of order. Sally turned to go back in, her body still shaking with emotion.

CHAPTER EIGHTEEN

She stood in the shower, water splashing down around her shoulders, tears mingling with the warm spray. She felt dirty, unloved, and stained. The anger of last night spilled over to her father and birth mother. It was because of their stupid, stupid affair that she was in this God-awful mess.

That's what people saw her as, Joe Taylor's dirty secret; she would always walk with that shadow over her. Why had it happened to her? No matter how many showers she took, she would feel the scar of his affair on her. Had her father only loved her because Lillian didn't? Did he see her as an issue to be dealt with, rather than a daughter he was proud of? God, where would all this mess lead? Lacey was at an all-time low; motivation and hope seeped out of her.

Her fury towards Willow had not dimmed. Her sister's behaviour at the restaurant had been unforgivable. How could Robert have stuck up for her? Using her drinking as an excuse was not good enough. The others were mourning their mother, too, but they didn't behave outrageously like her.

Lacey dried herself off then paced the apartment in her dressing gown, searching for reasons that would make sense of it all. It was all too obvious that Robert was on Willow's side. Indicating to her to leave had been the last crushing blow for Lacey. Well, her brother could go jump off a cliff! He was a wimp; a real Mummy's boy. Instead of telling Willow to sober up and apologise, he had planted the blame on Lacey's shoulders. Even if he was afraid of Willow, he could have stayed silent. Well, hell would freeze over before she would reach out to either him or Willow for advice or comfort!

Gathering up her clothes that lay where she had discarded them on the floor last night, she threw them into the wash basket and sighed as she looked about her. What now? Mr. Sherman had been forced to cancel their planned meeting the next day, as he had been called into court unexpectedly for a case.

She went out to her balcony. This was her space; her place to clear the troubled mind she was living with. The sounds of the city calmed her, reminding there was a world of possibilities still to be discovered.

She checked the two flower boxes and inhaled the scent of the colourful sweet peas growing along the trellis supporting the blooms. The sheets of rattan against the balcony railings were in need of urgent repair, bringing her dear Milly to mind. It was almost two months since her cat had walked out of her life, and she missed her company. Had she neglected her pet amidst all the upheaval? Is that why she had disappeared? The vet had assured her that cats often wandered off, and some could return days, even weeks, later. But it had been too long now; sadly, there was little hope of Milly returning.

The sun's warmth offered a little comfort. It travelled through her body and she stretched out, long and lean. As she took a deep breath in, a voice inside her told her to let go, to breathe out gently and let all her negative emotions out.

She did this a couple of times and felt strength spread through her. The heat tingling her arms and face caressed her and penetrated deep into her bones. Sunshine always brought positive vibes. Lifting her face to the rays, she closed her eyes and soaked them up some more, the heat on her body reassuring her like a comforting hug. Enough of the lows and depression, she thought determinedly. She still had an agenda, she still had a fight on her hands, and it was one she intended to win.

"Act now," the voice within her whispered. "Take back control and take action. Remember, seek and you shall find."

* * *

Aoife wasn't sure her boyfriend was telling her the whole story. There was no doubt he was extremely annoyed with his family and still shocked at Lacey's outburst. "She actually struck her sister! It was so reckless and uncalled for," he grumbled, "and the language she used within earshot of other diners!"

But something didn't sit right with Aoife. Lacey must have had a reason for such behaviour; it seemed so out of character. She recalled the quiet and soft-spoken girl she had met with Robert a few days before. Clearly disappointed by Aoife's presence, his sister had nevertheless been pleasant and polite.

The Taylors were a private family; airing their troubles in public would be uncomfortable for them. Robert was so worked up. He paced around his office, slamming drawers shut and barking instructions. Aoife allowed him his tantrum and held off asking questions. He would tell her more if he wanted to.

Later that evening, over dinner – his apology for his outburst – Robert finally opened up.

"It is all falling apart," he admitted. "Our lives are in tatters and I need to take charge before there are any more public displays. I'm the man in the family, after all."

Over a few glasses of wine, the whole story tumbled out. Aoife listened in silence while his mind churned over question after question. Had his mother really needed to reveal all? Why hadn't she kept her mouth shut? What had she hoped to achieve? For the first time ever, he was angry with his mother. Maybe she had a side to her that he had overlooked because she was his beloved mum. He should make a point of meeting Mr. Sherman and enquire a bit further about the whole bloody saga.

"Why didn't you tell me this before?" Aoife laid a comforting hand on his when he paused. But she knew the answer. Robert needed time when it came to discussing his family; unlike hers, where everyone knew what the other thought at any given moment. They came from such different backgrounds.

She tucked her hair behind her ear and placed her chin on top of her palm, while her elbow rested on a table as she listened.

"I guess I wasn't taking it all in, or else just burying my head in the sand." His smile was weak as he gently squeezed her hand.

"But, Robert, Lacey must be devastated. I mean, her whole life has been a lie! Well, sort of, you know what I mean."

"I know, I know, but why must she be the only one to get sympathy? We lost our mother."

Aoife stared blankly at him. Had she heard him right? Where was the strong independent man who threw out orders and made brave decisions every day in a tough business world?

"Did you hear yourself right now?" she murmured softly. There was no point in raising her voice although she longed to give him a good shaking.

"Yes, ridiculous, isn't it? I knew as soon as I said it that it sounded weak and pathetic. Lacey has lost a lot more than her mother. Aoife, what am I to do? My father was someone I looked up to, someone I admired and now, now I see how he cheated on his family and manipulated his wife."

His brown eyes had lost their sparkle, his skin was grey, and Aoife saw how troubled he was. She sensed a definite shift in their relationship. It had progressed to a more intimate level. They were spending more time together, and taking her into his confidence on private family matters proved their new closeness.

"Look, Rob, your father was human. Sure, he made a mistake, but Christ, don't we all? I mean, he looked out for his family. He didn't abandon Lacey, like a lot of men do after they've had their fun. He didn't change; you have. You had him up high on a pedestal and, while that's okay, remember you put him up there. He didn't ask you to raise the bar so high."

Robert listened, remaining quiet for a few moments. "You're right, of course." He smiled properly, her words providing the comfort and reassurance he needed.

They enjoyed the rest of their meal without any more soul-searching, and Robert hugged her warmly as they left the restaurant.

"You're good for me, you know," he confided, as he took her back to her apartment. "I wish...I mean, I'd like..."

She looked at him, waiting to hear what was troubling him now. His next words came as a huge surprise. "What I'm trying to say is, would you consider moving in with me, Aoife?"

Her beaming smile left him in no doubt of her answer. Tonight had moved their relationship up a gear, and being held in his arms confirmed her desire to spend her future with him. She slept soundly that night and her dreams were the sweetest she'd ever had.

CHAPTER NINETEEN

SEPTEMBER

Lacey was excited when Mr Sherman's secretary phoned to ask if they could meet at his golf club for coffee the next morning. She grabbed the chance to meet him again. Her determination to find her birth mother had grown within her and she thought of little else in any twenty-four hours, the Taylor side of the family pushed aside for now. She rehearsed again and again how she would greet her mother when the time came. Her real mother! There was no room for any "if not" or "she doesn't want to". In Lacey's eyes, her mother would want to meet her as much as her daughter wanted to meet the woman who gave birth to her.

"Have you news for me?" Lacey demanded impatiently, as soon as she saw the solicitor sitting at a quiet table in the corner of the bright, welcoming lounge. She couldn't tell from his demeanour whether good or bad news awaited her. It had to be good, she reckoned, her positive streak jumping to the fore.

"Hello, Lacey," he said with a gentle smile, and gestured for her to sit down.

"Sorry. Hello, Mr. Sherman." She blushed at her bad manners and sat across from him, trying to still her excitement and appear calm.

"I've been looking up old files and have some minor details that may help you," he began, taking a pair of reading glasses from his pocket.

She jumped forward in her chair, eager to hear it all, no matter how minor. "Anything at all would be great. I mean, any

94

information you can give me will be welcome."

"Lacey, before I tell you anything, I must advise you maybe to seek help professionally." His tone was cautious, an even timbre that deflated her positivity a little.

"You mean a private investigator?"

"No, my dear, I mean perhaps some counselling." He saw her stiffen and push back in her seat.

"I'm not crazy, I just want to find my mum," she whispered innocently, the brightness from earlier dimming slowly from her eyes.

"I'm not suggesting you are crazy. What you're about to do will affect you immensely and you may need some guidance or help dealing with it all," he consoled her.

"I see. Well, I can address that issue when I find out something. Right now, I'm waiting." She knew she was overly snappy and rude, and didn't mean to be. The man across from her only wanted to help, but she was running before she could walk. The fight in her returned.

Lacey's emotions were all over the place, and maybe there was some sense in his suggestion to seek help. Truth was, she didn't trust herself to keep calm and together to handle all the new information that would come her way.

Cautiously, he continued as the woman before him squirmed in her seat in anticipation. "Okay, your mother was in her early to mid-twenties. She's Irish, from County Cork. What town, I don't know. She and your father met through business meetings, or so he told me once. I remember the more I rattle this old brain of mine. I wasn't ever told her full name, except he let her first name slip once or twice and it sounded like Karen or Carley, I'm not sure. You see, I didn't handle your father's affairs regarding your adoption. I advised him about contracts and business dealings. He never told me who he dealt with regarding personal matters, so I can't help you with that."

The sad tone of his voice surprised Lacey. He looked older than when she had first met him. She got the feeling that remembering his old friend was upsetting for him.

"Would you like some coffee?" Lacey surprised herself by offering him refreshments in his own golf club.

"A good idea, Lacey." He smiled, his shoulders relaxing as he looked at the troubled daughter of his dear friend.

* * *

That evening at home, Lacey took out a new notebook she had bought, with a pale green cover. This would be her diary of events; the journey she would travel over the next few months. Or possibly years? So many questions crowded her mind. Flipping open the diary, she began to write a biography of sorts for her mother:

Name: Karen/Carley – Sounds like these

Nationality: Irish, County Cork

Age: Mid-twenties

Career: Business, but what?

It looked so meagre on the page. Not much to write really, it almost looked lonely. But Lacey was determined to follow through. This book would record her memory of events to show her children. It would be the start of her true family tree.

In bed that night, she remembered Mr. Sherman's advice about counselling. Maybe she should look into it. Since her siblings wouldn't understand what she was trying to cope with, at least a professional would be good to have as a listening ear. Lacey got out the notebook from her bedside locker and switched on her lamp. She would write down the many questions in her head. It might help her straighten her thoughts, put them in order, so that she would know what she wanted answered if she did seek help.

How would she react when she finally met her mum? What if her mum didn't want to meet her? Could she, Lacey, cope with yet more rejection in her life? She shuddered with that dreadful thought. It would be like losing her mother all over again. She pulled the duvet up around her protectively, her mind whirring. What if she was ashamed of her mother? What if her mother was ashamed of her? Was she prepared for the answers she might receive from the woman who hadn't wanted to raise her? What makes a woman give away her baby?

Mr. Sherman had mentioned contracts. What was in those contracts? Had Joe Taylor paid her mother off to leave and keep quiet? All the questions went into the small book. She poured her heart and soul into her writing.

She needed to go back home, to the house where she grew up. There might be something there –letters, photos, anything that could give a clue to Joe and Lillian's life almost twenty-four years ago.

She put her diary away and turned out the light. In the morning she would phone Sally to apologise for her behaviour at the family meal, and ask if she could search the house for anything that may help her piece her true identity together. Of course, it meant telling Sally about her search for her mother. But she would not lie. There had been enough lies already – and all they ever caused was heartache.

Sleep avoided her. She lay awake and imagined all sorts of encounters with her mother. The whirring of the washing machine in the upstairs apartment was comforting, as were the odd shouts of late night revellers heading home. She didn't feel so alone in the world. Listening to the machine change cycles and go into a top spin, she decided to sort out her own washing.

This is madness, she thought. Washing clothes at two am; maybe old Sherman wasn't far off the mark when he recommended a counsellor! Putting on the kettle, she made a cup of camomile tea and looked out onto the street below, watching the amber-coloured night. By four am, Lacey had nodded off, curled up on the sofa, until the banging of car doors of workers leaving for their offices awoke her.

Her journal lay open on the coffee table. Nothing had changed magically during the night. The contents were the same, a few scribbled lines with simple words, not giving much life to her unknown mother. So many questions waiting to be answered. Sighing, she reached for the portable phone.

When there was no answer, she decided to leave a message. "Hey, Sally, I want to say sorry for last time we met. I know I shouldn't have slapped Willow. I don't suppose we could meet? I

97

mean, could I call over to see you, at home...your home. Can you ring me when you get this message please? Thanks."

She laid the phone down gently, afraid she would hurt Sally if she just placed it back normally.

Somehow Sally seemed to have remained neutral in all the high-jinks. It was as if she detached herself from the altercations and created a boundary wall that protected her from all the hassle. Lacey wished she could build the same wall and keep certain people outside it.

Like her, Sally had been in awe of Willow growing up, but did she still have the same respect for her now? The older sister was supposed to be watching out for all of them and directing them, but really she had been a bully. Yes, Willow had been a clever tormenter, manipulating them in everything, even in the games they had played, the music they listened to. Her influence was stamped over their childhood.

What she and Sally had thought was sisterly love, was really Willow getting her own way. She was such a sly, cunning person. Lacey would point that out to Sal if she tried to defend the old battleaxe when they met.

Lacey's anger gathered in her stomach, a tight knot of annoyance and hurt rising in her throat. To hell with Willow, she thought, I'm going to put her out of my life forever! It was laughable really that she had mistaken her sister's concern all those years as love, when it had only been the bitch's way of suiting herself. Did Sally feel that way, too? Did she go travelling overseas to escape from the reality of her sister? Was that why she was always so quiet in their company? Maybe Sally felt her opinion didn't count; Willow always had the last word.

Desperate to keep herself occupied and avoid the building frustration, Lacey headed out to the nearby express supermarket. Throwing bread, bacon, sausages, apples and teabags into the basket, she joined the slow-moving queue at the checkout. Despite the express sign over the checkout, the customer in front of her held a basket which overflowed with much more than ten items.

"Excuse me, this queue is for ten items or less," she said to the big man standing in front of her.

"So?" he replied sarcastically. He flexed his well-worked muscles, hinting at her to back off, then turned away. When she tapped him on the shoulder, all six foot of him turned to face her again, his eyes flashing annoyance at being accosted in this way.

Lacey squared her shoulders and spoke firmly, keeping eye contact at all times. "So? So move your ass to another checkout, you have almost two baskets there."

The man just stared at the angry young woman before him, and was about to turn away from her when she continued to berate him.

"Want me to call the manager? Or is it like most men, you're a bit thick at times?" she continued to stare him down. Shoppers around them stopped what they were doing and watched. It was High Noon time in the supermarket.

The big guy was now reddening in the face, as he took in the muttering and whispering of the other shoppers. Leaning in to her personal space, he stared right back at her but Lacey stood on tip-toes and smiled. She was determined.

The whispering got louder around them. After a few minutes of stand-off, he stepped away, muttering "hormonal bitch" under his breath. Lacey smiled at his words, and watched as two other people in the queue quietly slipped off to take their overloaded baskets to another checkout.

CHAPTER TWENTY

Sally returned Lacey's call as soon as she got the message, and suggested her little sister come over for lunch. She had the kettle on and sandwiches prepared when she heard the gravel outside crunching as Lacey pulled into the driveway.

Greeting Lacey at the door, the two hugged.

"Hey, how are things? Glad you made it."

"Hi Sally, you look great."

Her sister was wearing a cream jumper and pale blue summer skirt, with a small Paisley-style detail. Her auburn hair was sun-kissed, with blonde and caramel strands poking through, and her blue eyes looked so kind and soft.

"Okay, are you going to stand there all day or are you coming in?" Sally felt a little embarrassed at her sister's silent stare. Without warning, tears gathered in Lacey's eyes and she began to blubber out words, her breathing too quick to make her understood.

"Oh Sal, help me please. My life is such a mess," Lacey cried, and her sobbing grew stronger.

Taken aback by this sudden outburst, Sally gathered Lacey into her arms and led her to the familiar kitchen and sat her down. While her little sister got her breath back and finished crying, Sally made two cups of tea and placed them and the plate of salad sandwiches on the table. They ate in silence.

"Have you been sleeping okay?" It was Sally who spoke first. She stood up and placed her cup into the sink, then turned and rested against the counter.

"Some nights," Lacey replied. "I'm sorry for the whole thing at the restaurant," she continued "but Willow pushed the wrong buttons that night."

"Yeah well, she often can, can't she?" the older woman sighed. "I was a bit taken aback sure, but look, no worries, okay?" Sally was all for leaving the past in the past.

"Thanks, Sal. I know you're all missing your mum. I mean, I miss her, too, even though...well, you know. But I feel like I've been hit by a large, very fast moving train." She slammed her fist into her other palm to emphasise the collision.

Wondering whether to continue on the sensitive subject of their parents, Sal took the bold step and probed further. "Had you any idea, Lacey, about Mum, I mean Lillian? Did Dad not say anything or even hint at it?"

"No, not a clue. I always felt that Lillian didn't approve of me, that I could never please her. I thought maybe she was a bit jealous that I was a daddy's girl. You and Willow were in boarding school and there was a large enough age gap. I thought maybe my arrival had ruined some plans Lillian had."

"Did you really feel left out? I mean, how did you cope? Did you ever question Mum about it? Or even Dad, for that matter?" So many questions for everyone to have answered, but who would?

"When you and the others were around, things were okay; good even. I did tackle Lillian once about how she often didn't bother to turn up after we arranged to meet for lunch. I'd sit there like a fool in the café and wait. She would laugh and say she forgot, it was old age coming on and she would make it up to me, but she never did. I always felt it was me, I was the disappointment, the black sheep, you know the way they say there is one in every family." Lacey grew silent again.

"Hey, why not go upstairs and have a few hours rest? When you've had a nap, I'll make dinner and we can talk some more, unless you have plans for later?" Sally began to clear away the dishes.

"That would be heaven, Sal, are you sure?" The smile on Lacey's face showed how nice it was to be looked after.

"Go before I change my mind." Sally pushed Lacey gently out

into the hall and watched as she climbed the stairs of their family home, pausing to glance at photos on the stairwell. The house was filled with many memories and it was the good ones she took to sleep with her as she snuggled beneath the duvet.

Back in the kitchen, Sally picked up her book and went into the sitting room. She was reading Diane Chamberlain's book, *Secrets She Left Behind*; Sally smiled at how apt an epitaph it would make on Lillian's headstone.

* * *

The evening sun was setting when Lacey woke again. She stretched, satisfaction filling her, and looked around the familiar bedroom. The soft blues and pinks of the patchwork quilt were both delicate and feminine. There were prints with flowers, hearts, and some with fluffy-looking clouds. What it would be to live in such an ideal world with those gentle blue skies, clouds as soft as cotton wool, flowers to enjoy and inhale their exquisite scent, and where no hearts would get broken. Yes a dream-world indeed! She snuggled back down; the remnants of sleep fading from her body.

"Hey, sleepyhead, dinner will be ready in twenty minutes." Sally stuck her head around the bedroom door and smiled to find her sister looking rested and more relaxed.

"Coming. Smells good. I don't remember you ever being able to cook!" Lacey stuck her tongue out in a playful way.

"Cheeky, what about respect for your elders, young lady?" Sally chirped back.

In the kitchen, she had the table ready and was putting the final touches to the meal when Lacey wandered in, yawning.

"Seriously, Sis, it smells divine, what is it? Takeaway?"

Sally playfully thumped Lacey. "I've been busy while you were snoring," she remarked. "It's chicken chasseur with some fresh vegetables and baby potatoes. Do you cook at all, or are you a ready-meal girl?" she asked Lacey, while she grabbed some plates.

"Depends on time. Some days I'll take the short cut and use ready-made, then others I'll get stuck in and start from scratch."

"When I was travelling, money was always tight so I ate a lot of fresh fruit and vegetables, whatever was in season. It worked out cheaper and I would experiment with spices and stuff. It was better than any Home Economics class with that old bat Mrs. Bolton. Remember her?" Sally asked, placing the vegetables into a warmed serving dish.

"Do I ever! Her idea of the perfect housewife was turning out the best brown soda bread and sewing a seam with an invisible stitch. I still have the apron I made in her class. Pink checked material."

Both girls laughed out loud at the memory as they settled down to enjoy their dinner.

"I've never made brown bread since," Lacey sighed, looking at her sister, the perfect hostess tonight. "You don't...You do! Sally Taylor, are you telling me you make your own brown bread. Well, well, Mrs. Bolton would be proud."

"It was the only thing she taught us, so I suppose it stuck!" Sally said in an almost apologetic way.

The two women enjoyed their meal, with a comfortable silence every now and then as the conversation ebbed and flowed. Having cleared up the table and stacked the dishwasher, they strolled through to the living room to relax.

Lacey decided it was time to broach the subject of recent events.

"It's been such a hectic time. I don't know where to start, Sally. I mean, I've so many questions and, to be honest, I need help getting the answers; any answers at all. Why didn't Dad say anything to me? Write a letter even? Leave me some clue as to the truth? Did he know Lillian was going to divulge all? There is just so much I must find out!"

She looked towards her sister and waited for a reply. For a few moments it looked as though Sally had nothing to say.

"It's okay. I'm sorry, Sally, to heap this on you. I mean, it's not your battle–"

"Do you ever stop talking or jumping to daft conclusions? Also, you say 'I mean' a lot!" Sally grinned at her and continued, "I don't know where to begin really, Lacey. I suppose, break it down to smaller steps. Like, list what's most important for you to know first. Is it, did Dad leave any letter of explanation? Or is it, whether there was some agreement between him and Mum, you know, whoever died last would break the news sort of stuff?"

"Yeah, I could do that, that's a good idea. When you put it like that it seems it's more manageable."

"You sound like Rob. He said something similar to me a while back. You're definitely a Taylor," Sally said.

"Yes, I am, but who else am I? Sally, the first thing I need to know is who my mum is. Who is she and do I have other family out there? Will you help me? I mean, will you help me find my real mum, please?"

The older sister looked shocked. Sally had totally overlooked the issue of the other woman, Lacey's real mum.

CHAPTER TWENTY-ONE

Willow was in no mood for anything today. After Lacey ran from the restaurant that evening, she had sat there with Robert and Sally and pretended nothing had happened. But, of course, soft sensitive Sally insisted on following the spoilt brat to check on her. It was good of Rob to stand up to Lacey and send her packing. Willow was the head of the family now and she deserved respect.

Lacey's behaviour only showed up her true colours, her true pedigree. A stupid little tramp! Willow smiled as she thought of what her dear mum used to say, "What's in the cat comes out in the kitten". So true; Lacey was obviously like her sordid, real mother. No real breeding, just a rough cheap tart, Willow reckoned. She thought about it as she twirled her pearl necklace around her fingers. What kind of woman has an affair with a married man? Especially men like her father; he hadn't exactly been George Clooney, but of course he did have wealth – one of the most powerful aphrodisiacs ever.

That had to be it. That whore of a woman had only slept with Joe Taylor for money, no doubt. She wasn't even interested in her own child, for goodness sake. Willow wondered if Joe paid her off. But why did Lillian agree to raise the child? Willow couldn't deny she was secretly intrigued by it all. Glancing at the clock, she realised it was time to leave for her hair appointment. Arranging a taxi to pick her up, she wondered if she got the opportunity to cheat on her husband would she take it. Could she resist temptation? Would Derek?

She grabbed her coat and stepped outside just as her taxi pulled up. She had taken to travelling by taxi more now as it was less hassle than trying to find parking in the city. It also meant she could enjoy a glass of wine or two at lunch. Of course, Derek moaned about the expense, but she was adamant she would have a good lifestyle. She had been raised in one, she would remind him with venom when he protested.

Charlie's Salon was busy today, but Willow had a standing appointment each Thursday at two-thirty.

"Any refreshments while you wait, Mrs. Taylor-Shaw?" the young assistant on work experience asked, while taking Willow's jacket.

"A coffee, please," she replied, as she took her seat next to the window. It was very plush, customer comfort was a priority. The whirr of blow-dryers filled the air, the phone ringing and the raised chitter-chatter of the stylists, their clients all competing with each other to be heard.

She sat in the red leather chair and looked out at the world. It was September and the good summer weather seemed to be continuing. The people were dressed in shorts and t-shirts, summer frocks and short-sleeved shirts. Groups of students strolled by, all chatting enthusiastically. Shoppers weighed down with bags filled from the end of summer sales, and various couples, boyfriends and girlfriends walked past. Mothers and children in buggies; mothers with daughters, too, Willow guessed.

I miss you, Mum, she thought, as she watched a woman of Lillian's age link a young girl's arm as they crossed the road. A tear slid down her cheek and Willow surprised herself by the aching that overwhelmed her. She discreetly wiped away the tears and blew her nose. To be caught crying in public would be so juvenile, she thought, and sipped her coffee as she turned away from the street scene.

It was nice to be pampered. The short bob style complimented her rather full face. She liked the deep red that caught the light, and it was a simple cut to manage when she showered. Very little blow-drying was needed to keep it looking well. Willow was relaxed as the stylist prepared her for her hair to be shampooed.

"Why, Willow, how are you?" A voice from behind her shoulder caught her unawares. It was Mrs. Thornton, a nosy old wagon, albeit an important old wagon at the golf club.

"I'm just in for a quick tidy-up. I suppose I shall see you at the golf fundraiser on Saturday night?" Mrs. Thornton asked. Before Willow had a chance to reply, the woman continued without pausing for breath, bending in closer near to Willow's shoulder, she spoke in a conspiratorial voice, yet loud enough to be heard.

"I heard about the drama at The Sea Horse. Maggie Heffernan told me you were assaulted, it must have been so upsetting." She leaned out again so her kinder words were sure to be heard. "Oh, and I'm sorry to hear about your mother, dear, a lovely woman. Must dash, I'm meeting Maggie actually for afternoon tea."

The stylist stood speechless, holding a cape she was about to put on Willow's shoulders. But Mrs Thornton sashayed away without a backward glance to Willow. The woman was on a mission and Willow wasn't important enough to spend more than a civilised minute or two with.

Willow reddened with anger. The cheek of that old bat. How dare she humiliate her like that! She could have at least lowered her voice and allowed Willow the chance to let her explain the restaurant incident. Willow was mortified; she would never forgive Lacey now. She must be the talk of the golf club. Thinking about the club, Willow thought it strange that she and Derek had not received an invite to the fundraiser. She must talk to him about it at dinner tonight.

The young stylist got to work on Willow. After spending time cutting and blow-drying, she finally got her chance to talk to her client. Pulling off the cape, the stylist shook it with a quick snap before launching into a hundred questions for Willow. She loved a bit of gossip that involved her customers.

"I heard Mrs. T say you were assaulted Mrs. T-S, how horrible! Were you hurt? Were they trying to mug you? It happened to my brother's girlfriend once outside a betting office. Scared her silly it did, emotionally scarred like," the hairdresser chatted on at top speed. It irritated Willow, especially her habit of calling the customers by their initials but there was no point in making a complaint because somehow this young one was loved by the other customers and staff.

Willow paid and left no tip. Her good name was ruined and now she would be the gossip of the salon. She knew by the time the stylist finished today, the story would have grown legs. She would probably have a broken jaw and black eyes by the last report of the evening.

CHAPTER TWENTY-TWO

"Crikey, it's so dusty here." Sally coughed to clear her throat, but it didn't work. "How about we open the skylight so we can actually breathe?"

"Good Lord, look at all the stuff packed up here, where do we even start?" Lacey asked in bewilderment.

She had seemed a lot happier since Sally had agreed to help her, and had jumped at her idea to come back this morning and go through the attic to try and unearth any letters or documents that might be useful.

Surrounded by boxes and bags, the two women each took a corner and settled into looking for evidence. Sally reckoned it was going to be a tougher job than Lacey thought. In her innocence, she probably expected there would be an envelope or a file with her name written on it, just waiting to be opened. Sally hoped she wouldn't be too disappointed.

The cobwebs clung to their hair and clothes as spiders dashed away into the shadows, annoyed at their homes being invaded. Sally took a large cardboard box that was sealed with brown tape. She tried opening it but failed. Then she saw her dad's old toolbox and grabbed a screwdriver.

With the container opened, she discovered all of Rob's old school reports, drawings, and even some birthday cards. The school photos were delightful: how cute Rob looked in his short pants and school tie. She must give him this treasure chest of memories to keep. Opening another box, she found newspapers, lots of copies of the same yellowed and tatty-looking local *Chronicle*. Why were these stored away? Had Dad's affair made the papers? Surely not!

"Hey, Lacey, look here, this one contains loads of newspapers. They are about twenty years old or so, do you think we should study them or will we come back to them?"

"Wow, interesting. How about we bring them downstairs, then we can go through what we find?"

Lacey sounded more optimistic. Until then she had found old clothes and baby stuff that had Willow's name on it or Sally's, but nothing related to her. They continued to search, and found a few other little treasure chests with baby photos.

By lunchtime, they were both shattered and covered in dust. They headed down from the stuffy attic and washed their grubby hands and tidied themselves up before preparing a bite to eat.

"Goodness, Sal, there's a lot to go through in that load of papers."

"Yeah, they must be important in some way. I wonder if it was Mum or Dad that saved these."

The older woman washed some tomatoes while Lacey made a pot of tea.

"How about staying here tonight, and that way we can take some time going through the stuff?" Sally took a variety of cold meats and salad ingredients out of the fridge.

"This is exciting. What will we find?" Lacey's excitement was infectious, but Sally felt obliged to caution her.

"I hope it's going to be good news for you, Sis, and not disappoint you. Have you thought about what if its bad news or something you don't like?" She looked at the young woman whose facial expression clearly revealed her apprehension.

"Mr. Sherman asked me the same thing, the last time I saw him. He recommended I consider some counselling."

"And have you?" Sally was impressed at Philip Sherman's way of thinking. She totally approved of this idea.

"Not really. I mean, what's the worst that can happen? My mother's a druggy, or some low life, or she doesn't want to know me or see me?" The young girl looked out the window. A wistful mood had overtaken her, her mind struggling with such scenarios.

The sound of Sally putting a large bundle of newspapers on the table brought her back to the present and she watched her sister spread the old yellowing papers across the table top. A stale smell of musty paper clung to the air.

"Okay, these are going back eighteen years or so. Will we divide them up and just sort of glance at them first to see if anything jumps out at us? What do you think, Lacey?"

"Sounds like a plan to me," she replied.

The two women took a paper each, and started to go through them, page by page. Headlines of murder, interest rates rising, and politicians or sportspeople misbehaving, were repeated again and again. Nothing seemed to stand out. After two solid hours of scanning, both of them were tired and agreed on a break. It was hard not knowing what to look for. There had been no mention of either their father or Lillian in any of the papers so far. Not even an advert for their father's business. They tried to recall what interests Joe or Lillian had, and whether or not that would lead them anywhere. Everything seemed to be building up to a dead-end.

"I don't suppose Willow would help out?" Sally asked, weary from the search. Her neck and shoulders ached from being bent over the print. She stretched and longed for a hot soak.

"Are you for real?"

Sally saw the disbelief in Lacey's eyes and shrugged her shoulders. "Well, she knew Mum best. She might know something that could at least give us a lead."

"Honestly, do you see her helping me out? I'm enemy number one in her book. She would rather walk over hot coals barefoot than help me, I reckon."

Lacey cupped her face in her hands as she leaned on the table. She looked drained and demoralised. "Maybe if *you* asked her, Sally, she might talk to you. It would be good to have some sort of direction." She picked up a paper at random and leafed through it, adding, "There must be something in these. I mean, why keep them? I'll get on to Mr. Sherman and see if he has found out any more."

"Okay, so our plan of action is you talk some more to Mr.

Sherman and I'll chat to Willow. We'll meet back here on Wednesday seven-thirtyish, what do you think?"

"You make it sound like a top secret military operation, Sal," laughed Lacey.

"Let's take a look at the photos and have a laugh at our wonderful fashion sense back then," Sally was over by the mantelpiece and sipping some water. She didn't feel as confident as she sounded about getting answers, but she would not reveal that to Lacey.

The two women spent the evening pouring over photos of their childhood. Sal stole a few glances at her sister to see if she had noticed the strange family set-up captured in the pictures. But her happy demeanour suggested she had not, and Sal didn't intend to burst yet another bubble for Lacey by breaking that story to her. Some things were best left alone; Sal decided that the photo dilemma would be one of them.

"Hey, have you looked closely at Willow in these, Lacey? More her teenage years really, who does she remind you of?" Sally enquired.

"Ah, a prim and proper young lady! Gosh, did she ever go out without being groomed to perfection? She's a real mini Lillian, isn't she?" Lacey was amazed at the resemblance.

They passed a pleasant evening chatting and recalling stories of their escapades as they grew up. When Sally went to have a hot bubble bath to ease her tired muscles, Lacey watched some television, allowing herself time to unwind mentally with some cheap entertainment on the *Comedy Channel*. It was late when they both retired to bed, tired but content.

CHAPTER TWENTY-THREE

Robert and Aoife were seeing more and more of each other. They hoped they were being discreet at the office, yet it was hard to hide their true feelings from their co-workers. He felt in control of life again, now that he had someone to share it with. He even slept better. But at work the gossips noted the lingering looks between them and the gentle touches when he would lay his hand on Aoife's shoulder, or she would playfully hit his arm when they shared a conversation.

He had called to see Willow a few days after the meal fiasco. He'd dreaded it, but felt obliged to check up on her. She had that way of making those around her feel guilty when really she was the person who stirred things up.

He met Derek instead, as his sister was out with some friends from the flower club. Relieved at the chance to speak openly without worrying that Willow would hear them, Robert was taken aback to hear how concerned his brother-in-law was.

"I know it is still early days in some ways, but surely she should be in better shape by now," Derek said. "I don't seem to help her, Rob. I try, but I end up saying the wrong thing, well, according to her anyway. It's like she couldn't care less about anything or anyone."

"She did do a lot with Mum. So it must be strange for her to do those things alone." Robert tried to reassure the older man.

"But that's just it, Rob. I thought it would be an ideal opportunity for us to do stuff as a couple. No offence, buddy, but your mum was in our life a lot, you know."

Derek paced over and back in the garden. He had been tidying up outside when his brother-in-law dropped in. Robert watched him pull up weeds and snap off dead flower heads with vigour. He seemed wound up, on edge, Robert thought.

"But she's out with friends from the flower club, you said. So that's good, isn't it?" Robert suggested.

"Only because she has turned against the golf set."

Robert raised his eyebrows in a questioning manner. Derek stood up and shrugged.

"We didn't get an invite to some fundraiser they were having. She took it as a personal insult and was muttering on about how they were gossiping about her. How her position in the community was damaged beyond repair, would you believe? I don't know why she would think that or what it's about, though. She'd a couple of glasses of wine drank, so I couldn't get much sense from her."

Derek sounded like a beaten man. He clearly loved his wife, but was struggling to know how to cope with her.

"What gossip would they have?" Robert realised the answer almost as soon he had asked the question. He shot his brother-in-law a look. "She did tell you about the incident at The Sea Horse, didn't she?"

Derek's eyebrows were raised in complete surprise and he shook his head. "Nope, not a word. What happened there, or do I really want to know?" he sighed wearily.

"Well, in a nutshell, she was after a few red wines. Mum was the topic of conversation and Willow was speaking. Lacey took offence and slapped her. I sort of hinted at Lacey to leave and I've not spoken to her since." Robert was still amazed by what had occurred at that meal.

Derek stopped gathering the grass-cuttings and stared at the other man.

"Are you serious? Lacey slapped her? Good Lord, that's not like her. What did Willow say?"

"I can't remember, but it was Mum-related." Robert felt a small pang of annoyance that Derek seemed to blame Willow without knowing the full story. But why had Willow not told her husband? What else did she not say? Was their marriage in danger?

"Fancy a beer, Derek?"

Derek didn't look too good. His face registered trouble. His eyes narrowed and the tight clench of his jaw spelled frustration. Rob wasn't sure now if he should have told him about the incident; maybe he should leave.

"I don't have any in the house. I'm trying to keep the alcohol around here to a minimum." He sounded so tired as he rubbed his fingers through his thinning hair. He threw down the weeds he'd taken the time to gather. Without looking at Robert, he started in towards the house, like a man desperate to escape from everything

"What do you mean 'to a minimum'?" Rob asked, as he followed Willow's husband inside.

"Nothing, nothing," Derek stuttered. "Let's go to the local for one."

* * *

Changed out of his gardening clothes, Derek left a brief note for his wife, explaining that he and Robert were off to Tipson's, then placed it on the kitchen table where she would find it. He doubted whether it would bother her, but he was happier letting her know.

Tipson's bar was busy. They sipped their beers in silence for a while, enjoying the cold alcohol. They watched some of the sport on the big screen and cheered along, forgetting their troubles with the rest of the punters whenever there was a goal scored, or a good effort made. Their conversation was mixed, a bit about sport, some work, some politics, all general chat. Neither smoked.

After two beers each, their chat returned reluctantly to Willow.

"Does she need counselling? Would it help her? Would she even go? She can be so stubborn and bloody private." Derek sounded like he was at his wits' end with his wife.

"She was very close to Mum. Derek, you said earlier about having no drink in the house, why is that? Is it Willow?"

"Have you noticed it, too? She's been having a bit too much at times. Every lunch she has at least two, if not more, glasses of wine. And, on at least one occasion that I know of, the whole bottle. I'm worried about that, too, Rob. Now I know she is holding stuff back from me. It's like her whole life has collapsed, like I don't count. As if she has built a wall up and no-one is allowed near her."

Derek hung his head low. He was relieved to have shared this burden. But was Robert the right one to tell? He was Willow's brother, after all; maybe he wouldn't take kindly to hearing him moan about his sister. Had he just made things worse? It was all so stressful, so bloody annoying.

The men finished their beers and decided to head for home.

"I'll leave the car tonight, Derek, and come get it in the morning," Robert said.

"Grand, Rob. Come in and have a coffee before you go. Willow might be home by now."

They saw her coat in the hall and her handbag on the stairs, but the downstairs of their home was in darkness. Derek got no response when he called Willow's name, so he went up to their bedroom and saw his wife stretched on top of their bed. She was fully clothed and asleep.

When Derek tried to move her, Willow just moaned and rolled over, the smell of wine on her breath. He took her shoes off and managed to get her cardigan off, then took a spare duvet from the linen cupboard and put it over her. Happy she was safe and asleep, he returned downstairs.

"Kettle's boiled if you want a coffee," Robert said. He looked at Derek, "Is she okay?"

"Yeah, sound asleep. Looks like she had a good night." His face betrayed the concern he felt for her and the frustration of not knowing what to do next. He yawned with exhaustion.

"Maybe we can have coffee another time. You should get some rest," Robert said. "I have a taxi arriving any minute and we can chat again tomorrow. Remember, Derek, you're not alone, okay? Keep in touch." They shook hands at the door and Derek locked up and went to sleep in the spare room.

* * *

Back at his house, Rob went straight to his bedroom. He sat wearily on the bed and text Aoife goodnight. She replied in seconds and his heart did a little jump as he read her message. On his way to the bathroom, he stared at the photo on his bedroom wall – his parents and him at his graduation. He reached up, took it down and placed it in a nearby drawer.

Where will this all end? he wondered.

CHAPTER TWENTY-FOUR

The following morning Robert decided to arrange a meeting with Mr. Sherman. Putting away the photograph last night had been a strange moment in his life. He was unsure whether it was his mum or his dad that he was most uncomfortable with. Deep down, it all scared him. No two days were the same any more. Christ, no two hours were the same. It was one hell of a rollercoaster he was riding right now. He decided to deal with one parent at a time, and visiting Sherman's office might sort his father's story out first. He was bothered by the way Joe Taylor had apparently manipulated his mother into accepting Lacey. This mystery needed to be solved; Robert needed answers.

Sitting in his office, he phoned the solicitors and scheduled an appointment later in the week. Maybe it would help Willow to deal with the issues too, if she were to know more about it.

Aoife came in and Rob got up from behind his desk. He kissed her gently, realising how her presence calmed him. He felt better knowing this wonderful woman was in his life.

"I've arranged an appointment to meet with Dad's solicitor, and I'm thinking about asking Willow to come with me. Do you think it would help her?" he asked warily. "I mean, if she had any questions of her own."

"Well, it can't hurt, can it? Like you say, it is giving her an opportunity to voice any concerns she has. Go for it, Rob, ask her to go with you."

Handing Aoife some files from his desk, he went back to his chair and sat down to call his eldest sister.

"Hi, Willow, it's Rob. How are things?"

"Oh, hi. Everything's grand."

"Good, I missed you last night when I called over to yours."

"Is there a reason you phoned, Rob?" He detected impatience in her voice.

"I'm meeting Sherman later in the week, thought you might like to come with me."

"Yeah, whatever. Text me the details, okay?" she grunted down the phone.

"You okay, Willow? Is there anything wrong?" Robert was concerned with her couldn't care less attitude.

"Look, what's with all the questions? I'm just not feeling good, okay? See you during the week, bye."

That was it! Robert found himself cut off; left with nothing to hear but silence. He was already regretting including his eldest sister in his plans. He knew, even without seeing her, she was hung-over.

Anything he discovered he would share with Sally and Lacey, and then maybe, just maybe, they could all return to life as it was before Lillian's death.

* * *

Robert picked up Willow the morning of the meeting at Sherman's. Determined to be pleasant, he found himself being made to feel more like a chauffeur. Willow had waited for him to open the car door for her, and then asked him to turn off the radio as she didn't feel like listening to anything this morning. They drove in silence.

As they entered the solicitor's office, Robert squirmed a little as memories of the will reading flashed into his mind.

"Thank you for seeing us, Mr. Sherman. My father thought a lot of you, sir." Robert settled into the office chair after shaking hands with the elderly gentleman.

"Please, call me Philip. I thought a lot of your father. We were good friends, I must say." Mr. Sherman seemed happy to be helping the family with their queries. "Now, what exactly can I do for you?"

"Well, as you can guess, since Mum died, we have a lot of

questions without answers." Rob gestured towards his sister to include her in his words. Willow sat stern-faced, clearly in no mood to help out her brother.

Robert knew that for Willow, it was plain and simple. Her mother was a saint; the wronged party in this horrid saga. She held her handbag on her lap, like a barrier against anything offensive which Sherman might say.

"Yes, it has been a serious shock for everyone, especially Lacey. How is she? The poor girl must be totally confused."

Robert noticed Willow's shoulders stiffen at the mention of her sister's name. Her face betrayed no emotion, so it was difficult to read what was going through her mind, but there was a noticeable tremor and agitation in her.

"Lacey is very upset, as we all are," Rob replied, glancing uneasily at Willow. Why did he feel she was a time-bomb waiting to go off? Would Sherman push Willow's buttons? Hopefully not.

"So tell me, what is it you want me to discuss with you exactly?" The older man was giving nothing away.

"I'll be blunt, Philip. How did our father get Mum to agree to raise Lacey?" Rob asked with genuine interest. He had leant forward in the chair, throwing weight behind the earnestness of his words.

His sister immediately turned to look at him, venom overflowing from every pore; the bomb was about to explode. She did not wait for Philip to answer, but shot in with her own statement.

"Really, Robert, I think that is rather obvious. Mum is, was, a great woman, full of strength and patience and love. I'm disgusted you could ask such a question, to be honest," Willow spat her words out to the room.

The fuse was lit. Robert sank back in the chair, the scolded schoolboy.

Philip Sherman looked at the cold, bitter woman. "Is that all?" he asked in a low tone, returning to the question in hand. Willow crossed her arms and turned icily away, clutching her handbag tighter.

"For now, I guess. I mean it was some feat on my father's part.

Like my sister says, Mum was a strong lady and it seems a tad out of character," Robert said, a slight blush caressing his cheeks. He felt like he was going behind his parents' backs, searching for secrets and hidden skeletons in the closets.

"As I told Lacey...Robert, Willow," he looked at them both, "I didn't handle Lacey's adoption by your mother."

When the two Taylors remained silent, Philip Sherman took the silence as a sign for him to continue. Joining his hands together, he rested his arms on the file before him.

"It was another firm who dealt with all the contracts. I was your father's friend and I only advised him. He was adamant at the time to keep Lacey's birth mother out of the picture. I mean, this was what she wanted, too, and he respected that so he–"

"Oh, wasn't he the gentleman? He respected *her* feelings?" Willow was seething. "Oh, how in love they must have been! He and his bit of fluff, but who cares if he respected his wife? She raised his– what's the word they use nowadays, *love child*, isn't that it? Can't use bastard any more, can we?"

She rose from her chair and pushed it aside. "I've heard enough of this crap.' She pulled on her coat and glared at Robert.

"Are you coming," she barked. It was an order and not a question; she had finally exploded.

"Willow, please, we need to know more. Mr. Sherman is telling us the story as he knows it. Will you sit down and stay quiet?" Robert was annoyed now. He gestured to the chair before her but instead she stepped towards him.

"Stay quiet? Are you serious? You drag me along here 'to get closure' and instead all I get are insults to my mother's memory. Really, Rob, grow a pair. I'm leaving and I suggest you do the same."

She stormed over towards the door and waited, furious with her brother, daring him to go against her in front of Sherman.

"I assure you, Willow, I did not intend to disrespect your mother's memory," Philip spoke quietly, trying to soothe the agitated woman. He stood up, hoping to appease the woman.

"Mrs. Taylor-Shaw to you, Mr. Sherman," was the icy reply.

"And whether you did or didn't is not an issue I wish to discuss. Rob, are you going to take me home or do I have to get a taxi?"

Robert had remained seated. He was dying of embarrassment. His sister had attacked full-force and he was sure those outside the office had heard the heated outburst. He got slowly to his feet and held out his hand to Philip, a look passing between them that shared an understanding of the irate woman in the office.

"Excuse me, Philip, I'm sorry to leave like this but I must take my sister home. Maybe we can re-schedule for some other day?" Rob felt about ten years old.

"Give me a ring when you are free to meet, Robert. Give my regards to Sally and Lacey, won't you?" The older man closed the file before him and buzzed to his secretary for the next client as they left the room.

Robert was sure the solicitor had often experienced clients having meltdowns; Willow's outburst did not appear to have alarmed him one bit. He, on the other hand, was embarrassed.

His throat tightened and his pulse raced. It reminded him of the day he had got caught in school throwing stones at the windows, and been marched up to the headmaster's office. His mother had been called in and when she was informed of his behaviour, she had twisted it around that it was the other boys' fault. Her Robert would never dream of taking shots at school windows. The headmaster made it clear that Rob had been caught red-handed. Not at all, she'd said, he had obviously been covering for some other boy and that had been that. His mother had stormed out, taking her son with her. She had even gone a step further and written to the school asking for an apology for wasting her time. It was months later before the taunts of "Mummy's Boy" had died down. The incident replayed in his mind as he drove Willow home.

The atmosphere in the car was icy. The heavy silence felt like a physical force around his shoulders and his throat, and he opened the window. This need for air was suffocating him, he couldn't get enough. He dare not speak to his sister; what would he say? How could she humiliate him like that? He had stood up for her in the past, but no more, he promised himself. His driving reflected his anger, speeding up as they approached amber traffic lights instead of taking caution, blasting the horn at other motorists who annoyed him. How could Willow sit there, all calm and content and acting the victim?

They had not spoken since they left the office. Her steely presence dominated the small confines of the car. Robert's emotions were so mixed up right now, and she was acting like she was the injured party. He just wanted to get her home and put distance between them until he calmed down. He didn't want to speak now; he couldn't speak, he was sure his voice would squeak like a child. Drawing up outside her home, he veered with a sudden swerve into the driveway.

"What a morning! Wait until Derek hears about the scandalous behaviour of that solicitor. What a stupid, stupid man. I'm sure there is somewhere we can lodge a complaint about his conduct. I need a lie down, so I won't invite you in, Robert. Oh and Robert? Don't ever pull a stunt like that again."

Willow stomped out without waiting for a reply, slamming the car door behind her. Robert sat stunned. He took in the anger blazing in her eyes as she haughtily nodded her goodbye. Then, turning back towards the house, she walked purposefully away.

He had been dismissed. Rob's outrage was eating him up and he pulled out into the traffic, not knowing where he was headed for. Was this the type of man he was? One whose mother and sister could dictate his life? Was it true what Lacey had said, that Willow was a mirror-image of Lillian? It certainly seemed that way! Maybe Joe Taylor had good reason for his carry-on. Life is never black and white, only many shades of grey. Slight appreciation for his father and what he may have endured began to creep into his heart.

Robert phoned Aoife to explain that he would not be in the office today, but promised to tell her more over dinner later. He drove the car aimlessly, eventually heading towards the coast. His disgust had softened a little, and a walk on the beach would be welcome.

The salty air filled his lungs as he stepped from the car. He took a deep breath in and the loud exhale disappeared into the open space. He watched the usual high jinks of the seagulls twirling over the foamy waves, shrieking their calls to each other as the sky filled with their exchanges. An elderly couple walked hand-in-hand along the strand.

Rob set off for the cliff path. He needed to feel the strong sea breeze on him; it would clear his thoughts and sieve out the good from the bad. Climbing higher on the moss-covered path, the thundering waves crashed with anger beneath him, the taste of brine on his lips from the fresh spray distracting his thoughts from Willow to more pleasant memories of family day outs when they were small. "When we were still a family," he said aloud.

CHAPTER TWENTY-FIVE

The old newspapers, the yellowing corners tattered in places, were spread out on the sitting room floor. Drinking her morning coffee, Sally was looking at them again. There must be a reason why these papers had been kept. They were all from the same year, but various months, so what was the common denominator?

As Sally laid each paper in its own spot on the floor, she took note that it was only the front page and the features section of the broadsheets that had been saved. She reckoned the front page was to verify the dates of the papers, and whatever part of the puzzle they were not seeing was in the features section. She settled down to read the scattered pages once more, from top to bottom, inside and out.

Lacey had arranged to call over that afternoon and they were going to comb through them again together, but Sally continued to make notes while she pored over the pages. The date on them was the year after Lacey's birth. There was nothing major on the front page – Government news, a suspicious death in London, an advertisement for some gents' outfitters. Checking the other front pages, they had similar stories; nothing that would connect to Joe Taylor or Lacey. Sally was convinced she was right in thinking the front pages had been saved just to verify the dates. There must be something inside – an article, or photo, or whatever. If only they had something to go on.

Sipping her coffee, she flicked through the old papers – a spread of wedding dresses; a new shop opening; latest styles from abroad now available in Ireland. There were photos of designers and models enjoying champagne, the top business people of the day all attending.

As Sally read about pearls and sequins, chiffon and lace, she became lost in thoughts of her own. She had always thought she would meet the man of her dreams while on her travels. She believed in a soul-mate; 'what is for you won't pass you' was her motto. But so far, she had not met anyone who ticked all the right boxes. Had she set the bar too high? Some of the men she had encountered so far had been lovely guys, but as a couple they had lacked chemistry. She enjoyed their company, they had made her laugh; others had wined and dined her, and really romanced her; some she had truly given her heart to. But always, a niggling doubt about the next step of commitment held her back. Was this a throw-back from her parents? Had she seen something in their marriage that had slipped into her psyche unawares? She had always believed her parents' marriage to be solid, and in ways it had been. But the secret that they shared must have hung between them every day.

Alongside thoughts of settling down, Sally felt a different pull on her emotions. Not feelings of love or longing for companionship, but a longing for freedom. She was getting itchy feet again; living in one spot for too long was closing in on her. She needed change.

Shaking herself, she concentrated once more on the pages before her. Opening another section, she saw again the news spread about the new shop, with photos of VIPs and dignitaries. "I wonder..." she muttered, and grabbed another paper. Yes, there it was, "Blushing Brides" again, staring at her. A similar article ran in another paper, and in another.

Was there some connection between the shop and Lacey? She felt a frisson of excitement tingling her fingers and toes, but Sally wouldn't allow it to take over. Should she phone Lacey with her suspicions? What if she was wrong? But it made sense, it was the only thing that connected all the papers and it was close to Lacey's year of birth. Definitely, "Blushing Brides" was important.

Maybe Mr. Sherman could shed some light on the subject. Of course, she could just Google the shop and see if it was still in existence. No, better to wait until Lacey called over. It would be wonderful if they uncovered a part of her birth mother's identity together.

Sally was thoroughly enjoying playing detective. Travelling alone had heightened her sense of observation. With her, safety was always paramount on her trips and she was naturally attentive to her surroundings. That same perception and vigilant eye was proving useful now.

She was starting to fix some lunch when her phone rang.

"Hey, Sally, are you able to talk?" The words gushed out at her before she could even say hello.

"Rob, what's up? Yeah, I can talk. Are you okay?" He sounded agitated, his voice breathless.

"Could you meet me here at the office? I'll get a sandwich in for you."

It sounded important; worry edged its way into her mind.

"Can't do I'm afraid, I'm waiting on Lacey to call over, and I don't want to miss her. Can we meet later?" Sally could tell he was anxious by the way he spoke. *Not more bad news, please*, she prayed in silence.

"Okay, I suppose so. You'll drop by this evening then, 'bout six? How is Lacey? I haven't seen her since the restaurant debacle."

Rob's guilt at not contacting his young sister could be heard in his voice.

"Still fretting about things. This has really shaken her. Willow doesn't help, and she's been really unsettled since–"

"God! Don't mention Willow! That's what I want to talk to you about," he snapped.

"Oh, is she okay? What's happened?"

"I'll fill you in tonight. I'm beginning to think she really is deranged." Robert's voice was a secretive whisper, but Sally realised he probably didn't want to be overheard in the office.

"Oh God, this should be good," groaned Sally. "See you tonight."

She wondered what Willow had been up to now. Robert's reaction had surprised her. He could normally handle Willow, so it must be something big if he was calling her a nut job. What an entertaining day lay ahead! The bridal shop thingy, if she was right, and Rob's tale of woe about Willow – that should keep her occupied. Between playing detective for one sibling and counsellor to another, Sally felt her career options shifting continuously. She chuckled at her own humour.

* * *

The bundle of newspapers Lacey had taken home with her had yielded nothing. Well, nothing she could detect, anyway. They were dated two years after her birth, but she couldn't figure out why they had been kept. Travelling over to Sally, she hoped her sister might have discovered a clue.

The afternoon was bright; the sun blazing in the sky, children laughing and playing outdoors, a positive energy and buzz in the late summer days. Lacey thought about the task ahead with Sal. It was a shame to be locked indoors on such a lovely day. Maybe they could break off for a while and have a stroll in the local park.

As she parked and got out of her car, Lacey was in an upbeat mood.

"Hi, Sally, I brought some fresh strawberries with me. With the sun out and the fruit, I still feel really summerish." Successive warm days were a rarity in Ireland. The people were more in tune with wet, gloomy, damp weather.

"Great! I have some ice cream but no cream. Any luck with the papers?"

Sally didn't want to mention her own thoughts yet, in case Lacey had discovered anything. The more her little sister discovered on her own, the better. It would help give her control over her life and regain confidence if she was dictating her circumstances, after suffering such a terrible shock.

"Not a thing, Sal. Then again, I didn't know what I was looking for. I think I over-scrutinized everything, if that's possible." Lacey's voice held a tone of weariness and frustration.

While Sally filled two bowls with the fruit and ice cream, Lacey grabbed the spoons. They strolled out to the garden, the sunshine soothing, a soft breeze tickling their bare shoulders.

"What about you, any luck?" Lacey asked, scooping some dessert onto her spoon.

"I may have." Sally glanced at her sister for a reaction. The spoon fell from Lacey's hand onto her lap. Ice cream smeared her clothes.

"Really? Oh Sal, what? What have you discovered? Tell me, please tell me."

"It's only a hunch, but did Mr. Sherman give you any idea about your mum's career?"

"No, nothing." Lacey's eyes sparkled with excitement.

"Finish your ice cream and we'll take a look then," Sally teased.

Watching Lacey gulping down her desert, Sally realised her young sister was still growing up. The poor girl had had more to contend with already than most would ever endure in a lifetime.

"Finished. Please, Sal, tell me." Lacey was bouncing with enthusiasm, like a five-year-old being offered a treat for being good. She had ice cream smeared on her chin, and her face was alight with excitement. Sally couldn't help but laugh.

"Well, as I was going through the papers, one particular event was in all of them," Sal explained, leading the way back indoors.

Grabbing some kitchen paper, she gave a piece to Lacey and indicated to her chin.

"Go on." The young girl wiped her face and followed Sally into the room.

"There's an opening of a designer bridal shop, and all the VIPs and dignitaries of the day attended." Sally found the feature in one of the editions and showed it to Lacey.

"Wow, a designer," muttered Lacey, as she sank into the armchair. Her eyes searched the photos. Was this her first clue to her birth mother? Could this be the link that would start the chain of events to find her mum? Her eyes were glued to the papers, scouring each page, and letting it all sink in.

CHAPTER TWENTY-SIX

By the time Willow woke from her previous night's sleep, it was almost dark outside again. She felt funny. The sleep had been more like a coma than a snooze.

"Derek?" she called out to the silent house.

What time was it? She searched for her watch on the locker, but it wasn't there. She tried to focus, but her thoughts were all jumbled. She was half-dressed and light was fading fast outside her window. Her stomach rumbled. When had she last eaten?

Throwing her dressing gown on over her clothes, Willow decided she needed some coffee.

"Derek, are you home?" she called out again. Still no reply.

On the kitchen table was a note in her husband's handwriting, *'Gone out for a bite to eat, back later, x.'*

She made a pot of coffee and sat alone in the dark kitchen. The silence in the house seemed to scream out at her. It had an empty, lonely feeling about it that unsettled her. How often had she sat alone here before and never been bothered by it? This felt different. A strange uneasiness was present and for the first time ever, she worried where her life was heading. The house was too damn big, yet it still felt claustrophobic.

Was this the life she had waiting for her? Empty years filled with nothing? She knew she was slipping into a depression, but the ache inside her from Lillian's death was growing each day. The empty space in her heart was filling with longing and it hurt. It hurt so badly.

Was there any need for her to go on? It would be so easy to close her eyes forever and then this misery would cease. Derek would cope. She believed that without question. She could be with her dear mum again. Lillian's smiling face flashed before Willow.

"Mum, I need you so much," she cried out to the silent house. Her voice echoed in the bleakness of her surroundings.

"I don't want to stay here," she mumbled, and quickly dashed upstairs.

A change of clothes and fresh make-up, and Willow stepped out into the night air. It took several deep breaths to settle her and she started to walk. This was exactly what she needed: to be outside, to clear her head and settle her emotions.

Derek could wait. She was annoyed with him. He could have wakened her and the two of them could have gone for a meal together. He hadn't shown an ounce of interest in including her in his plans for the evening, so she could do the same. Strolling along, she checked her phone. No missed calls. So he definitely hadn't intended to include her. There was one text message from Robert; a brief *We need to talk* flashed on the screen.

Robert. There was another man who needed a strong woman behind him. Aoife was a nice young lady but did she have the stamina needed to push Robert in the right direction? Willow had doubts. The events from the solicitor's office blazed in her mind, and the rubbish that awful man had spouted about her mother. The few shots of vodka she had downed when she returned home had calmed her anger a little.

Love child? Talk about turning a sow's ear into a silk purse. There had been no love involved, she was sure of it. Her father's head had been turned by some jumped-up tramp who wanted a sugar daddy for herself. Nothing more!

She must have been a smart jumped-up tramp, all the same. After getting pregnant, she obviously persuaded the old fool to raise the child! Willow almost smiled when she realised that Lacey's mother may have been shrewd in her actions. Maybe she was another woman who was strong, like Lillian and Willow. Why, if she squeezed hard enough into her heart, she even found an inch of admiration for how the tramp had pulled the sordid thing off. The lit-up sign of a taxi caught her eye. Climbing in, she told him to take her to a bar suitable for a woman of her age and standing.

Arriving at the bar, she thought she really should text Derek. An entire day was almost over and she had missed most of it. Looking around her, there were couples chatting and sharing the night together. Taking out her mobile phone, she text the name of the pub to him and asked him to join her. She waited, sipping her drink.

* * *

Finding the house still in darkness on his return, Derek didn't bother to check on Willow. The highlights from the latest Open Golf tournament were on, his phone was in his coat pocket on the hallstand, and his wife must still be asleep upstairs. If he was honest with himself, he was relieved at not having to deal with her now. He was also ashamed at even having that thought.

* * *

Robert was waiting for Sally to call over. It had been a crazy few days, although the walk on the beach had cooled his temper. He was not used to having his whole life view challenged but, since the will reading, the world as he knew it had changed beyond recognition.

The family was disintegrating at breakneck speed. He needed to take charge and find out what they needed to know, or at least clear the air between them. His family was crumbling and he was determined to stop it. He and Sal could decide on an agenda and tackle matters together. It felt good to him to have focus again

He couldn't recall what time Sally said she would call over. Maybe he should phone Derek and include him, too. He would probably be the best one to handle Willow and he'd already said he was desperate to understand his wife. Good luck to him on that one! Willow had shown what a force of strength she could be when challenged.

Derek's phone rang three times and then cut out. Strange, it was like he had cut Rob off. As he put the phone down, he heard a car pull up outside. Preparing to greet Sally, he opened the door and found himself facing his flustered-looking brother-in-law. Derek was definitely on a mission.

"I was just phoning you," Rob said, not liking the troubled face facing him. "What's up, Derek? You look agitated. Is something wrong?"

"Your sister, she's not well. I mean, mentally."

"What has she done now?"

"Where do I begin?"

Both men sighed; Derek in total frustration, Robert in wary trepidation.

CHAPTER TWENTY SEVEN

The "Blushing Brides" fashion show had certainly been the event of the year, but the coverage did not provide much information for Lacey to go on. She dissected each article and picked through photos, but there was no mention of a woman with a name like Karen; the owner was named Stella. Sally was sorely disappointed.

"I'm sorry, Lacey," she apologised, looking at her sister. "I really thought I was on to something."

"Its fine, it was worth a shot." Lacey shrugged her shoulders, disillusioned.

"You have checked your birth certificate, haven't you?" Sally's expression signalled that she knew she was asking the obvious, but they both knew people often ignored what was right under their nose.

"Yes," Lacey replied, "and my mother is named as Lillian." When Lacey had first discovered this written lie, she had known then that both women must have agreed on the deceit together. How else could they name Lillian as her mum? She dare not think of how they had managed the whole thing. Her birth mum must have used Lillian's name throughout the pregnancy and the birth.

"How did they manage that? Is it too outrageous to think they both were named Lillian?" Sally asked.

"Unless there are two Lillian Taylors, I have no idea." The younger girl stretched her arms in the air, keeping her views on the deceit to herself. She closed and folded the newspapers, and put them in a tidy pile on the floor beside her.

"So what's next?" Sally asked, not sure of the next step.

"Philip Sherman is next. He must know more than he's telling me. I've contacted the adoption authority, too," Lacey told her.

"Really? What can they do?"

Sally stood up to stretch. Being hunched over the papers had her neck and back aching.

"Not a lot, as I've not got my mum's name. If I had that, it would solve so much. But I'm in touch with another group called National Adoption Contact Preference Register and they were very helpful. They have my name and details, so if my mum is looking for me then there is a good chance of us finding each other." Lacey flicked the corners of some pages of the newspaper in front of her, her frustration evident.

"I'm meeting Robert shortly, if you want to come along." Sally knelt beside her sister. "Maybe going over to talk to Rob will take your mind off things for a while?"

"Nope, don't think so, Sal." Lacey shook her head vigorously.

"He's worried about Willow, he rang me earlier. I'm sure he wouldn't mind you coming along, too."

"No thanks, I have absolutely no desire or intention of wasting time on Willow at the moment. She has her husband and the two of you willing to pick up after her, so I reckon there is nothing to worry about." The younger woman was bitter, but she was not going to fall out with her sister over this.

"We're here for you, too, Lacey," Sally assured her. "Don't be so angry. Willow's taken Mum's death really badly and right now she's lashing out, that's all. She'll come round when she settles."

Lacey took Sally's hands in hers, and spoke with gentle understanding. "Sally darling, you are amazing. I am so grateful for your support and I know life will calm down again. But right now I'm not, nor have I any intention, of wasting energy on Willow. Like I said, she has plenty of people running after her."

Sally nodded in understanding. Her eyes looked tired as she directed her gaze to the pile of newspapers.

Lacey lifted her bag and got ready to leave. She turned and swept up the papers she had folded, as if she had suddenly realised something.

"I'll take these, if that's alright. I might go over them again. Enjoy your evening with Rob. I'll catch up with you over the weekend or next week."

The two women hugged each other and Sally walked her sister to the car. Lacey felt a bit guilty about not going to Rob's; she didn't want Sal to think she was ungrateful.

"Thanks, Sal. I really mean it."

"No thanks needed. Mind yourself, okay?"

Lacey headed for home, stopping only to pick up an Indian takeaway meal. It was disappointing about the bridal shop and that they still had no definite leads, but all was not lost yet. Lacey decided to contact Philip Sherman and try teasing more information out of the man.

After she had wolfed down the spicy meal, she pulled out her journal, looking again at the sparse information. There were so many gaps to be filled in.

Once she had changed for bed, she got down to tackling the bundle of newspapers. She was convinced that the bridal shops held a clue. In every edition, there were photos and articles about "Blushing Brides". In the older papers, there were photos of the shop celebrating its first anniversary along with fashion shows that were held.

Lacey scrutinised each photo in detail. The owner, Stella, was always centre-stage, yet Lacey couldn't see any family resemblance to anyone in the photos. Determined to dig deeper, she turned on her laptop and Googled the business.

"Blushing Brides" was a popular name in the wedding business. The shop that appeared in print was no longer operating, so Lacey searched the owner's name. Although the name was fairly common, she couldn't locate a match for the woman in any of the papers. Nevertheless, she wrote down "bridal shop" and "Stella" into her notebook, and placed a question mark beside them.

So, what next? Lacey phoned Philip Sherman. It was a chance she had to take and hoped he wouldn't mind her contacting him at home.

"Mr. Sherman, it's Lacey Taylor. Sorry for disturbing you, but

I really need to talk to you."

"Lacey, how are you? I was wondering when you'd phone." She could sense his smile in his voice. He really was a kind man. Not stopping to answer his question on how she was feeling, she ploughed into her reason for phoning.

"Sally found a bundle of newspapers in the attic, and we came across a lot of articles about a bridal business. Does that ring any bells with you?" Lacey held her breath, awaiting his reply. She knew she was being slightly rude again, but she really couldn't help it.

There was a prolonged silence. Playing with her hair, wrapping it around her fingers, Lacey kept her mouth shut for a few moments. She didn't want to push the solicitor, but she felt she would burst with anticipation.

"Well, does it?" Her impatience gained the upper-hand. He didn't deserve this impolite intrusion on his private time yet she needed answers.

"Lacey, I'm not sure. Your mother, I mean, Lillian, was a very fashion conscious woman; would she have kept the papers? Some of her friends did own boutiques, I remember." Slight annoyance rang in his voice, Lacey needed to remember he did not have all the answers.

"Oh right." She felt so discouraged that she regretted the phone call, regretted disturbing him.

She had never allowed for the fact that Lillian may have stored the papers for reasons known only to her. Not everything from the past in the attic would relate to Lacey. She was acting selfishly, and admitted that to herself.

"Thanks, Philip. Sorry again, I'll talk to you some other time." Sad and disheartened, she realised the call had been a waste of both their time.

"Lacey, if anything comes to light I'll contact you, I promise. Okay?" The elderly man sounded upset, too. "Before you go, how's Willow?"

"Willow?" The question surprised Lacey. "I'm sure she's fine. Why?"

"Good, good. Tell Robert I said hello and to contact me again if he needs to."

Now Lacey was thoroughly confused. Why the fuss about Willow? Had something happened to her sister? Robert and Sally were meeting tonight to discuss Willow, and now Philip Sherman was asking for her.

Lacey tried to push it out of her mind. Her older sister could look after herself, couldn't she? Lacey had more important work to do, and so once more delved into the old newspapers with vigour. She wasn't letting this go.

Two hours later, she was shattered. Her head could take no more. Closing up her journal and tidying up the sitting room, she decided it was bedtime. In the morning she would ring Sally and solve the mystery of Willow's well-being. Maybe it was time to take her head out of the clouds and remember there were others who may need help, too. All of the Taylors had been surprised about Lacey's parentage, so she needed to stop being self-absorbed and think of them as well.

But the photos of brides and dresses from the old yellowing papers pushed all her good intentions aside, and she fell asleep to dreams of weddings, and churches, and confetti that fell from the skies.

Stella appeared in her dreams. She was standing at an altar as Lacey, dressed in cream lace and heavy brocade, walked up the aisle by her father. But as they approached the altar, Stella wasn't standing there alone; another woman was near her. When this woman turned towards Lacey, her face was missing. A complete blank.

CHAPTER TWENTY-EIGHT

"This must be serious, Derek, for you to call over to me." Rob followed his brother-in-law into the kitchen.

"I came home yesterday afternoon and she was thrown across the bed asleep. She was well out of it, Rob. I covered her with a duvet and headed back out for a bite to eat. I left a note," Derek added quickly, when he saw Robert was going to interrupt.

"When I came back home later last night, I watched some telly and when I went upstairs to bed she was missing."

"Missing? Is she still missing?" Robert's eyes were wide with disbelief.

"She arrived home this morning. I tried to phone her last night when I realised she was gone, and only then saw a text that she had sent earlier, asking me to join her." Derek was upset, his arms flew about the air as he explained, his voice steeped with emotion.

"Is she okay? I mean, she isn't hurt or anything?" Rob asked.

"She has the mother of all hangovers and refuses to tell me where she was, or what happened." Derek didn't try to hide his despair. "I couldn't face going home straight after work today, so here I am." He slumped down into a nearby chair at the table, and held his head in his hands.

"Look, she definitely needs counselling. She lost it in the solicitor's office, totally flipped–"

Derek's head jerked up, startled by Rob's words. "Hang on, the solicitor's office? Why was she at a solicitor's office? Why didn't she tell me she was going there?"

He was angry now. He didn't know whether his wife was losing it or just deliberately pushing him out of her life.

139

"Derek, Sally is on the way over here. I asked her to call because I felt Willow might listen to her about seeking help. The solicitor's office was my idea. I needed to chat with him and thought Willow could, too. I thought by talking to Mr. Sherman, she might find closure over Mum's death and Lacey's revelation—"

"Hold it right there, Rob. You decided what was best for my wife without talking to me? Now you're arranging for Sally to talk to her, again without consulting me in events. What is this? Derek obviously can't handle Willow so I'll take over the job? Robert, the big man of the family, will sort it all out and the rest of us will fall into line, is that it?" He stood face-to-face with Willow's brother, his rage barely controlled, his closed fists clenched by his side.

"It's not like that, mate, not at all." Robert's voice was calm. He had the height advantage, but Derek wasn't going to let that intimidate him.

"Oh, but I think it is, MATE! Stay out of our lives from now on. I came here hoping you could maybe help me, but it's you and the others that are pushing her over the edge. Do not include Willow in any more bright ideas you have, do you hear me?"

His voice dripping with sarcasm, he pushed past Robert, shouldering him as he went by.

"You Taylors have always interfered with our marriage," he shot back, and then stormed out of the front door, not bothering to close it. Derek's fury at the Taylor family annoyed Rob. Grabbing his car keys, Rob followed his brother-in-law out and drove to Aoife's.

* * *

Sally was surprised her brother was not at home. She tried the doorbell again, then walked round to the back garden and peeped in the windows; there was no sign of him. She took out her mobile and received only his voicemail. After leaving a message, she thought maybe he was over at Willow's, so she drove towards her sister's house.

It was now almost seven in the evening. For the first time ever, Sally felt tired and fed up of the family's dramas. It seemed an age since she had actually indulged herself. At a standstill in the evening traffic, cars and taxis all around her, the constant drone of engines, some revving eager to be moving, Sally decided to hell with it all. She changed direction and drove to the beach.

Sitting on some rocks, Sally composed herself and, after some long deep breaths, felt more settled. The crashing of the waves further out brought to mind memories of good times; nights she had spent sleeping near a beach in campsites. Heaven, she remembered sadly.

Taking in the serene scene before her, she realised how she missed travelling; the freedom of each day being her own to do what she wanted; the peace of knowing any decision she made affected no-one else, that there would be no fall-out from something she said or did. Claustrophobic was what she felt.

Maybe Lacey was correct. Willow had Derek to lean on; Robert was a strong businessman who should be capable of sorting himself out, and he had Aoife; and Lacey…Well, life's a bitch and unfortunately her little sister had found that out at a younger age than most, that's all!

Yet, deep in her heart she worried for Lacey. Where would this hunt for her birth mother lead her? Would it be a disaster, or the start of something special?

'No, no, no,' Sally murmured aloud. 'I'm here for me, not others. This is my time, right here, right now.' She shook herself and gazed out to the dark sea. She needed to focus on her own desires in life; her needs were important, too. Being torn apart by all her siblings was not healthy.

The tide was out and there were only a handful of people about. While dogs chased sticks which their owners flung into the water, children collected shells and inspected rock pools. It was all so idyllic and tranquil, so different from her ruffled home life.

Sally strolled along the beach. The strong high cliffs were peppered with seagulls resting for the night. Only the odd screech of a gull broke up the soothing sound of the waves breaking. She remembered the evening she had come here with friends for an impromptu sing-song around their disposable barbeques. They had gone exploring in the caves and been mesmerised by the many colours mirrored in the cave roof from the water-pools beneath their feet. It was the rippling of these wondrous colours and the dark shadowy corners, teasing you to venture a little bit further, that had encouraged her to travel. There was a whole world out there waiting to be explored, just like the caves of her teenage years.

Darkness was starting to close in.

Reaching the car park, Sal felt refreshed. The salty sea air had cleansed her troubled mind. After Christmas, she would leave, regardless of how the Taylors were. There were areas of deep forests and open oceans waiting for her footprints, and she could not refuse their calling to be explored.

She drove home. Robert, Willow and Lacey could wait until the morning. The world would not collapse in one night just because she, Sally Taylor, had taken time off.

CHAPTER TWENTY-NINE

Lacey and Philip Sherman took their seats in the café, Tea for Two. A popular place, the busy shop was perky with the sound of music and chit-chat. There was a vibrancy about it that would lift even the darkest of thoughts or feelings. The red gingham-patterned tablecloths were cheery and the bold modern prints on the walls kept the tearoom fresh and welcoming.

While Philip was taking what he apologised was an important call, Lacey ordered tea and cream scones. She hoped he would be able to give her something definite to work on, but she also needed to apologise for the way she had handled their last phone call.

"Sorry about that, Lacey." He returned to the table and sat down.

"I ordered some tea and scones. I hope that's okay."

"Perfect. Okay, let's get to the business at hand," he muttered.

"Look, before we start, Philip, I need to say sorry. I was rude and selfish the last time we spoke, and you have been nothing but kind to me."

The solicitor smiled gently. "I know what it's like to be young and impatient. I accept your apology and thank you. Now, have no more worries about it."

He cleared his throat and fetched a small moleskin notebook from his inside coat pocket.

"So you've news?" Lacey was excited to see him produce the jotter.

"I asked my wife about the bridal boutique story. I hope you don't mind, but fashion is not my forte." He stopped as the waitress arrived to their table. A pot of tea and scones were placed in front of them, along with a pot of jam and some fresh cream.

They both thanked the young girl who served them.

"I didn't reveal any names, Lacey. I only asked her if she remembered anything about that shop."

"It's alright, I don't mind," Lacey assured him. "Anyone who can shed light is welcome. Did she recall something?"

"Apparently, the woman who owned 'Blushing Brides' is the wife of some ambassador, she supported a charity of sorts, for those starting off in business. My wife said Stella was only a front for the business. It was the designer of the dresses that was the real star. A young woman, mid-twenties, had had some minor success before the charity trust got behind her. After that night, she became very popular. All the top boutiques and shops stocked her designs and, after being in business here, she also sold dresses abroad."

Lacey sat enthralled. Was the designer her mum? Her stomach was doing somersaults with both fear and excitement. Did she dare interrupt him? Ask the one question that was burning within her?

Philip Sherman paused and calmly buttered his scone. He hadn't noticed her silent stare, willing him to say they were on the road to finding her mother. The noise of the café melted into the air. Lacey's thoughts were floating on her own cloud of possibilities, and reality around her had disappeared.

"Anyway, as I was saying, the designer moved abroad. My wife remembers that a group of the old golf set attended one of her many fashion shows. I asked her if Lillian went, and she said no. Lillian had no interest in the designer and she was very touchy about the big deal that was being made of her." Philip looked up and caught Lacey's intense expression. "Sorry, Lacey, I'm rabbiting on. I suppose you want to know who she is?"

She nodded vigorously, unable to speak. He actually had a name? She could not believe it. Her cloud of joyful images was about to fill the whole sky.

"Her name is Cora Maguire. I know I said her name began with a K and this is a C, but my memory is shaky with age. So, what do you think?" He picked up his cup and calmly drank it, seemingly unaware of the importance of the news he had just shared.

Lacey's eyes were like big saucers on her slim face. Big, hot tears fell silently on her cheeks. Her hands were clutched to her chest and she had not touched her scone or tea.

"Oh, I'm sorry, pet. I never meant to upset you. Here, take this, it's clean." He looked around the cafe, clearly embarrassed and a little uncomfortable by the scene.

Lacey blew her nose on the crisp blue handkerchief. This was so overwhelming – going from nothing about her mum to finally knowing a name. She started to shake. This was a definite concrete clue at last. Oh my God!

Finally, after composing herself and drying her tears, Lacey smiled at Philip and watched his shoulders sag with relief. Settling herself again, she smiled at a woman sitting nearby, who had been throwing dirty looks at Philip, probably wondering what he had done to upset his young companion.

"Do you think Cora Maguire is my mother? I mean honestly, do you think it?" Her hands were clasped to her chest like in prayer.

"Maybe seventy-five percent sure, Lacey. Not one hundred percent, but I do recall your dad saying he put aside money as a business investment for your mum. Maybe that was the business. Look, Lacey, your dad and your real mother were not some quick fling, I do know that. There was an age gap but he really did care for her. Times were different back then. Respectable people did not up and leave their families, it wasn't like now."

The woman who had stared at Philip was leaving. Passing by their table, she grunted her displeasure at his behaviour and smiled sympathetically at Lacey.

"So you think if it was nowadays, Dad might have considered leaving Lillian?" Wow, this was a whole different level to deal with.

She was totally flabbergasted. This was a completely different light on events. But somehow she didn't see Joe Taylor leaving his three other children. Whatever he had been, he was a family man.

He had loved all of his kids; there was no doubt about that.

"Let's go for a walk." Philip Sherman put a finger to his short collar to loosen off the tightness; he seemed uncomfortable in the busy cafe. Once out in the fresh air, they walked together towards a nearby park.

"Can I ask you something?" Lacey stopped and paused. "Would you have told me this if I hadn't pressed you on it?"

He stood silent for a few minutes, the cool air refreshing them both. He could only answer honestly. "No. If you hadn't returned and asked questions, I would have let it rest. Why would I tear a family apart? I thought Lillian's letter and your father's would have explained everything—"

She grabbed his arm roughly. "What did you say about my father, a letter?" Her grip was tight as she held on to him. Gently, he took her hand and held it.

They stood and stared at each other, the colour draining from both their faces. This had been a morning of incredible revelations. Philip let go of her and Lacey held her head in shock. She twisted from side to side, not knowing what to do next.

"Lacey, we need to sit down. Over here, there's a bench, come on." He held her elbow and directed her to the timber park bench, then sat beside her.

"You never knew your dad left a letter for you?" he asked in a hushed tone. "Please tell me Lillian did not withhold it? This is significant, Lacey. Are you sure you never received it?" He was pale and his eyes showed disbelief.

Her hands were shaking, her breathing came in gasps. "Received it? This is the first I've heard of it! Dear Lord, where is it now? Would she have destroyed it? Surely she didn't hate me so much to do that?"

She stared at her companion in total disbelief. Philip appeared uneasy, his hand on his chest with shock.

"But she may have hated your father enough to do it," he whispered sadly.

Lacey saw the horror in his eyes, the perspiration on his brow. She felt dizzy. Her stomach was in knots; she really didn't know how to react. Right now, her legs were weak and she couldn't summon the strength to stand. Flashes of Lillian and her father appeared before her. There was so much to take in, Lacey wondered if she would ever be able to think straight again.

Glancing at Philip, he appeared just as worried and upset as her. What can of worms had opened between them this morning? Sitting on the hard bench, they both realised the horrors of Lillian's actions by not disclosing Joe's letter. What was next for them?

CHAPTER THIRTY

Lacey sat in her sitting room and stared at the walls closing in around her. The tightness in her chest hurt, her head was fuzzy and dizzy, and her legs trembling and weak. She lay down and pulled the bronze throw over her as she started to shiver. Wrapping the blanket more tightly around her, she didn't realise she was crying until big teardrops wet her cheeks and flowed down to her chest. She gave in and her sobbing grew stronger until her body shook all over.

She couldn't control it; a release valve had opened and every raw emotion that had been pent up inside sought its escape.

Philip Sherman had insisted on bringing Lacey home to her apartment block. She had been so pale, her breath coming in short sharp gasps, that he'd pleaded with her to call a doctor. Lacey didn't think he had seemed too well himself.

She lay wrapped in the comforting wool blanket and cried herself into a fitful sleep. Each nerve in her body ached and tingled; her eyes were puffy. In her sleep she tossed and twisted on the sofa, nightmare after nightmare tormenting her, visions of Lillian looming over her, laughing menacingly and pointing at the fireplace. In the centre of a lively fire, burning vigorously, were sheets of paper. Lacey could make out her father's handwriting but as she desperately lunged to save the letter, it would disappear into ashes.

In other dreams she would be reaching to stop Lillian striking a match to start the fire. Even her father stood laughing, then he and Lillian would turn their backs on her and walk away hand-in-hand.

It was late evening when she finally woke. The dull sky was leading into night and it was cold in the apartment. Her head had cleared a bit and her thoughts settled on what she should do now. Finally, she summoned the strength to get up from the sofa and make herself something to eat.

Opening a tin of tuna, she mixed it with some shredded lettuce and diced peppers, then spread it on a sandwich, savouring each bite as she gathered her thoughts together. Breathing in deeply and twisting her aching neck from side to side, she slowly began to feel calmer.

Before going to bed, she took out the journal and paused a few moments before writing her latest news inside. Beside "Name", she wrote "Cora Maguire" and beneath that she put "Career: Fashion Designer".

It was soul destroying to think that her search for her real mother was taking her down a path of deception and lies. Should she share the news with the others, or was it better to let sleeping dogs lie?

But what if her father's letter was hidden somewhere at Sally's – their old home? She would have to explain to Sal why she wanted to search her parents' bedroom.

In Willow's case, Lacey knew she would not divulge anything to her oldest sister. After all, Willow would probably accuse Lacey of lying, making it all up to further discredit Lillian. Robert wasn't proving to be the support she'd thought he'd be either. If Sally wanted to tell him, then she could, but Lacey had no real thoughts on it either way.

Tomorrow she would phone Sally and explain the latest plot twist to her. Then she would phone Mr. Sherman and ask if he could recall definitely giving Lillian the letter at the reading of Joe Taylor's will.

Staring into the bathroom mirror, she took in her appearance. The puffiness around her eyes was reducing, but her damp hair stuck to her ears. Her head was like mush, her life a rollercoaster, and she may as well smile because she was all cried out. Having satisfied her hunger, she brought her coffee into her bedroom and hopped into bed.

First thing next morning, Lacey set about making her calls.

"Mr. Sherman, please. It's Lacey Taylor."

"I'm sorry, Ms. Taylor, but he isn't in his office today."

"Well, can you tell me when he will be in, please? It's important I speak with him." Lacey couldn't hide her disappointment.

"I'm not sure when Mr. Sherman will be back in the office, would one of his associates be any help to you? I could arrange an appointment for you in the morning with–"

"No, no, no, I need to speak with Philip." Lacey was getting cross with the secretary. "It's urgent, is he on holiday? Maybe I can catch up with him at home?"

"Mr. Sherman is not at home and is not in a position to handle any work right now."

"What do you mean?"

The assistant at the other end of the phone delayed answering. Lacey realised that she was deciding whether she should tell her any more, so So Lacey pleaded with her again.

"Please, we are family friends. I have his home number so I can ring his house or you can tell me, what is it?"

"Mr. Sherman is in St. Martin's Private Hospital. Thank you for calling."

"But how? When? Hello? Hello?" The phone line was dead.

Shaking, Lacey placed the phone down on the table. Philip Sherman was in hospital? He couldn't be. She had been with him just yesterday; he had driven her home. This was awful. Worse than that, it was dreadful news.

Was she the reason? Had the meeting yesterday upset him that much? Maybe Willow was right, maybe the secrets and clandestineness of her family history was taking its toll – first on Lillian and now the family solicitor. What if, by trying to find her mother, Lacey had brought misfortune or bad luck to her or her designer business? What if the press took up her mother's love-child story, it might damage the goodwill she held in the trade?

Should she abandon it all? Just walk away and accept the cards life had dealt her?

Questions, nothing but questions, yet the answers eluded her. Every time she did manage to prise open a door in this messy puzzle, it didn't lead to a resolution, but just a more tangled web of bloody questions!

"Blast it, damn it, curse it anyway!"

She threw a cushion across the room in frustration and watched in horror as it expertly hit the vase of dead flowers and sent it toppling onto the floor. Stagnant water spilled out and dead leaves and petals stuck to the mess on the carpet.

"Bloody effing hell," she roared, as she went to find a cloth to clean up.

CHAPTER THIRTY-ONE

Willow was out and about doing what she did best – spending money. She felt a little groggy, as she had stayed up late watching a film on television. It was easier than going to bed and risking conversation with Derek. Relations between them were strained at the moment, ever since the misunderstanding; it was easier to call it that than the night she went out and forgot to come home until the morning.

Why was he making such a fuss? It wasn't like she had ever done it before. He had picked on her about drinking, too. She was angry that he found so many faults with her and yet never looked in the mirror. If she were to point out his failings, it would make for exhausting reading. He hadn't exactly been particularly understanding since her mother died. After all, grief had no time limit to it. He put more effort into his bloody meetings and business trips than he did to making sure she was coping with her sorrow. Plus, he was always quick to offer his services to others but she was never a priority, as far as she could see.

So she enjoyed a few drinks more than normal? It was a short term issue, for God's sake. Why, last night she only drank two glasses of wine while watching the film. It was madness at her age to be counting her drinks as if she was a young one sneaking alcohol from her parents. Briefly, she recalled Lacey had drawn attention to Willow's drinking that night they'd all been at her apartment, even though the point of them gathering was to read the letter. Saint bloody Lacey!

No, she would not allow her day to be ruined by Derek and Lacey. She rummaged through the shop rails without much thought. There were sales all over town yet Willow wasn't excited by any of them. Shopping just wasn't the same without her mum; the whole ritual had lost its gloss. Derek would be happy to see their credit card bill reduced. Maybe that would get him off her back. Yes, that was it, she'd play the good wife role and soon her marriage would be back on track.

Throwing her Chanel bag over her shoulder, she walked confidently out of the shop. It was twelve-thirty, almost lunch time. Absentmindedly fingering her pearl necklace, she decided to grab a bite to eat. She would phone and invite Sally to join her.

Sitting at the table nearest the door, Willow pulled out her phone. She ordered a white wine while she tried to contact her sister. There was no reply at her home; the phone rang out. She tried Sal's mobile instead, but that too went to voicemail. Willow wasn't sure when she had seen Sally last. It was weeks ago, if she remembered correctly. Had it been for lunch or shopping? A lot of her thoughts were jumbled lately; she was finding it difficult to recall things at times.

"Thank you," she said, as her lunch arrived.

Eating alone was not enjoyable for Willow, but she forced herself to tackle the sandwich and salad. It would soak up her glass of wine if nothing else, and she could excuse herself from eating dinner with Derek later; she had thought about doing a roast today. She wouldn't be surprised if he ate at lunchtime to avoid their evening meal together.

This bickering would have to stop. Willow felt lonely, and Derek was the only constant in her life. Even Robert hadn't been in touch since...when? Had her family abandoned her? Maybe Derek was right. Since her mother's death, her behaviour had possibly been a tad unacceptable. Her siblings needed to be sorted, too, along with Derek. She would make a gesture of peace and then she would decide...what? What would she decide?

But why pick on her? All Willow wanted was her mum back. Lillian had always known how to soothe Willow's worries. A calm word from her and everything was settled. With every day that passed, Willow wanted her mother more and more. She knew it could be only a good thing if she were to join Lillian. Then her mother could explain all this silly business about Lacey and Joe Taylor.

Her mother had been good at keeping secrets, and Willow would keep secret anything that Lillian revealed to her. Sighing with grief, she glanced around her. There wasn't any reason for her to remain here now. Life was a true bitch and she would be damned if she let it dictate to her how to live.

Sitting in the busy cafe now and drinking a coffee, made her remember the restaurant shouting match. Perhaps she had been too harsh on Lacey, but Rob had supported her at the time. Was that the last occasion she had seen Sally? Were her sister and brother still angry with her? They wouldn't be that petty, surely? After all, she had been provoked; Lacey had been disrespecting their mother.

At home tonight she would sit and talk everything through with Derek. It was time for an adult conversation between them and she would set out the boundaries to keep it so. Willow would show responsibility and maturity by directing the conversation and leading the way throughout. All would be sorted out, thanks to her.

Now she was sorry she had eaten a big lunch. She had originally planned a nice roast for dinner. Ah well, she would still cook the roast. Derek would see that all they had gone through recently was just a blip on their radar. Their marriage was as strong as ever; together they would reunite the Taylors and by the first anniversary of her Mum's death, they would be the close contented family they had always been. She just needed to convert the others to her way of thinking.

* * *

She was busy in the kitchen when she heard the car pull up in the driveway. Derek was on his phone as he came through the hallway. She smiled invitingly at him as he approached, and he winked.

"Something smells delicious." He gently kissed his wife on the cheek. It looked like he was making an effort, too.

He loosened his tie from around his neck and shrugged off his suit jacket, placing it on the back of a kitchen chair.

"I hope you're hungry, Derek, I have all your favourites ready," she said, busying herself with pots and dishes. Grabbing a pair of oven-gloves, she transferred food from the oven to the table. There were candles in their best silver holders, napkins of fine linen matched the beautiful tablecloth, and she had even set out the best crystal glasses.

"This is fantastic, Willow. Sweet potato and lamb, hmmm, smells divine!"

In the centre of the table was a large jug of iced water with sprigs of rosemary in it. No wine bottle.

"I'd like us to talk, Derek, really talk. See, no wine, just water. I'm...I'm sure our situation lately hasn't been fun for either of us. So maybe over dinner we can discuss how we made mistakes and how we can get back on track, do you agree?" Willow sounded positive and upbeat, she was in a forgiving mood. Why hadn't she thought of this sooner?

Cooking always improved her mood. She loved the whole ritual of preparing and cooking meals and then serving them to appreciative guests.

The food was excellent and they ate in almost silence.

"You really excelled yourself, Willow. So you want to talk? I think we need to, too. I've been worried about you. I know you're grieving and at times it has been difficult for you, but I'm delighted you've turned the corner and are back on track, so to speak." Derek smiled and gently laid his hand on top of hers. He knew he would accept the apology that she was going to offer next.

"Well yes, of course I'm grieving, Derek. It is still early days in my book and, as you say, life's been difficult. It was on those occasions that I felt most let down by you."

"Let down? What do you mean?" He sounded shocked, his tone was icy, a look of disbelief on his face.

"You appeared to put your work first. Some nights I needed you to be here at home, but I didn't have you to talk to."

"Willow, I have to work. I never put work first, you know that, but we are in a recession – you may have noticed. Any business we get, I need to grab with both hands." Derek stopped speaking and held up his hands. "I'm listening, Willow. Talk away, you go first. I'm sorry."

Willow poured some water for herself, wishing it was vodka. She glanced at Derek; he wasn't being as cooperative as she had expected. Her annoyance bubbled.

"I know there's a recession," she snapped, "but I need you, too. Look, Derek, I may have been a touch awkward at times since Mum's death, but at least I've had a reason. I don't understand why you have been so touchy and inconsiderate. I mean, Robert showed loyalty to me when Lacey accosted me at the restaurant. I have been stressed since that, too, and then not getting the golf invite. Our social standing has taken a knock. I'm not saying it's my entire fault, but Lacey, the little smug bitch, had her input there with that awful behaviour. I mean, I get assaulted and she plays the victim!"

She looked at Derek and he seemed to be listening. She wasn't sure from the expression on his face whether he agreed or not, but at least he was letting her talk. So she continued talking, desperate to get it all off her chest. Once she had, he would see sense and apologise properly. It was just a matter of getting her point across, she reasoned to herself.

* * *

Derek looked at his wife. He didn't know the woman sitting across the table from him; this was a stranger. So far, she had blamed everyone around her. It was all so bloody ridiculous.

With a heavy heart, he sipped his water and let her ramble on. Should he see the evening through, or get up and walk now? It was late and he really didn't want an argument. For an easy life, he would see the night through, but he had a lot of serious thinking to do.

She was totally oblivious to any of his feelings, he realised. How had he not noticed her true character before? Had he turned a blind eye to it through love? What were his feelings for this woman now?

He sighed. He found his life tiresome; the constant struggle was taking its toll on him. He would phone Robert and apologise for his outburst, let him be the big man and worry about his sister. She was all Rob's; Derek would be hassle-free.

CHAPTER THIRTY-TWO

OCTOBER

He woke to the sound of gushing water; a sweet scent filled his bedroom. Relaxing back on his pillows, Rob Taylor felt good. He smiled as he listened to Aoife's soft quiet humming as she towelled herself. Their relationship had moved forward and both were happy, it felt right.

"Morning, honey." He admired the beautiful woman who stood before him. "I could get used to this," he added, with a wicked smile playing on his mouth.

"Used to what, Rob?" Aoife was busy moisturising her shoulders, the towel slipping a little as she sat on the edge of the bed.

"Waking up to a gorgeous woman in my shower, and then she proceeds to seduce me as she sits on my bed." He reached over and tenderly ran his fingers down her arm.

"Some of us must get to work," she laughed. "Not everyone has the perk of using 'I'm the boss and I'm allowed to be late', you know." Slipping on her grey pencil skirt and cashmere sweater, she busied herself in getting ready. He watched as she carefully applied her make-up and then put on her black kitten heels.

"True, so true," he murmured, again admiring the delicious curves of her body.

Driving to Aoife's house the night he argued with Derek had been the best decision he'd ever made. She had been there for him while he opened up about his fears and anger, and anything else that came to mind. He had been so raw after it all, and she'd held him as exhaustion took over. Her arms had been comforting; her gentle soothing words reassuring him it was okay to have such a mixed bag of emotions.

Their kisses that night had been of longing, but she'd refused to sleep with him. She explained he needed to sort out his confused thoughts with a good night's rest. But last night their hunger for each other had taken over and their relationship had moved to another level.

He hadn't been in contact with any of his sisters, and the world had not collapsed because of it. No messages, no visits, no anything. It was so stress-free that he decided he should take Aoife abroad on a quick trip next week. Then he could face his family again, knowing this time he was not alone in facing any demons that awaited him.

* * *

Sally tried reaching Lacey again. It was unlike her not to reply at some point. She'd tried to contact Robert at his office and been told he was unavailable. When she phoned Willow, there was only an answering machine. What was with the Taylor family? Had they all disappeared or taken a vow of silence? Not so long ago they'd all been banging on her front door, falling apart, and pleading for help. She took one evening out to herself, and they abandoned her.

Taking herself into town to stroll amongst the shoppers, she found a café and sat outside with her iced-tea. The outdoor heaters were in place, as the days had begun to shorten and a chill peppered the air. So many people rushed by, hurrying to wherever they needed to be, some on mobile phones, others striding at a fast pace, barely moving to avoid others.

She admired the buildings around her, looking up at the different styles of architecture. There were clocks, large and small, alcoves hidden beneath rooftops, and carvings peeping out from eaves of other buildings. Such a wealth of history yet no-one was taking the time to look up.

It stirred up the feelings she had experienced on the beach, the yearning for the open road and open country. She could rent out the house to give her an income while she travelled; Rob could keep an eye on it for her. The winter ahead didn't seem so harsh now Sally knew she would be leaving. She would get her affairs in order and head back out into the world.

The New Year, a new journey, and the prospects of discovering what the world had yet to offer, was both comforting and exciting. But the feel-good factor fizzled instantly as her brother-in-law appeared in front of her. Derek was unshaven and he had lost his polished appearance.

"Good God, Derek, you look appalling. Here, sit before you fall down." Her surprise at his appearance registered on her face.

The man pulled up an empty chair and sat while she ordered him a coffee and a sandwich. His pale face was gaunt and there were stains on his tie. The shirt was crumpled, and it was obvious he had neither showered that morning nor slept in a bed last night.

"Okay, Derek, want to tell me what's happened? You look terrible, to put it mildly." She indicated to him to eat the sandwich. People passing would probably assume she was helping out a person who was down on their luck, and who could blame them? He looked awful.

Derek managed a weak smile and ran his hand through his ruffled hair.

"Thanks, Sally, you were always the thoughtful one. I married the wrong sister," he laughed gently.

Ah, so Willow was behind this shocking appearance. Sally sat quietly. After a few mouthfuls, he looked more composed and a little colour had returned to his face.

"I didn't go home last night, Sal. I couldn't. She has made it impossible to be there. I can do no right by her. I slept in my car," his voice was a whisper full of shame. This morning, when he'd tried to go into their home, she had left her key in the inside lock to prevent him from getting in.

"Derek, how bad are things? I mean, is this a once-off, the car last night? You should have called over, or even gone to Rob."

"Yeah sure, like Rob would be happy to see me," a slightly

bitter tone came through. He looked thoroughly fed up.

"Look, is Willow sick, or just being awkward? What exactly is happening? I'm sure Rob would be happy to help Willow." Sally thought briefly back to The Sea Horse incident.

"He and I had a row – over Willow, surprise, surprise! Haven't seen or heard from him since. Anyway, my wife is my priority, not Rob's." Derek's angry look as he spoke convinced Sally not to mention her brother again.

Mentally making a note to contact Rob later, she pushed the conversation back towards the current problem. "So, what was so bad at home that you couldn't return?"

"I went back to check Willow at lunchtime. She has been drinking a lot lately, so I've kept an eye on her. We had a talk not so long ago. Well, Willow did all the talking, if I'm honest. She is oblivious to the mayhem her actions are causing. I mean, provoking Lacey, her outburst at Sherman's office, her boozy lunches and more boozy dinners. Anyhow, she copped that my visits home for lunch were more to observe rather than for her company. Yesterday she threw pots and vases at me, and accused me of pushing her to drink. I was the cause of everything, apparently. If she had a happy, loving marriage, she wouldn't need her wine or vodka." Derek ordered more coffee from a passing waitress. "Need I go on?"

Sally nodded. She was trying to remember what the outburst at the solicitor's office was that he'd referred to. There had been so much happening, she couldn't keep up. So mental note number two, ask about the solicitors.

"So, having ducked some cooking pots at lunchtime, I came home to find her passed out on the sofa. I tried to put her to bed, but she woke up and went for me. She verbally abused me, I'll spare you the descriptive language she used, and then she started with her shoes." He shook his head in disbelief at the memory.

"Her shoes?" Sally asked, puzzled.

"Throwing them. So I left the room and she followed me, her Jimmy Choos and Louboutins are in a heap at the end of the stairs. She screamed at me to get out and not return and I thought '*not a bad idea*', so I did. I left and slept in the car last night. She was screaming how her mum would have understood her and that she would tell her when she saw her what we were doing to her! Weird, or what?"

"Oh, Derek, what can I say? Dear God, talk about losing it. But Mum is only gone, what, three months or so, and the family is at each other's throats." All she could do was sigh.

Their coffee cups sat untouched and cold. Sally looked across the table at the worn-out man before her. He wasn't coping very well and, from what he told her, neither was Willow.

CHAPTER THIRTY-THREE

Mr. Sherman would make a full recovery. He'd suffered a mild heart attack; a warning to slow down and watch his stress levels. Lacey sent a large basket of fruit and a card. She also phoned the hospital, but only family were allowed to visit.

She felt responsible for his illness. She would call at his house once he was discharged, to apologise in person, and promise never to bother him again. In the meantime, she would press ahead with looking for her birth mum.

She had tried to research the designer Cora Maguire but amazingly there was little known about her. The young designer from Cork had attended college in Dublin but was now living abroad. She lived a private life and never attended her own fashion shows, believing her dresses spoke for themselves. That accounted for her not being photographed in the press.

Lacey desperately needed to find the missing letter from her father. She still had difficulty accepting that Lillian would have kept it from her. It would explain so much and save time, and surely it would hold the most important fact of all – the name of Lacey's mother. She still had no confirmation that Cora Maguire was definitely her real mother.

Sally had mentioned going through her mother's belongings, so Lacey hoped that the letter had not been destroyed. If it had been, what had the letter taken with it? All the details of her birth and contacts for her mother, or the secret that Lillian refused to reveal as to why she'd agreed to Lacey living with them? Lacey feared another Taylor revelation. But if it had survived with Lillian, wouldn't her sisters have found it when they'd cleared out her room? More blasted unanswered questions.

Maybe Lillian hadn't kept it at home? Had she a safety-deposit box somewhere? If so, had she ever told anyone? No, Philip Sherman would have mentioned that at the reading of the will. More visits to Sally were on the agenda. She might be able to recall their father's arrangements when he died. Life was a bloody knotted mess right now, but Lacey could not rest easy until the answers were out and the loose ends in her life tidied up.

"Sally, will you be home for the evening? I'd like to call over, if that's okay?" Lacey was getting ready to head over as she called Sally on her mobile.

"Sorry, not tonight. I've to go to Willow's, she's not doing too well. Erm...is it important, or could it wait until tomorrow?" Sally was keen to check Willow out for herself. She knew her elder sister could be volatile, but maybe her brother-in-law had been exaggerating events. Derek's account of her behaviour was frightening, and Sally wanted to help if possible.

"I was going to ask if I could have a look at some of Lillian's stuff you kept. Philip Sherman mentioned another letter, that's all. He's going to be okay, too, by the way. Thank goodness. I understand if you're busy...What's up with Willow anyway?" She was curious now.

"Oh, long story for the phone. What's wrong with Mr. Sherman?" Sally couldn't keep up with her younger sibling's conversation.

"Heart attack. Listen, I'll catch up with you over the next few days, Sal, okay?" Lacey didn't want to hassle her sister. She couldn't recall Sally ever taking much time out for herself.

"You have your own key for my place, Sis, so use it and go through what you like. If I'm home early from Derek and Willow's, I'll see you later. If not, I'll call you tomorrow."

* * *

Lacey let herself into her old home. Sally had left a note on the hall table telling her to search wherever she wanted, so she went straight to Lillian's bedroom. The room was immaculate. Her dressing-table was filled with her favourite perfumes and some photos. Two lavender sachets in soft muslin bags hung from the wardrobe door knobs. A heart-shaped cushion with purple trim sat on her bed. Embroidered in the centre in a softer purple was "World's Best Mum".

Lacey felt like an intruder. She sniffed some perfume and in an instant felt Lillian's presence. She padded on tip-toe around the bedroom. Sally had told her most of the stuff was stored in the walnut double wardrobe, so Lacey took a deep breath and opened the doors. Pulling out box after box, she decided to return each one to the wardrobe as she finished with it.

Focusing on the job, she sorted letters and documents into piles – stuff that looked official, and bits that were not so important looking. There was paper everywhere. Old photos, receipts, programmes from Robert's sports events, and loads of articles that Lacey could not make any connection with. Two hours later, she had not found anything of importance. Her heart sank with disappointment.

Glancing at her watch, it wasn't too late so she would wait for Sally and see how her evening had gone. She was watching TV when her sister came home.

Throwing her bag and jacket onto the chair, Sally plonked down on the sofa. She stretched her lean body to relax it. "Hey, Lacey, any luck?"

"Nope, nothing. Tell me, how is Willow?"

"In a bad way. Derek is all out of ideas and patience with her. The drinking is seriously an issue and because of her constant hangovers, she's eating paracetamol by the packet. She refuses to see a doctor or counsellor, and honestly I can see Derek walking away from the marriage. I met him yesterday by chance and he looked homeless. He told me everything, but I had my doubts until I saw the evidence for myself tonight." Sally's voice was tired and she looked drained. She kicked off her shoes and curled up on the sofa.

"Why was he so homeless-looking?" Lacey was puzzled.

"Because our dear sister had locked him out and left him with no choice but to sleep in the car, then she refused to let him in to shower or change his clothes."

"So, what's next?" Lacey was shocked at Sally's words.

"Drag Rob into it, I guess. She might listen to him. Apparently, she and Rob were at Sherman's office recently and she lost the plot there. It bugged Rob and he ended up arguing with Derek, or something like that. Which reminds me, how's Mr. Sherman? He's in hospital you said?"

Philip hadn't mentioned to Lacey that Robert and Willow had visited him. Maybe that had played a part in him being ill, too, maybe it wasn't all her fault. She might as well tell Sally what Philip had revealed to her.

"Yes, we met for coffee and he mentioned that Dad left a letter for me, and when I told him I never got it, he was shocked, upset even!" Lacey threw her arms up in the air. "What a family, eh?"

"Oh God, not more surprises," Sally groaned.

There was silence, not a word was spoken, both women lost in thought, their eyes betraying both bewilderment and tiredness. Eventually Sally took the lead.

"I'm shattered, Lacey, so I'm going to bed. Stay here tonight and things may be clearer in the morning."

"Suits me." Lacey too was weary. She hoped the letter from her father was only misplaced, and not destroyed.

CHAPTER THIRTY-FOUR

Robert's life – both at work and at home – was going better. So the latest phone call from Sally, requesting an "urgent meeting", irritated him. Some recent fallout, no doubt, he thought. He was getting fed up with his bloody family; this would be the last urgent meeting he was agreeing to. Derek had made it clear he was taking charge of Willow, and Lacey was plodding along with her own task. He wanted to make time with Aoife his priority now. He saw her in his future for sure, which pleased him.

Thinking back, he remembered he had gone running to Sally when he had been annoyed over the antics in Sherman's office. He owed her this one meeting. But this one, and no more. He wasn't letting his life get dragged down again.

Sally greeted him with a warm hug when he arrived, and he followed her through to the kitchen of their old family home.

"Well, Sal, what's the latest drama that has unfolded in order for you to summon your brother?" He sat by the door facing the garden window, fingers tapping on the table.

"Willow."

Holding his hands up, Robert protested, "Derek made it clear she was his problem." His voice was firm. "Next issue on the agenda." He knew he came across as being mean, but enough was enough.

"I'm leaving after Christmas," Sally replied quietly.

"What? Why?" He hadn't expected that. His sister pulled out a chair and sat down near him, hugging herself tightly as though she was struggling to speak.

"I'm drowning here, Rob. I can't do the normal living-in-one-spot thing. I'm going to rent out this place and head off to pastures new."

Seeing her nervous and vulnerable, he softened his tone and nodded gently towards her.

"Fair enough, Sis. I suppose it was inevitable. Don't blame you, really. Maybe Aoife and I might visit," he said, smiling at the thought.

"Rob, that would be great. She's a lovely a girl. I'm happy for you, honestly."

Even though he didn't need it, Sal's approval of Aoife meant a lot to him. It felt good to be part of a couple, to belong somehow.

"So that leaves Lacey. Any word from her? How's the hunt for the mother going?"

"Why not ask her yourself?" Sally answered. "She's standing behind you."

Robert turned in the chair and saw his sister leaning against the kitchen doorway. She looked sleepy and wasn't even dressed, a dressing-gown wrapped around her.

"Ask me what?" Lacey said, as she yawned.

"Lacey, how are you? I haven't seen you since…" Rob's voice trailed off as he recalled the restaurant scene.

Lacey picked the kettle up and went to fill it with water. Making some toast and fresh tea, she busied herself about the kitchen, ignoring their brother.

Sally pressed on. "Our main concern is Willow right now. I've been over to visit and…hang on Rob, let me finish." He nodded his acceptance to listen. "Like I said, she is in a bad state. Derek is a complete wreck and I'm thinking we need to admit her somewhere for help and counselling."

"How do you propose to do that?" Rob asked. Did they not realise Willow was a woman of iron willpower?

"Shouldn't Derek be here if we are discussing his wife's future?" Lacey pulled up a chair to the table and joined the others. Munching on her buttered toast, she looked from one to the other for an answer.

"Derek is happy to accept whatever we decide. In fairness,

Willow isn't easy to live with when sober, let alone drunk. He really is wiped out with it all," Sally's voice was sad.

"Have you any ideas, Sal?" Rob's tone was considerate; it was not the time to be selfish.

This was the big sister who had always led the charge when they were young. The strong, "don't mess with me" girl who had always guided everyone along the way. Now Willow was a broken woman, as if she too had died along with Lillian. Willow needed them.

"What about the retreat house in Carlow? A lad I worked with attended there. He had a drink addiction and they really helped sort his life out. It's called something like *Succour House*," Lacey suggested, knowing the difference the treatment centre had made to her work colleague's life.

"Perpetual Succour House?" Sally spoke.

"That's it. Beautiful grounds, top class doctors and counsellors. Maybe they could help Willow. Will we suggest it to Derek?" Lacey looked at the two of them for their response.

"I think the three of us should be with him when he talks to Willow about it. A united front, and she might understand we mean it for her own good." Sally seemed determined that the family should stand and support each other.

"Okay, let's do it. Why not today? Get the ball rolling." Rob stood up, urging the girls to move. They agreed that Rob would contact Derek to make sure to have Willow at home, and they would all meet at four o'clock at Willow's house.

* * *

"Don't worry, Lacey. We'll sort you out, too," Sally hugged her, as they heard the front door close behind Robert.

"I have a name, Sally," she whispered, clutching Sally's arm.

"Really, that's great, what is it?" Sally seemed excited to hear the news.

"Cora Maguire. Oh, Sally, if I could just get Dad's letter, it might solve everything. I can't believe Lillian would be so nasty as to destroy it." Her bottom lip quivered. She didn't want to cry, not again; her life seemed like an endless river of tears. Anyhow, Willow was the priority for them right now. Her search could keep for a bit longer.

"No, no, she wouldn't have done. Look, how about we sort Willow, and then you and I come back here and go through Mum's stuff together?" It was as though she had read Lacey's thoughts.

The sisters knew a tough mission awaited them this afternoon. Their project to sort Willow out would be tricky. Willow might agree, or she could scream her way through their meeting. But whatever they said, they needed to say it together. The united front would prove to Willow that all her family were concerned, that they all loved her.

CHAPTER THIRTY-FIVE

"What's this, the Taylor Annual General Meeting?" Willow snapped.

They were all gathered in her sitting room; she was uncomfortable with them in her private space. Derek and Robert each sat in an armchair, Sally and Lacey were side by side on the sofa. Willow sensed a ganging up against her, so her defences were up.

"Would someone care to tell me what's going on? I hadn't realised we were all such bosom buddies." She threw a sneering look at Lacey, but the youngest Taylor didn't take the bait.

"Sit down, Willow. We are all here to talk about your behaviour lately. There is no point in beating about the bush, we're worried and feel you need to seek help," Derek spoke up.

"Straight to the point, Derek, I like that. So what exactly is my problem then?" Willow walked around the room slowly. By remaining standing, she could look down on them, it gave her a sense of advantage.

It was like a film scene, where the suspects of a crime were being interrogated. Only this time, it was the suspect who was asking the questions. Her hands tingled and a slight sweat broke out on her forehead. Her breathing quickened, and only by pacing the room could she keep it under control.

"We think you need counselling. Since Mum died, you've lost it a bit, coupled with the extra drinking and–" Rob looked sheepish, like he was telling tales out of school.

"And what, Robert? I've gone crazy? It's called grieving. But then, none of you loved Mum like I did. She was my best friend.

We did everything together, everything, and you expect me to live my life like nothing's changed? A whole chunk of my life has been wiped out." Her anger flared now.

Sally stood up and placed a hand on Willow's arm, but she shrugged it off like something filthy had touched her.

"Sit down. We know you were the closest to Mum. It's because you loved her so much that this is so hard on you." Sally's words soothed Willow a little bit. She allowed Sally to gently guide her to the sofa.

Willow sat down and sighed. Sally sat on the armrest and kept an arm around her. "Willow, we are concerned, that's all. Do you think you need help?" Willow saw the men glare at Sally, unhappy with the question, but she jumped at the chance to tell them her own view. It was the opening she had looked for to enable her to be honest.

"Maybe, just a bit. I don't like being angry. The pain never seems to go away." Her voice broke as she started to cry and her shoulders shook. The room descended into silence as they all let Willow's tears fall. The mantel clock ticked time by. A palpable relief settled in the room.

Willow looked at Lacey, and spoke quietly. "Have you anything to say in all this?"

Lacey got up and knelt before her eldest sister, then hugged her in a tight embrace. "I want my loving big sister back," she whispered.

Many hugs and tears later, it was agreed that Willow would book in to the retreat centre and receive help. The decision was made and they all appeared happy with the result. Her tears ran freely; it was good to let go in safe surroundings. Derek hugged her hard and kept whispering to her how proud he was of her, while Robert and Lacey tidied up the cups and plates and got ready to leave.

Sally held her close and reassured her that she would pull through this; by Christmas, she promised, life would be brighter. Willow smiled, much weaker now. She looked at her family around her and knew they all wanted to help, but only she knew what truly lay ahead. This mess she found herself in would end soon – for them all.

As they gathered in the hallway to leave, Willow called Lacey over. They stood awkwardly for a few moments before she opened her arms to her little sister.

"I'm sorry, Lacey. I hope you find what you are searching for. Look in Mum's metal box. We found it when cleaning out her room. It might help."

"What metal box?" Lacey asked, puzzled. But Willow turned away from her and stood apart from the group gathered on the doorstep. Derek thanked them all for their support and promised to put the wheels in motion first thing in the morning.

Willow and Derek strolled back into the sitting room together, his arm around her.

"Derek, I'm sorry. You do know I love you. Anything I said to hurt you was the drink spewing poison. Will you forgive me?" She could barely speak between sobs.

"Of course I know you love me. And it's because we all love you that we want you to get better. You can pull through this, Willow, I know you can." Derek held her hands and looked into her eyes.

She wondered if he could sense the fear she felt, the deep grief she had buried in her heart. "Can you forgive me, Derek?" she insisted.

"I'd forgive you anything , Willow. I love you."

"Anything, Derek, do you really mean it?" she asked in a hushed voice.

"Of course. Now, go up and have a rest. You have been so brave, Willow. This dark cloud will soon lift, I promise. Can you give me some time alone to sort some paperwork for meetings that are due, and then I'll come up and see you're okay?" He placed a gentle kiss on her forehead, and she nodded as he walked with her to the staircase.

Willow walked slowly up the stairs and turned to smile at her husband, but he was already heading to the study to work. She was forgotten about already. Work would always win with Derek, she thought, bitter resentment returning.

She went to the bathroom and stood by the door. She could hear Derek on the phone discussing meetings. So they thought they knew what she needed, did they? She needed her mum, not bloody therapy. They were all happy to have her locked up, out of sight, out of their hair. She had been happy to play their game, make them think she agreed.

She stepped into the bathroom and closed the door. A warm bath and a drink or two would do the job that lay ahead. She found the vodka hidden behind the bath panel, and then she collected up her sleeping tablets. Settling into the bath of bubbles, she raised her glass to the Taylor family. Then, without hesitation, she swallowed the tablets washed down with the vodka and fell asleep.

Soon she would see her mum – they would be together again.

CHAPTER THIRTY-SIX

Gathered around the graveside of their parents, this time it was Willow they lowered into the ground. By the time Derek had found his wife, it had been too late.

It was a dry but cold day, and a stiff breeze whipped around them. Robert and Aoife stood on each side of Derek; Sally and Lacey hugged each other. The same murmurs of prayers said at Lillian's funeral were being recited.

Derek could not believe that his strong resilient wife was gone. When he had gone upstairs to check on her later that evening, he had thought it strange that she was still in the bathroom. He'd called out to her a few times and put his ear to the door, his armpits growing damp as anxiety crept over his body. He could hear no movement; something wasn't right. The silence alerted him into action.

He had shouldered in the locked door and found Willow motionless. The vodka bottle rested empty on the side of the bath, and the tablet container had rolled against the radiator. Lying in a bathtub of cold water, Willow had been pale, her face without expression. Her body had slipped along the enamel of the tub, leaving her half submerged.

Frantic, Derek had clutched her as he lifted her out, hoping against hope she hadn't meant to do this. Begging her to wake up, he rubbed her in the soft towels, arranged on the heated rack nearby. Making the 999 call would forever be etched in his mind. Watching Willow's face being covered in the paramedics' blankets on the cold floor would haunt him eternally.

The sight of the pale oak coffin being lifted out of Willow's home had shattered what remained of Derek's broken heart. Willow was finally at peace. He had done his best, everyone assured him. He could not have known.

It was Robert who had broken the news to Sally and Lacey, after Derek contacted him. Both men had cried without restriction or shame when they saw Willow laid out in the funeral parlour. Sally found the ornate mother-of-pearl box that Lillian owned and which Willow had taken as a memento. Placed inside were some of the pearls they had played with as children. With reverent silence, Sally positioned the precious memory into the coffin with her sister, before she said her goodbye.

At the graveside, they were all lost in thoughts of sadness and despair. The day passed in a blur. Each compared it to Lillian's funeral; only the weather had changed.

A week later, Sally asked Lacey to move in with her. She didn't like the empty rooms and the silence she woke up to each morning. Eventually they agreed that Lacey would sell her own apartment and live in the house. Sally explained she would not be settling there, but would like it to be kept within the family. Robert was happy to go along with both of them.

Lacey had protested at first, but she felt nothing much any more. Her mind was numb. In the space of five months, her stepmother had died, she'd lost her sister, and seemed no further down the road to finding her birth mother. Willow's mention of a metal box had been pushed from her mind by the past week's events. They couldn't get over the shock of Willow's death, something none of them could have foreseen.

It did, however, waken in Lacey a new determination to find her mum. Life was short and full of the unexpected, so she needed to seize these coming weeks and make them count.

* * *

While both sisters were watching some late night telly, Lacey decided to broach the subject of the metal box.

"Sally, the night over at Willow's when we were all talking, she mentioned a metal box. What was she talking about, do you think?"

"A box? I don't know, Sis. I don't recall her talking about it, to be honest."

"No, it was just to me. She hugged me and said Mum's metal box might help me." Lacey didn't want to sound too enthusiastic; her sister had lost all sparkle and gusto since the second funeral.

"Oh right." Sally didn't take her eyes off the television. Lacey fell silent. Maybe another day would be better to mention it again.

In the morning she would visit Philip Sherman and enquire as to his health. He was still off work but he had phoned her and asked her to call for a chat. He had also attended Willow's funeral, but the cemetery was not an appropriate place for a conversation about her dad's letter.

She went to bed that night wondering what both items might reveal – the letter and the box. She lay listening to Sally walking around in the bedroom next door. Sleep seemed to elude her, and she appeared to be taking their sister's death the hardest.

Lacey hesitated before turning off her bedroom light. Should she go and talk to Sally? Did she need company? She worried about her. Slipping under her duvet, she snuggled down and found comfort in the warmth of the covers. Lacey finally dozed off and her dreams were filled with reunions, but all the time the woman with no face was present.

* * *

Sitting at her bedroom window, Sally looked out at the back garden. The moon was almost full and it cast a silver glow over the flowerbeds. Lillian had loved the privacy it offered. The apple trees stood sentry at the bottom near the shed. How many times had they played their childish games in that garden? Swinging from the trees, planting flowers in the beds with Lillian, breaking other plants with footballs playing with their dad. They had enjoyed a happy childhood. Life hadn't been so dreadful, had it? Had Sally missed something and let Willow down?

"Oh Willow, why? Why? Why? Why?" she whispered into the darkness. Could Willow hear her? Were they together now, her mum and her sister?

Had it been her fault Willow had taken her life? Had the idea of a retreat house pushed her over the edge? Did the others blame her, especially Derek? No wonder sleep was proving so elusive.

* * *

On the drive over to Philip Sherman's house, Lacey stopped and bought some ginger biscuits. She had noticed that he always had a packet on his office desk, so they must be his favourite. She bought some flowers for his wife, too.

"A cup of tea will be fine, thank you, Mrs. Sherman." Lacey thanked the elegant, middle-aged woman who led her into the conservatory. Sitting there, relaxed and composed-looking, was Philip. Lacey automatically bent down and kissed his cheek.

"Hello, Philip. You're looking good." She settled into the armchair opposite.

"Nothing like taking it easy, Lacey. I'm seriously thinking of retiring," he chuckled. "Anyway, how are you? Have you news for me?"

"Nothing really. Willow's death really knocked us all. Today is the first day I've really thought about getting back on track with matters. She mentioned a metal box before she... she died," Lacey faltered a little. She couldn't say the word suicide yet. She tried to remember the kind Willow, the caring older sister, rather than the bitter nasty woman Willow had morphed into.

"A metal box? Do the others know anything about it?" Philip looked thoughtful, as though he was trying to recall any mention of it in his chats with Joe Taylor.

"Nope, well, I've not really brought it up much. Sally isn't thinking very straight at the moment. So I don't want to hassle her too much."

The morning sun streamed in through the windows as they sat and drank their tea in silence. A firm friendship had grown between them and they were relaxed in each other's company. Sneaking a look at Philip, Lacey was happy to see him looking well. There was colour in his face and he even had a sparkle in his eyes; he looked so wise.

"Philip, I have to ask you. Your heart attack, was I part of the reason you got ill?"

He laughed out loud. "I'd love to say yes," he teased her. "But no, I had been warned to cut back long before that. It was just bad timing, Lacey, that's all."

He put the folded newspaper that lay on his lap onto a side table. He had been tackling the crossword when Lacey arrived. He took in her worried look and smiled warmly at her, his own concern for her had evaporated now that he knew Willow's death had not set Lacey back in finding her birth mother.

"I guess I feel to blame for everything that's been happening. Willow reckoned it was the secret of Dad's affair that killed Lillian, and then I was questioning you and you got ill, and then Willow died because of Lillian's death, I think." Lacey sighed.

"All just horrible events in a short space of time, that's all, my dear. Think no more of them," he reassured her in a calm voice.

"Why did Dad not want me at the reading of his will?" she asked, as she picked at the fringed cushion next to her, oblivious to her own actions.

"He wanted to spare you the heartache. I know he wrote the letter to you after you were born and left it in our files. Lillian was insistent she would handle the issue of your birth and I had no reason to doubt her."

"Why with you and not with the company who handled my adoption?"

"He wanted it placed with his will. To be sure you would receive it, I suppose," Philip replied.

"In her letter to me, she mentioned there was other stuff in their marriage that had an influence on the decision to raise me. Do you know about that?"

"Robert was asking me about that the day he and Willow

came to see me. I'm beginning to think she knew more than she told you, Lacey. Willow lost her cool that day in my office. She was very defensive of Lillian. Maybe that metal box she told you about will give you the answers. Maybe it was her way of making peace with you before she...died."

"So if I find the metal box, my questions will be put to rest?" Lacey could feel excitement daring to grow inside her again.

Philip smiled kindly back at her. "Let's hope so."

CHAPTER THIRTY-SEVEN

Back home, Lacey again went to Lillian's bedroom and searched. She pulled out every drawer and placed them on the bed. There were treasures of all sorts, keepsakes from different events the family had attended. Carefully going through every scrap of paper, hoping they would tell her about a safety deposit box or a letter, she had soon covered the bed with Lillian's mementoes.

Next she went to the wardrobe and gave it a thorough search. There were few clothes hanging up, as her sisters had recycled most things to charity shops. Lacey stood in the familiar bedroom and gazed around her, perplexed as to where to look next. The dressing table and wardrobe had offered up nothing. The bedside locker yielded even less, the book Lillian had been reading still lay there undisturbed.

Lacey dropped to her knees and looked under the bed. Not a trace of a box or a letter was to be found. She sat on the bed and thought where else she could search.

She climbed the stairs to the attic and began exploring each cardboard box and combing each paper for something useful. The attic was stuffy and she could see the dust motes dance their way around in the air as she threw open the skylight. During her search she found plenty of childhood toys and old photo albums, but put them to the side for reminiscing at another time.

After what seemed like ages, her tummy rumbling reminded her that it was time to eat. Cobwebs and dust were sprinkled and tangled in her hair and on her clothes, and she was so disorientated she couldn't remember if it was lunch or dinner she should be having.

Returning down the attic stairs, she blinked in the bright

sunlight on the landing. Her eyes strained for a few seconds after the dimness of the attic room. Sally had gone out earlier that morning and had not returned home since. Lacey glanced at the kitchen clock, with her mind in turmoil. What if Sally had snapped like Willow? What if she felt as bewildered as their dead sister? It was now five-fifteen and Sally had not made any contact. Lacey's worry grew; Willow's death had left them all edgy and a little paranoid.

The evening drew in and Lacey, having tidied up in the kitchen after her meal earlier, went up for a bath. She sent Sally a text asking her if she had eaten, or should Lacey get something ready for her? The message didn't deliver. Lacey forced herself to stay calm. She mustn't jump to conclusions. The bath would help her relax.

She added her favourite lavender oil and lit some candles. Sitting into the warm, welcoming water, she lay her head back on the inflatable pillow and closed her eyes. Peace at last, she thought. The warm bath was like a giant hug for her weary mind and body.

* * *

Sally arrived home late. She heard her little sister walking around upstairs, but didn't feel like conversation. She had gone out to the cemetery that morning and met Derek there. He visited the grave each morning and still could not grasp that his wife had gone. They had stood there in silence, their minds both filled with unanswered questions and a lot of guilt.

Sally watched as he tidied up the wreaths of flowers, picking off the dead flowers and leaves. His tears kept falling, wetting his hands as he busied himself with the task of sorting the garlands that lay neatly together.

She stepped over closer and hugged him. Holding each other tightly, they wept together. Although they drew comfort from each other's presence, neither of them found it any easier to answer the big question: why?

Linking arms, they walked slowly around the cemetery grounds, finding solace in their peaceful surroundings. So many headstones marking death of all ages; old, young and in-between, and death by so many ways – illness, accident, and by choice.

They spoke in hushed tones as if they would disturb those resting beneath the earth.

"Sally, what did I do wrong? Did I push her away so much that she felt alone and abandoned?"

"Of course you didn't, Derek. We all know how much you loved each other. She was in an unhappy place in her life and we did our best. It's an upsetting thing, suicide, but those of us who are left will never fully understand or never have the answers, only the questions."

"Everyone handles grief in different ways, I guess, and differently again by males and females, would you think, Sal?"

She sensed he needed to understand so much, his emotions tearing him up inside.

"I'm so lonely without her, Sally. I don't think the physical ache that is pulling and tugging at my heart will ever go away."

"I don't have the answers, Derek. But yes, grief is different for everyone. Talking to each other and being together will help us through these dark days."

Had they all abandoned each other since their mother's death? She was deep in thought as she linked his arm tighter and they continued walking.

They lunched together and chatted some more, but Sally didn't reveal that she would be leaving Ireland after the New Year. It didn't feel right or appropriate to announce her departure when he was still so upset and lonely.

She had no idea where she would go. She'd no plans or put any thoughts into organising her itinerary or what route she would take; all she knew was she had to leave. She and Derek eventually parted – he to return to his empty, dull house; she to a house waiting for her to decide her future.

Once home, Sally went to her bedroom. She needed to sleep. The restless, uneasy nights had caught up with her.

* * *

Relief washed over Lacey when she heard her sister eventually return home. Sally was the most grounded person she knew but, having lost so much lately, everyone seemed to be on high alert.

Lacey lay awake for a while. She needed to move on with finding her real mum. She could not allow her grief at losing Willow to interfere with her mission to locate Cora Maguire. She must not allow any distraction to breathe distance between her quest and reaching its answers.

Maybe Willow had spoken to Robert about it. After all, Philip Sherman said they had visited him earlier. She didn't want to push Sally on the missing box, so instead she would talk to Robert.

Perhaps if she could discover why Lillian had agreed to raise her, it might help with finding her birth mother. How different life would have been for her as Lacey Maguire; the name rested uneasily on her tongue. Had her mother married? Was she still using her maiden name, and did Lacey have other siblings? So many questions; she was tired of them, tired of all the wanting to know and never finding the right answers.

CHAPTER THIRTY-EIGHT

Aoife and Robert were having a lazy Saturday. They were sitting in their dressing gowns eating breakfast when Lacey phoned. Robert was happy that he and his little sister were back on track. Willow's death had been a real wake-up call to them all.

Aoife was so calming and strong in helping him to handle all that had been thrown at them recently. She kept him grounded, reminding him to sort issues into different priorities and then decide what to tackle first.

"Hey, Lacey, what has you up at this early hour?"

"Robert, it's eleven in the morning! Gosh, being in love really has changed you, you're all marshmallow and sweetness," she laughed, as she ribbed him.

"Who said anything about love? This is the real me. I'm always sweet, you cheeky monkey," he teased her back and smiled across at Aoife.

"Listen, can we meet for a chat? I know I've asked you this before but I need help with some stuff about my quest for my real mum. Would you help me, please?"

She waited as he paused before answering.

"How about we meet tomorrow? Aoife is meeting her parents then, so I'm free. Is that any good?" Robert wasn't really up for soul-searching today, but he would meet Lacey tomorrow and chat then. He winked at Aoife and smiled. She was the best thing in his life by a long shot; work was no longer his number one priority after the loss of his mother and sister.

"Perfect, thanks, Rob. Say hi to Aoife."

Rob switched off his phone and turned his attention back to Aoife.

"My sis says 'hi'," he smiled across the table.

"I'm glad you're meeting her tomorrow. It's not good to be angry with each other," Aoife said, as she munched her cereal.

"One thing I've learnt, Aoife, is life is too short," he sighed, "and I don't want to lose any more family from my life."

* * *

The following morning Rob drove over to the girls' house. He was in an upbeat mood and was determined to stay that way. Lacey, greeting him with a hug, said Sally was showering and would be down later. So, grabbing a cup of tea, Rob and his youngest sister went to the sitting room.

"Okay, let's hear about it?" he asked, as he settled on the sofa.

"Do you recall in Lillian's letter, she said there were other circumstances in the marriage – other than me – that had taken place?"

"Yes. Willow and I were asking old Sherman about it at his office, but she lost the cool altogether and that ended that," he remembered. Thinking of her outburst in the office, he remembered Willow so full of energy and fight. But now she was gone from them, lying still and cold.

"Did Willow know, do you think? Was she protecting Lillian by throwing a tantrum and putting you off the scent, so to speak?" Lacey asked.

"Maybe. Have you found something in your searches that can help us?" Rob was curious.

Since he had read Lillian's letter, it had bugged him what the other circumstances were, too. It was a puzzle he longed to solve.

"Philip told me there is another letter. One that Dad wrote for me, but Lillian never gave it to me. And we don't know for sure if she destroyed it or not." Lacey's voice grew quieter until she was almost whispering.

"What? She'd never, surely not?" Rob was amazed. "When was this?"

"At the reading of Dad's will, apparently Philip gave it to her to forward to me but she never did." The sadness in Lacey's voice filled. "Like I said, I don't know for sure. But then before Willow died, she whispered to me that Lillian's metal box would help me."

"A metal box?"

"Yeah, you don't know anything about one, I suppose, do you?"

Robert shook his head. "Good God, talk about opening Pandora's Box." He let out a sharp whistle.

Sally joined her siblings in the sitting room. She sat by Rob on the sofa and leaned in to greet him with a kiss on the cheek, while he hugged her in return. Willow's death had brought the three of them closer.

"What Pandora's Box is that?" Sally asked, looking from one to the other.

"I was filling him in on the latest twist in the neverending saga of my increasingly complicated life," Lacey sighed.

"You have searched through Mum's stuff?" Rob asked. The idea of a mystery box stirred his curiosity.

"Yes, I went through it a few days ago, and nothing." Lacey's spirit seemed to be dissolving quickly with each disappointing thought.

"What about you, Sally? When you and Willow packed up her clothes, did you see anything in her closets? Or maybe it's a second safety deposit box in a bank which Willow was referring to," Rob was feeling stirrings of excitement now.

"I thought it may be that, too, but Philip Sherman said he knows nothing about two boxes, only the one Lillian kept her jewellery in," Lacey sighed again.

"Willow and I packed her clothes off to charity. Her private papers, receipts and bank statements, we burned, and– Oh my good Lord!" Sally shrieked and jumped off the sofa.

She ran from the room leaving Rob and Lacey looking at each other in amazement, shocked by her outburst. They heard her thumping back down the stairs before she stopped in front of them, breathless, holding a metal box in her shaking hands.

Finding her breath, she offered the box to Lacey. "I'm sorry, so sorry, we found this in Mum's room and I put it away to open some other time. I completely forgot."

The air was buzzing with anticipation.

"Is there a key? Have you opened it?" Lacey's hands trembled as she held the black box.

Could this be it? Could this box hold the answers for her, and her siblings?

"No, no, we couldn't open it and that's why we put it away for safe keeping." Sally was near tears. "I'm sorry, Lacey, it never really clicked with me."

"That's okay, Sally, we've all been distracted."

Robert went to the kitchen and returned with a screwdriver. "Give me that," he said, as he took the box from Lacey and proceeded to unscrew the cover. It was a struggle at first, but the screws finally came free. Inside were envelopes and documents and some photos.

* * *

Kneeling by the low coffee table, Lacey's heart was in her mouth as she emptied out the box contents. She gently handled each piece of paper, placing them one by one onto the coffee table. No-one spoke, anticipation crackled in the air. All of them were aware that this was a special moment.

She looked at the photos – two of them taken in a hospital, a baby's nursery. A tiny bundle with a pink knitted hat and big bright eyes stared back at her. Turning it over, she saw her father's handwriting. Written in pencil: *Lacey, four days old.*

The other photo was of a young, dark-haired woman, holding the baby. Lacey's hands trembled more as she turned it over to read: *Lacey and her mum.*

It was too much for her; she sank down on the armchair. She so wanted to cry, but something was stuck in her throat; her chest tightened and her breathing became difficult. Oh my God, she thought, I've found my mum. The photo showing her as a baby in her mother's arms proved that Cora Maguire did exist.

She felt faint. She could hear mumbling somewhere around her, but could not make out what was being said. The voices seemed to be in the distance. Lacey was floating, her mind light with the drama of what she had discovered.

Sally quickly moved her onto the sofa and told her to lie down, then ordered Rob to get a damp cloth. Speaking quietly and calmly to Lacey, she said, "It's okay, breathe in slowly, now out slowly. Close your eyes. Think about your breathing. You can feel it slowing down."

* * *

Rob hurried back into the sitting room and gently placed the wet cloth across his sister's forehead while Sally continued to soothe her. When Lacey's breathing seemed calmer and more controlled, he turned his attention to the box once more.

Sifting through the papers, he found a document that looked like a contract. He unfolded the sheets of paper and saw his parents' signatures. The headed paper was titled *"Agreement between Joe Taylor and Lillian Taylor, re: Monthly Payments"*.

Robert's mind was in turmoil. Here was the reason that his parents' marriage had lasted.

It stated that Joe Taylor agreed to pay into a bank account, held in Lillian's name only, the sum of two-and-a-half thousand each month. Robert's stomach turned; his mother had been paid to raise Lacey.

But why? Why had she been willing to stay and play happy families? Was it all about money? Status? Had his mother been so shallow and easily bought off? His eyes misted over as he thought of the mother he loved. The times he had taken her to lunch and they had shared secrets. Secrets, that's what had them in this awful mess.

He fumbled through other documents and uncovered, underneath, an envelope with Lacey's name on it. This was it. This must be what Lacey wanted, and maybe held the answer she sought so badly. As he recognised his dad's handwriting, a lump rose in his throat.

"Lacey, how are you feeling?" His voice was gentle, he wasn't sure if he should say anything or just let his sister rest.

"Much better, Rob." Lacey was still lying down with her

eyes closed. Sally, kneeling nearby, looked over at Robert. He gestured towards the envelope in his hands but Sally shrugged her shoulders. She didn't know what to do, either. Robert decided for both of them.

"Don't sit up too quickly, Sis, but I've found Dad's letter to you." Lacey heard the emotion in her brother's voice.

"Easy, Lacey," Sally whispered.

The young woman swung her legs off the sofa and stared at the envelope in Robert's hand. It was bulky, but the handwriting was recognisable, their dad's familiar script across it.

As Robert handed the letter to her, she took it hesitantly, her hand shaking.

"I'll make some tea." Sally stood up and went towards the kitchen, beckoning Robert to follow.

"Let me help you, Sal." He followed his sister out.

CHAPTER THIRTY-NINE

L eft alone, Lacey sat holding the letter. Should she open it now? Would this answer all her questions? Carefully and deliberately, she peeled the sealed envelope apart, keeping her focus on her breathing as she slipped the pages slowly out.

Unfolding the sheets, she saw the familiar writing, and as she read, the tears pricked her eyes.

My Darling Lacey,

I hope what's written in this letter will clarify how you came to be here. I'm writing this, not to hurt you, but to reassure you how much you are loved and wanted. Lillian, I am sure, has explained to you the special circumstances surrounding your birth. Your mum – your real mum, Cora – was young and starting out in her life.

Cora and I were not a quick fling but a real relationship. We met through friends, and even I was surprised when she asked to meet me again. There were no secrets; she knew I was married and had a family. But how often do you hear that you can't help who you fall in love with?

Lillian and I were growing apart but I could never leave my children, and Lillian knew this was the trump card she held against me. I'm not claiming to be a saint; Lillian had her problems, though, and she needed me, so we came to an agreement.

But then, my sweet little one, you came along and changed our lives and plans forever. I would not be without you. Cora was only starting her career and too young to take on four children. Yes, I was leaving Lillian and taking the others with me. But Cora found it difficult. I do not judge her, Lacey, and nor should you. It is easy to condemn until you remember it was a different Ireland you were born into.

I hope Lillian has been honest with you. She is a woman who seeks acceptance, and status is everything. Yes, she can be harsh, but she is a strong woman who has fought her own battles through the years. But even the strongest person has a weakness.

You do not need to know every detail, but just that you are a wanted, cherished little girl who has brought me so much joy and love, as indeed your sisters and brother have through the years.

I pray Lillian has the heart to be honest. She hated that she depended on me so much, but the agreement we made suited all parties. Over time, we did become a family in the real sense, and for the most part your special birth was put behind us. It was Cora's request that we cut ties with each other, and although I offered her photos and letters, she declined.

Cora did not take one penny from me, I may add, in case you think she was with me for my money! No, she was not like that.

Lacey, this letter probably seems confused and hesitant, and maybe so, but I am trying to explain a complicated situation without making a villain out of the people involved. We all made mistakes but we all gained so much more.

I got another daughter to love; your mum, Cora, her chance to follow her dream; and Lillian, the income and stability she craved in society.

I cannot tell you how much you are loved Lacey. Your brother and sisters dote upon you; they fuss over you and watch you.

One last thing, my darling baby, it is I who chose your name. You were so small and delicate and fragile when you were born that you reminded me of the fine, elegant and dainty lace my own mother would crochet, and so I named you Lacey.

Do not judge me or the others harshly. Hold onto knowing you are wanted and loved, and always will be.

Forever,

Dad xxxxx

CHAPTER FORTY

She put the letter down. There was so much to take in, her head was pounding. The letter gave her answers, but not enough. She now had confirmation that the fashion designer Cora Maguire was her mother. She also knew that her father really had loved her and that she was by no means a mistake in their lives.

The rattle of cups and cutlery in the kitchen reminded her she was not alone. Dragging herself off the sofa, she strolled out to join the others.

"Okay?" Sally put her hand reassuringly on Lacey's arm.

"Here, if you want to read it." She handed the pages to Sally, who took a deep breath and proceeded to read the words before her.

"It confirms Cora is my mum, but it mentions other stuff that I'm not sure of," Lacey explained, pulling out a chair. More bloody questions and apparently no answers, she thought, with confusion still surrounding her.

Robert placed a cup of tea in front her. He too placed a hand on her shoulder and gave a reassuring squeeze.

"Oh my God, Dad was going to leave Mum!" Sally's pale face revealed her shock. She grabbed the back of a nearby chair to steady herself.

"What! Hang on a minute." Rob took the letter from his sister, his eyes widening in disbelief as he read it through. Silence settled like a cloak around them.

"When did he write this?" Rob looked stunned. He turned over the page looking for a date or a clue that would answer his question.

"Philip Sherman said it was some time after I was born; I was only a toddler, I guess. He put it in their personal safety box and I was to receive it after Dad died."

"Did Mum know about this?" Sally asked, finding her voice again.

"Yes, Dad says so. And so does Philip," Lacey sighed, disgust at Lillian's behaviour seeping through her once more. Her stepmother's antics were unbelievable. How could one harbour such dislike for so long? Surely she hadn't lived her life in total hatred towards Lacey? Had she ever had even one ounce of good feeling towards her?

"What's next?" Rob wondered aloud.

"I'm going to look for my mum." Lacey stood up, ready for battle.

"But what did he mean about Lillian's weakness? What's all that about?" The letter had answered some questions but there was too much left unsolved and it needed to be clarified.

"What else is in the box?" Sally asked, heading back through to the sitting room.

There were other letters, bank statements, more old photos, and an envelope that had an official-looking stamp on it.

The bank statements were in Lillian's name and showed regular monthly payments into the account. Robert's trained eye straight away picked up that on the third Wednesday of every month, two-and-a-half thousand pounds was lodged and, when the currency changed to the euro, it became three thousand each month.

The money was withdrawn in different amounts and the account always emptied before next payment. It was obvious this had something to do with whatever arrangement had been made between Joe and Lillian.

Sally groaned as she lifted out an official document; it was a legal and binding contract, drawn up in the offices of Philip Sherman between her parents, and held the reason why Lillian agreed to raise Lacey. It also named the firm who had dealt with Lillian's actual adoption of Lacey.

Laying the document on the table, she went to the drinks

cabinet and poured a large whiskey. The others looked at her, questioning the unusual behaviour.

"Don't ask," she replied to their stares, gazing at the amber liquor glistening in the clear crystal tumbler. "Believe me! You'll both be joining me when you read that contract."

"What contract?" Lacey snapped up the letter Sally had been reading. "What the—"

"No, please, no more surprises," Robert raised his hands in defence.

"Want one of these?" Sally held her glass up and looked at Lacey.

"No, no thanks. This is just crazy. What else is hidden in this box?" Robert finally put his hand out for the contract. Lacey handed it to him and, as he read it, she saw his eyes widen in amazement.

"I'll have what you are having," he nodded towards Sally.

For the second time that day, the Taylor siblings fell silent. What an explosion of revelations they had discovered. Was there no end to what would be disclosed? The answers Lacey needed were indeed there in black and white. Her mum was Cora Maguire; her father and birth mother had loved each other; Lillian had despised her, but in order to satisfy her own selfish life, she had agreed to raise Lacey. It was a miracle that the Taylor children had grown into such well adjusted adults.

"Did Willow know about this, do you think?" Robert's voice sounded sad.

"It's possible. She was close to Mum. She was very protective of her," Sally replied.

"Is that why she did what she did?" he asked in a sorrowful tone that revealed how he missed Willow.

"What do you mean?" Sally's puzzled look matched Lacey's.

"Well, did she think she was like Mum with her addiction? Mum had her...her gambling," his voice trailed off, clearly embarrassed saying it aloud.

"Who would have thought it?" Sally whispered. "I guess it's possible. Anything's possible."

"But why didn't Willow seek help?" Lacey questioned aloud.

The contract revealed that Joe Taylor would make a monthly payment into an account in Lillian's name. She would have the freedom to do whatever gambling she wanted and, by Joe funding her habit, she agreed to raise Lacey. The bank statements they found backed everything up.

It all made sense now. If Joe had left Lillian for Cora, she would not have the finances to enjoy her habit. So the arrangement had been made. Joe remained with his wife and children, Lillian retained the life she had become accustomed to.

CHAPTER FORTY-ONE

When Robert filled Aoife in about the letters in the metal box, she was speechless. What a web had been spun! Who would have believed the secrets that lay behind the Taylors' front door?

Feelings of guilt overwhelmed him. He didn't know what bothered him most. How did his father settle for a life with a woman he didn't love? Or, were there many types of love? He must have loved Lillian when they married. Was it his mother's gambling that drove his father into the arms of Lacey's mother? Did she give him the affection he lacked from Lillian?

Robert was confused. He had thought his father must have been the villain but, in an odd way, he appeared now to have been the good guy. Joe had stood by his children, and remained loyal to Lillian by not abandoning her. But yet, instead of paying her money to indulge her habit, why hadn't he sought professional help for her? Maybe he had, who knew?

Grabbing the car keys from the kitchen table, he shouted to Aoife that he would be back in an hour or so. He didn't wait for her answer. Right now, all he wanted was peace and quiet, so he drove to the cemetery.

* * *

Kneeling by his parents' grave, and the fresh earth of Willow's resting place, he remained still. The leaves twirled downwards around him. The winter was making a grab to the days, with cold winds and black clouds. Pulling his coat collar up around his neck, Robert lightly touched the brown earth before him. Where

197

had it all gone wrong? Willow shouldn't be dead. She should be here, alive, with them; with Derek. Was life so complicated that seeking help was so difficult?

Robert cut a sad figure. His body sagged under the weight of his weariness, his head low and his face gaunt. His dark eyes had lost their sparkle. He didn't cry; he couldn't. He just felt numb. All that had happened had drained him.

He'd thought that the solitude here would ease his mind. Instead, he was more troubled by his thoughts. Thank God for Aoife. She was his one beacon of light in this long, dark tunnel.

Were they destined to be together, or was she just a comfort for him, a shoulder to lean on? Would they stand the test of time? When he didn't need her any more, would he still want her? Would she want him?

His father had loved two women; maybe Aoife wasn't the right woman, and later he would meet his soul-mate. He couldn't think straight any more, his mind was just a maze of jumbled thoughts.

The few leaves in nearby trees were rustling as a cold breeze gathered around him, making him shiver as he stood to leave. He looked around at the many headstones, a sea of black and grey that swept before him. Watching other visitors to the cemetery, he wondered what secrets had been revealed when their loved ones died. Was everyone hiding a lie? Slowly he headed home.

* * *

"Is that you, Robert?" Aoife's voice greeted him as he took off his jacket.

"Who are you expecting?" he teased, as he hugged her, the scent of her perfume filling his mind with pleasurable thoughts.

"I was worried about you," she said, and stood back to take in his tired face.

"I went to the graves. Aoife, everything seems so unreal right now. Kneeling there, I thought the stillness would calm my mind but it only filled me with more questions." He leaned wearily against the nearby worktop.

"Anything I can help with?" For her, they were a proper couple now and so should be there for each other.

Sighing, he shrugged his shoulders. Should he reveal his doubts about their relationship? What if she wasn't in it for the long haul? Or what if he wasn't? Should he cut her loose now? Allow her to go before either of them got hurt more than necessary?

Gazing at her now, he knew for certain he wanted her in his life, no matter what.

"Come here, I need another hug." He reached for her, smiling.

As he wrapped his arms around her, she kissed his neck and rested her head on his shoulder. Robert gently toyed with her hair and breathed in the scent of *Green Tea* by Elizabeth Arden. Holding her close felt good, it felt right. Would this bubble of happiness burst and his heart break? Again he kissed the top of her head, seeking reassurance in her arms.

She smiled at his tender touch and cuddled in closer. "We will be okay, Rob. The storm will pass soon. Remember, pet, you're not alone in this," she whispered.

His back stiffened. It was as though she had read his thoughts; her words of consolation hadn't soothed him, but surprised him. He suddenly felt uncomfortable.

"Better go in and do some work." He broke the hug and stepped aside.

"Work? It's Saturday!" she said, puzzled by his action.

"Need to catch up on some stuff. I've neglected it a bit with all the family issues turning up."

He couldn't look her in the eye as he shuffled off. He knew she was baffled by his behaviour, and promised himself he would explain it all another time.

* * *

Pulling out of the driveway, he phoned Derek. Robert allowed it to ring until the answering machine kicked in, but didn't bother leaving a message. Instead, he would call in to check on his brother-in-law. He had never really intended to go into the office; he just needed to be out and about.

He wondered what Derek would do now that he was alone.

Would he consider another relationship at some point? If he did, how would the Taylors handle it? This was crazy thinking, Robert knew. His sister was not long dead, for goodness sake.

Pulling into Derek's driveway, Rob noticed that the garden Willow had enjoyed was a little overgrown. The windows were grubby, and the whole house had a lonely feel to it.

He pressed the doorbell and waited. He tried it again. Maybe Derek was out with his golf buddies. Why should he be at home mourning? But then, through the glass panels, he noticed the shadow approach the front door.

"Hi, Robert, come in."

"Just popping by for a minute, how are you?" Rob said, following the other man into the kitchen.

Scattered around were foil trays and plastic containers, evidence of half-eaten takeaways abandoned on the worktops.

"Coffee?" Derek switched the kettle on.

"Sure go on, why not?" Rob pulled out a chair and sat at the table. "Any news?" he asked Derek, who was busy rinsing two cups and grabbing a tea-towel. Chaos surrounded him in the kitchen.

"Nope, same shit different day, that's all."

A silence descended as they waited on the kettle boiling. Rob looked at Derek. His brother-in-law was weary, the unshaven stubble showing his indifference to keeping up appearances. Was he even going in to work each day?

"I was at the graves this morning. I can't get my head around it all. How are you coping? I mean it, Derek, how the hell do you get through the day?" Robert didn't apologise for his directness, he needed to ask the question; he needed to know.

Derek placed two steaming cups of coffee on the table, and then sat across from his brother-in-law.

"I get up. I eat. I try to work, and then each night I try to sleep." Derek looked around the room, as if he was seeing it all for the first time. The stale smell of leftovers and beer cans lingered in the air.

"She would kill me if she were to walk in." Derek got up and opened the window and gathered up some of the rubbish.

"Whatever Willow was, she was a top-class housekeeper and cook." He tried to smile, but Robert knew tears lurked, waiting, ready to burst out any moment.

"I miss her. I miss her so bloody much." He stood by the sink, and then the tears began. He cried the tears of a man in deep grief. "I'm putting the house on the market. It's going on the agent's books next week."

Rob was not surprised, he could understand it. How could Derek continue to live here after all that had happened? Robert knew he wouldn't be strong enough to do so, if it were him.

"Have you somewhere to go, somewhere in mind?" he asked Derek.

"I'm getting out of the city altogether. I'm going to go over to Galway. My sister and brother are settled there and, well, it will be good to have family nearby. No offence, Rob," he smiled weakly at his brother-in-law.

"None taken. I understand. Aoife and I will be over for a visit. Sure, two hours and you would be there these days." Robert tried to lighten the mood but failed.

"I'm not abandoning Willow. She's with her mother, so I guess she is where she's happiest." Derek's voice had an edge of bitterness to it. Who could blame him? Rob thought.

"Do what's right for you, Derek. Life moves on." An awkward pause hung between them.

"Do you regret it?" Rob surprised himself with the question.

"Regret what? Marrying Willow?"

Robert nodded.

"No, never. We had our ups and downs, but we loved each other. Maybe if we had had children, it would have been different, but who knows? What about you? Do you think you and Aoife have a future?"

Rob stayed quiet for a few minutes. It was the thought that had played on his mind all morning. Now he was being asked outright what he was scared to give voice to.

"I hope so. I mean, I thought so, but with all the revelations lately...I wonder, can anyone ever be happy, I mean truly happy?"

"Rob, listen to me. Grab happiness anywhere you can. All relationships have rocky patches and doubts. But I don't regret one single day I had with Willow. Do what you have to do, Rob, whatever's right for you, but remember you are not the same man as your father. Don't let someone else's mistakes colour your life."

"True, and thanks. Look, I'd better head off. Let me know what happens with this place, okay?"

After a brief moment, Robert gave his brother-in-law a quick hug and walked towards the door. Rob turned and looked at Derek as if he was going to speak, but stopped himself. Derek held out his hand and Rob shook it. They would both be okay.

CHAPTER FORTY-TWO

The computer screen was alive with images as Lacey clicked on various websites. Now that she knew for definite that Cora Maguire was her mother, she wanted to contact her. She had Googled the name, and several sites mentioned the fashion designer's work.

Lacey discovered that her mother owned a shop abroad which was her headquarters, but no longer had a base in Ireland. She specialised in wedding gowns and special occasion wear. Some of her dresses had been showcased at red carpet events, and she had a respectable following. Several television celebrities had worn her gowns and been pictured in women's weekly magazines and monthly glossies.

Lacey's thoughts were scattered. She found it difficult to focus. Should she go to visit Cora, or write to her, or maybe phone her? Should she do it by herself, or could she ask Sally to travel with her if she needed to go abroad? Fixing herself a sandwich and a cup of coffee, she mulled over her options. She needed to be careful how she handled this. Philip had suggested caution when dealing with such a sensitive issue.

She printed out all the details she could find about Cora's business, and pasted them into her journal. The old photo she had found in the metal box was now displayed proudly in her bedroom. What a wealth of information that box had contained. The others had been shocked by their parents having a contract, and by what Joe Taylor's letter held. But Lacey didn't want to dwell on the paperwork. She was determined to find Cora, and then all the crazy details would fall into place.

Her dreams at night no longer featured faceless people. She marvelled at the beautiful gowns Cora designed and, while asleep, she saw herself striding down the catwalk in those very frocks. All eyes would be on her as she swayed her hips and swung her arms, dripping with diamond bracelets. She would be her mother's number one model. They would hang out together, going to posh openings of theatre nights and premieres of films. She, too, would be photographed for glossy magazines. People would be amazed that they were mother and daughter and not sisters, together they would laugh at this silliness.

The mornings brought Lacey back to earth. In her dreams, Cora was her best friend, but in reality the woman was a stranger she had yet to meet. Before she'd taken her career break, Lacey had worked her way up to a good position within the department. Having received her degree in business studies, she hoped it would show her mother how mature she was. She desperately wanted Cora to be proud of her.

Her main concern was how she should approach her mother. That was the awkward bit, the concern which filled her mind the most. Once again she turned to Philip Sherman for advice. A bit old perhaps to be her knight in shining armour – she giggled at the thought – but definitely her number one saviour!

"Hi, Philip, any hope of you being free to meet?" Lacey kept her fingers crossed on her free hand as she waited for his reply.

"You have news, I take it. I can hear it in your voice. What time do you want to meet?" Lacey knew Philip was fond of her and wouldn't let her down.

"You tell me, you're the busy one," she teased, knowing he was curious to find out what she knew.

"Call over about seven, is that okay?"

"See you then, and thanks." Lacey hugged herself with happiness. She decided to take the metal box with her to show him everything they had found. He might even be able to add more detail to matters.

* * *

At seven o'clock on the dot, Lacey pressed the Shermans' doorbell. Philip, greeting her with a warm hug, explained that his wife was out with her art buddies for an expensive dinner.

Lacey placed the metal box on the coffee table in his cosy sitting room, and said nothing. Now that she was here, she was unsure where to start and surprised by how nervous she felt.

"Do you recognise this?"

"No. Can I open it?" he asked after a few minutes, when he noticed she was hesitating. Lacey nodded.

"She kept everything in here?" he enquired, as he sifted through the envelopes. Both of them understood who "she" referred to. Again Lacey nodded.

He did recognise the contract. It bore his headed notepaper and his seal of office. He didn't need to read it, he was able to recall the details of that particular agreement in his mind. Lacey watched as he picked up Joe Taylor's letter next and smiled, as though the familiar handwriting churned up long forgotten memories. He left it in the envelope, signalling that he felt its contents were private between father and daughter.

Lacey remained silent. She had also brought along the photograph. Philip picked it up and sat back in the armchair. He studied it for what Lacey felt was a lifetime. His face revealed nothing, and she couldn't work out what his feelings were.

"How about some tea or coffee?" At last he spoke.

"No thanks, I'm fine." She felt a lurch of disappointment. Had he nothing more to add after what he had just seen?

"Well, neither do I really, but I will have a brandy." He went to the drinks cabinet and fixed himself a large one. Once settled, he took a long sip and then sighed with satisfaction. Lacey looked at him full of expectation.

"Well?" she picked up the contract and held it in front of him. "You knew about this?"

"I can't deny it," he whispered, "but that was a private matter. I cannot reveal confidential files, Lacey. I am never allowed to reveal what goes on between clients, no matter who it can help."

"This photo, do you recognise her? Did you ever meet her?" Lacey asked.

"I recognise her. I don't recall meeting her, but she could have been at functions and I wouldn't have noticed her." He paused. "So what do you need, Lacey? You know who she is now, and you know why, so what's next for you?"

"I want to meet her, Philip."

Her steely gaze left no doubt that she was determined.

"How do you plan on doing that?" he questioned gently, taking a sip of his comforting brandy.

"I hoped you could advise me. Any ideas?"

"Best to write to her, I guess. You can't just turn up on her doorstep. Remember, she may not want to meet you."

Philip, Lacey mused, always the voice of reason. She mulled briefly over his words, but chose not to dwell on them. In her mind, Cora would welcome her with open arms.

"Remember, Lacey, Cora didn't contact you after Joe died. She had an opportunity then but she didn't take it." Lacey bristled at his words, but he held up his hand for her to allow him to continue. "It's not all going to be a bed of roses; there will be some thorns along the way, that's all I'm saying."

His words startled her. Thorns! Was she nothing but a source of grief to everyone? Lillian had described her as a thorn in her side, and now Philip was telling her she may be the thorn in the side of her birth mother. Lacey was distraught. Why couldn't people be happy for her? Why were they only seeing obstacles? Surely Cora would be happy to meet her? She and Joe had loved each other, after all, and she would be a reminder of that great love.

"Lacey, I'm not trying to dissuade you or dishearten you, but I do want you to be aware of what could happen," his voice was gentle again. "I have seen too many families torn apart by wills; wonderful reunions with lost families are a rarity. Be realistic about it and then, if and when you meet your mother, it will be what you want it to be."

She settled back in the comfy armchair, still feeling deflated at Philip's sobering words.

Over the next few hours they agreed that Lacey should write to Cora, and Philip would also write a brief letter on his office notepaper to confirm Lacey's identity. He advised that she should keep her correspondence brief and not ask too many questions. The time for all the unanswered thoughts, he advised, should be when – or if –they met face-to-face. Since they had no home address for Cora, some quick and discreet phone calls to some of Philip's business acquaintances would be needed to reveal her personal whereabouts. Or they could contact her business headquarters, of course. That might be the better option to avoid upsetting Cora.

Lacey drove home to Sally, relieved that her next steps were planned out but almost overwhelmed by the feeling of huge butterflies taking over her tummy. It really was full steam ahead now, and there was no going back. Before the year was over, she would have found her real mum! She slept soundly that night. Her dreams were more colourful and filled with laughter, and she woke happy, convinced that those dreams would soon be reality.

* * *

Cora Maguire couldn't sleep. She was troubled and, though she couldn't put her finger on what exactly played on her mind, she felt disturbed. This heavy feeling of foreboding stayed with her, making Cora feel unsettled and downright anxious.

CHAPTER FORTY-THREE

NOVEMBER

"You're up early." Sally was surprised to find her sister up before her and sitting in the kitchen eating breakfast.

"Morning, Sis, I've a lot to do today. What are your plans?" Lacey tucked into her cornflakes.

"I'm going over to Derek to help him pack away Willow's belongings." Yawning, she poured herself a coffee.

"How's he doing?" Lacey asked.

"Surprisingly well. He's selling the house, had you heard?" Sal put on some fresh toast.

"Yeah, he mentioned it the last time I spoke to him."

"He is going to move to Galway, near his own family." Sally spread some raspberry jam on the warm toast and munched, her hunger obvious.

"Oh, I didn't know that! Well, good for him. It must be lonely over at the house now. Has he a time set for the move?" Lacey washed up her breakfast dishes.

"No, unless he has decided since," Sally replied.

"Do you want me to help?" Lacey offered.

"No thanks. We'll manage. You do whatever you're up to and we can chat tonight. I might ask Derek for dinner, though. Is that okay?"

"Sure. We can all catch up then. See you later so. I'm going to have a shower."

Lacey dashed upstairs. She was excited by all she had to do. Later she was going to her local library and there, in the comforting silence of the historic building, she would write her letter to Cora. She loved the old building. It had been a church in its early days, then it lay empty – so many of its parishioners having moved out of the area. But the local authorities had bought and converted it to the local library for the community; a way of saving a building that was steeped in history. The quiet corners of the converted structure always soothed her, as though the tranquillity of the church still remained there amidst the shelves of books.

* * *

Sally dumped her plate and cup into the sink. She would clean up later. Gathering her coat and car keys, she shouted goodbye to Lacey as she closed the door behind her. She was unsure what the day would bring. It would be tough and sad – no doubt about that – but it was something that needed to be done.

Rain poured down her windscreen, the wipers working furiously to clear her vision. She turned off the radio; she didn't want people interrupting her thoughts. Sally was tired of bringing closure to people's lives. First it was her mother, and now her sister.

When Willow had helped her with Lillian's stuff, it had been difficult but she could accept it. Losing your mother and clearing out her things was part of life. That day, she and Willow had shared the load. They had laughed, cried, and even shared long silent moments as bit by bit they sorted through Lillian's belongings.

But today, not six months since Lillian died, and she was going to be putting Willow's life into boxes labelled *Charity, Keep, and Throw Out*. It wasn't right. Willow was her big sister. They had shared a childhood together. They had laughed and plotted about boyfriends in their teenage years, sharing make-up, and secrets and dreams. Sally pulled her car over to the kerb and turned off the ignition.

Tears came slowly at first, as she tried to reason with herself that this was life. But they persisted and she gave in, allowing the hot salty drops to wash over her cheeks and fall into her lap. She wanted her big sister back; she wanted her mother, too. No longer fighting her feelings, she sat at the roadside and cried without constraint. The rain came stronger, and it was like the world knew how she was feeling and shared her pain. The heavy drops splashed against the windscreen and the day changed to a cold, grey, dull Thursday.

Looking through the windscreen at the heavy sky, Sally decided it was time to go abroad again. Maybe before Christmas, she thought, instead of waiting until the New Year as she had planned. But they were thoughts for another day. Sally had a job to do; Derek would be waiting. She turned the car engine back on and pulled out into the traffic.

* * *

The library was busy, but Lacey found a quiet corner where a desk and chair were not being used. Her hands were shaking, she was so nervous. How should she start? *Dear Cora? Dear Mum? You don't know me but I am your daughter?* That would be too forward and might frighten her, and Lacey did not want that. Now that she had discovered Cora, she didn't want to lose her.

After several attempts at writing the letter, Lacey balled up the latest draft and flung it down on the desk, where it joined the others. Her scrunched-up attempts taunted her, showing her efforts to write as futile.

This was frustrating. Why couldn't she just phone or visit her and get it over with? Take the chance, seize the moment. Okay, it might be a shock, but at least everything would be out in the open and that was what Lacey craved. She was sick of secrets and lies. Sipping from her bottled water, she knew that idea was not a serious option. It had to be this way, by letter. Stuff Philip Sherman for always being right.

She took up her pen and tried again to put into words what she felt, without causing Cora to run and seek shelter in the highest of hills far away from her. Lacey tried to put herself in Cora's shoes. What if she were the one receiving the letter? What would she want to read? Oh dear Christ, what a bloody mess! How could she even begin to imagine what it would be like to receive a letter from a long lost child?

Lacey wondered what she would have done all those years ago, if she had been in Cora's position. She didn't think she would have given up her child, but Philip Sherman kept reminding her it was a different Ireland back then, a lot less accepting of affairs of the heart and unmarried mothers, as well as other stuff like abortion, suicide and even homosexuality. Glancing at the many balled-up sheets of waste paper gathered near her, she believed she still would have taken her baby with her. It would have been a struggle, sure, but hadn't Joe been supportive? Lacey didn't think she would be content with abandoning her baby to another woman's care.

Traces of bitterness and anger seeped into Lacey's thoughts. Was her mother selfish? She had put her career first, hadn't she? Joe Taylor had been prepared to leave Lillian, so Cora would not have been a single parent. Why did she turn her back on her daughter? Or on Joe, who loved her? Lacey was haunted by so many conflicting thoughts. What did it say about her mother as a person? Had Lacey inherited some of that looking-after-number-one streak? Is that why she had been fed up with Willow, because the focus was not on her and her troubles?

An uneasy and painful feeling settled in the pit of Lacey's stomach. This was a new way of assessing herself as a person. She had never really questioned her motives before. Was she selfish, self-centred and unforgiving? Philip had been wise to stop her from rushing headlong into a reunion. He had realised that Lacey was looking at the situation in a romantic and idealistic way, pushing reality aside.

Sitting in the solitude of the former church, Lacey felt uncomfortable. In the clear light of this wet day, she wondered now if Cora Maguire and Lillian Taylor were more alike than she had first realised? Both had put their own interests first, not their children's – Cora had her career, and Lillian had her private fund for her gambling.

She was getting nowhere with this, not today anyway. She was too angry now. She didn't want to pen a letter where her resentment showed through in her words. It would have to be later, or another day, when her head was clearer. Lacey packed up her writing things and text Sally to say she was going home and would make a start on dinner for the evening.

Mindlessly chopping vegetables and washing up after the preparation gave Lacey time to reflect. The smell of the roast chicken wafted through the kitchen, as it slowly cooked in the oven and a bottle of wine cooled in the fridge. She would take tonight off from her exhausting thoughts and devote it to enjoying the company of her sister and brother-in-law. Some family time was required, and Derek certainly needed her support and full attention for the evening. She would prove to herself she was not selfish, that she could show concern and be caring for others.

With dinner under control, Lacey lit a fire in the sitting room. Placing coal and timber on top of each other, she soon had a welcoming fire blazing in the hearth.

CHAPTER FORTY-FOUR

Cora Maguire could not shake off the uneasy feeling she'd first felt some nights ago. She was distracted and making silly mistakes with orders in her shop. She was not happy with her behaviour but, not knowing the cause, was unable to resolve it. She had never felt so out of sorts before. Even hosting a red carpet fashion show did not bother her in this way.

Why was she so unsettled? Although there was a recession everywhere, people were still willing to spend money on a wedding day. Business was going well, and so far she had been able to keep all her staff on full-time hours. Whatever the problem was, it was not business-related; this was personal.

Maybe her biological clock was running out of steam, she thought to herself with a smile; she would be fifty in a couple of years, and time was marching on. Not that she had ever allowed her biological clock to interfere with her life. Cora enjoyed her success, working at what she would consider her hobby. Her privacy through the years had been sacred to her, allowing her to sleep soundly at night knowing her secret from the past had not haunted her. She didn't allow herself to give it much thought. If truth was told, she seldom wondered where her daughter was or what was she doing? In fairness, Joe had kept his word. He had raised their daughter without her help.

Joe, what a sweetheart he was. She sighed, a pang of nostalgia for those special memories. No-one had ever replaced him in her life. She gave herself a shake: time to get on. It was seven-thirty in the morning and she was working at her sewing table, putting last minute adjustments to bridesmaid dresses that were required for that week.

* * *

Lacey went back to the library, well supplied with paper in case she had a repeat of her previous efforts. She had asked Philip if she could maybe e-mail the correspondence and ask Cora to contact her, but Philip had firmly replied, "No way, *never!*" It was too impersonal, he pointed out, and what if the e-mail got into the wrong hands? A hand-written letter was more appropriate. So, like a scolded schoolchild sent to re-do their homework, Lacey found herself back at the library struggling to put pen to paper again.

It didn't matter what way she approached it, the words would not come. Philip suggested keeping it brief, not a long flowing autobiography; just enough to introduce herself and state her intentions in a clear and concise manner. It all sounded so simple, so why was she still unable to hold the pen without her hand shaking? This was torture. She wanted to scream out loud and let the frustration out of her system.

"Deep breaths," she murmured to herself, trying to keep calm. Just be honest, she thought, it will all come right somehow. Her hands trembled again as she gripped the pen a little harder than she meant to, and began to write the words that would surely change her life.

Dear Cora,

Writing this letter isn't easy, but I believe I must do this. I mean no harm or hurt to you, but I do need to make contact with you. Joe Taylor was my father, and he told me in a letter he left for me after his death, that you are my mother. Enclosed with this letter is another short note from my dad's family solicitors confirming who I am. I am Lacey, your daughter, and I would love if we could meet. Looking forward to your reply,

Lacey Taylor

There. That was brief and to the point. If she were in school, she should get an A for it! Now it just had to pass Philip Sherman's approval! She hoped she had said enough in the letter without sounding either pushy or needy.

Having left the library pleased with her letter, she strolled through the streets again lost in thoughts of dresses, and weddings, and coffee mornings with Cora. Maybe she would get involved in her mother's business, be her partner? She did have a business degree, after all, from University College Dublin. Lacey popped into the next newsagent she found and bought four or five bridal magazines. Pure madness, but what the heck? A little dreaming was okay, surely. Who knows, she might come across some of her mother's designs while reading up on the trade?

Before heading home, Lacey dropped her letter into Philip's office. He was working there today and she had already phoned to tell him her letter was ready. With that task completed – and a few silent prayers – Lacey prepared for an afternoon of magazine reading.

Settled in the sitting room with a pot of tea and some chocolate biscuits for comfort, she laid the magazines out on the table. Even though she felt like a glass of wine to celebrate fulfilling her difficult task, she declined the impulse. Willow had taught them all a hard lesson. So she flicked open a magazine and settled herself to learn all about the bridal business. The hot steaming mug of tea warmed her as page after page of glossy photos smiled out at her.

How did brides decide what they wanted? There were hundreds of shapes and styles – and the prices! It was amazing what a huge selection each magazine offered, and it was only the tip of the iceberg of gowns. New collections were being unveiled every few months, so what you picked for your wedding today could well be considered dated when the big day rolled around. What a ridiculous business the whole bridal thing was!

Lacey surprised herself when she realised she was tut-tutting the "must have" finest cotton handkerchief, and the delicate shell pink nail varnish with matching pink silk butterfly hairclips for goody bags for the female guests. The male guests got top quality tiepins with the wedding date engraved on them. Why would you wear a tiepin with someone else's wedding anniversary on it? Honestly, what a money-making racket! Cora had chosen the right business to set up in, Lacey thought, full of judgement all of a sudden. Flipping through the pages of another bridal magazine, she was immersed in an inane list of "Last Minute – Don't Forget!" when the phone rang and interrupted her bewilderment.

"Hello, Lacey here."

"Hello, Lacey, I got your letter. I've put my one in with yours confirming your identity, and they are in the post as we speak."

"Oh God, Phillip, it's finally happening, isn't it? It's actually happening!" Lacey jumped up with joy at his news. She was really excited, at last there was action.

"Are you okay? Is there anyone with you?" Philip sounded concerned.

"I'm fine. It's just that, well, I only just finished the letter and now it's all done and it could be in her hands very soon. Thank you so much," she was laughing as her words tumbled out.

"I told her any contact should be through my office, and that it should happen only when she felt it was good to do so. We must wait now, Lacey, and allow her time to absorb what's happened. Don't hold your breath for a quick response."

Lacey remained silent for a minute, she calmed her breathing and allowing her excitement to settle.

"Guess what I'm up to? I bought bridal magazines," she smiled as she said it.

"Oh? Is there something I should know about?" he teased.

"I decided to read up on the whole wedding scene so I might understand her more. Don't worry, I'm not planning on any elopement!" she laughed out loud. "Have you seen the prices they quote for this wedding business?" she chuckled, so positive now for a good outcome.

"I shall leave you to it. I'll be in touch if I hear anything."

* * *

By two o'clock that afternoon, at "Bridal Creations" in Chester, owner Cora Maguire had decided to head home early. The high profile business was just around the corner from the magnificent cathedral, so it attracted a lot of attention from young women imagining themselves floating up the aisle of such a majestic building. Leaving the shop in the capable hands of her manageress,

Cora grabbed her bag and headed out into the busy streets.

Was she getting old? She would be forty-eight on her next birthday. Maybe the early morning starts were taking their toll, especially since she rarely got to bed before one am. Troubled, Cora decided to go for a leisurely walk down by the River Dee and feed the ducks and pigeons. The fresh air might clear this foggy feeling she'd had for a few weeks now. She just wished she could put her finger on what was causing it.

CHAPTER FORTY-FIVE

The next few days were torture for Lacey. She jumped each time the phone filled the house with the shrill sound of its ringing. Waiting for acknowledgment of her letter was eating away at her; Philip had reminded her that it could be weeks, months, or maybe never at all. She knew there was nothing else she could do right now, except accept the agony of waiting.

She thought about redecorating the house to fill her day, but it was also Sally's home and she might feel it was too soon to change things. Instead, she and Sally went over to help Derek pack up for his move.

Boxes and plastic wrapping were scattered around the rooms; pictures and photos had been removed from the walls; the whole house had an abandoned feeling. There had been a good deal of interest in the house and several serious offers, so Derek was hoping for a quick sale.

Sally had been in a quiet mood for days. Lacey had noticed she seemed remote from what was going on. At Derek's, she worked in silence, only sharing an odd smile if someone spoke to her. Lacey wondered if her sister was finding it too difficult to cope with being surrounded by Willow's belongings and Derek leaving. The family was breaking up. The once solid Taylor clan was getting smaller, and their lives were heading in different directions.

Lillian's death had destroyed more than Lacey's life. She had ruined her own children's lives. Watching Sally wrap some ornaments in old newspaper, Lacey went over and hugged her sister.

"What was that for?" Sally was surprised.

"You look tired, drained in fact. Are you feeling alright?" Lacey's face showed genuine concern.

"Like you say, I'm tired. It's been a whirlwind of sorts the past few months. I don't think any of us will ever recover properly from this. You know, Lacey, I still don't understand why Mum – my mum, I mean – agreed to Dad's proposals after you were born. It would have been so much easier if he had left her and we had been raised by him." The weariness in Sally's voice filled the air. She was no longer the optimist of the family.

The empty sound of a deserted house wrapped its creepy atmosphere around them, echoing what they both felt. They finished the packing and stood at the foot of the stairs where they had said goodbye to Willow the night she died. Now they would be saying farewell to her house and, when it sold, to Derek. Looking at the empty coat stand, the bare walls, stripped of the paintings Willow had been so proud of, loneliness and sadness wafted in the air. It had always been a house Lacey thought, never a home.

All being well, Derek hoped contracts would be finalised in a week or two, and another chapter in the Taylor saga would come to an end. He was putting a lot of the furniture into storage before starting work in Galway at the end of the month.

Sally and Lacey had offered to organise a dinner later that week – one final family meal before their brother-in-law moved away. Lacey shuddered. It sounded a bit like the last supper, she thought.

* * *

"This is smashing, ladies, I think you should open a restaurant together and I would be your best customer." Robert stretched his arms in the air, full of contentment. The wonderful lamb casserole had filled him up, washed down with a full bodied red which Derek had brought.

Lacey and Sally looked at each other and laughed; cooking for a living was not on either of their agendas. They had pushed the boat out with their menu, offering a choice of starters and a trio of desserts. It would be a long time before they would all meet like this again, so they'd made a determined effort to make it special.

"Looking forward to Galway, Derek?" Aoife asked across the table. She was an accepted member of the family now.

"Yeah, I'm excited. It's not a million miles away so I'll be over and back, and sure you all will visit, too." He glanced around the table at everyone nodding in agreement.

"Try keeping us away. A free weekend," Robert laughed, "especially during racing week."

The evening was pleasant and relaxed. The pretending was over, no more secrets.

"Any news from the solicitors, I mean Sherman?" Derek enquired as he started into some tiramisu.

"Not yet. Maybe never." Lacey shrugged her shoulders as she spoke.

"Surely your mother will reply, one way or another. I mean, even if it isn't what you want to hear, it's only courtesy," her brother-in-law added, between mouthfuls.

"I would think so, but the ball is in her court now," Lacey replied, as she refilled their dessert dishes.

"Well, whatever the outcome, we're here for you." Sally squeezed Lacey's hand gently for reassurance.

They laughed and reminisced as the evening gave way to nightfall. Aoife was the driver for the night, so the men poured a few after dinner brandies and relaxed as memories of Willow and their parents were shared. As a family, they had suffered so much in such a short time that they knew only too well how important it was for each of them to be available for the others.

CHAPTER FORTY-SIX

Cora felt as though her life was in a downhill spiral. The uneasy feeling should have been a warning to her to expect trouble of sorts, but she had dismissed it. Now her hands trembled. A letter fell from her grasp onto the floor. She had difficulty breathing with the shock of it. She needed to lie down, meditate on something pleasant. Focus her thoughts. She started to count, "One, two, three, breathe in through my nose, out through my mouth."

She lay on her bed trying to sort her thoughts; her world had taken a massive and totally unexpected hit. How could this happen? Could she seek her out like this without any warning? The questions rattled around in her already troubled mind.

She had not slept well for a while, but now she doubted she would ever sleep again. Joe had promised this wouldn't happen, he'd said he would take care of it. This wasn't fair, why now? They had agreed all those years ago. No contact. Yes, she had loved Joe and having a baby together was fine, acceptable. But when he'd said he wanted his other three to live with them, too, Cora had been overwhelmed. She was young. Being a mother of four, when her career was only taking off, was not possible. But Joe was adamant he wouldn't leave his other children with their gambling mother.

Why did he have to be such an honourable fool? But a sweet fool. It had been so easy to fall in love with him. When they first met, neither of them had intentions on each other. They had talked business and Joe, already successful, had been happy to share advice with her on getting her name out there. It had been networking, long before it became the buzz word it was now. Their friendship had grown and when she'd leaned in to kiss him goodnight after a fundraiser event, he had willingly responded. He'd never put pressure on her. They'd fallen in love, their relationship no casual fling.

Even finding out she was pregnant – although unplanned – had been a delight for them both, once they got their heads around the idea. Joe had been unfazed by it; the age gap between them never came in to question for either of them. They had discussed setting up home together but Joe had struggled with leaving his three children with Lillian. He couldn't do it. His wife was unstable at times and he could not allow his children to be raised in that environment.

Cora remembered it all – the talks, the rows, the compromises. She recalled Lillian's shouting and hysterics when Joe told her of his plans to leave. She did not want to raise the children alone so he had told her he would happily take them with him. But Cora's designer star was just beginning to shine, with offers to travel abroad for fashion weeks – and four children wouldn't allow that. So, reluctantly, it had been agreed Joe and Lillian would remain together, and Cora got her career. But at what price she wondered now. And Joe raised the four children he adored.

Oh, for goodness sake, stop being sentimental and think, woman! She gazed up at her bedroom ceiling, desperate for guidance. What should she do? Reply, but say what? Should she contact a solicitor about this? Dear God, what a bombshell.

"*I am Lacey, your daughter...*" The words stood out for Cora, "*your daughter*". Her flesh and blood; this was her own child. It was incredible to acknowledge that there was family out there that she had chosen to ignore, but for how much longer? She went to her home office and retrieved a folder from the back of a filing cabinet, holding it to her chest for a few moments before opening it.

Did she want to go there? She had not looked at its contents in over twenty years. But this letter had made it an impossibility not to look through it now. She walked over to her desk and put the file on the table before her. This is silly. I can ignore it, she told herself, no-one says I have to do this, and I'm not going to.

Picking up the still closed folder, she walked back to the filing cabinet and tucked it in its original place. Then she slammed the drawer shut and went to work.

* * *

As the days turned to weeks, Lacey did her best to keep positive. She had badgered Philip about where her mother lived until he gave in and told her. She decided that if there wasn't word by the end of the month, she was going to visit Chester. She knew Philip would be firmly against it, and Sally would think her mad. But it wasn't their lives which were in limbo. So she didn't tell them.

Sally and Lacey decided to visit all the tourist spots in their home city of Dublin. Pretending to be visitors, they spent several days sightseeing and lunching in all the recommended bistros and cafés. Although the miserable month of November meant the weather was atrocious at times, they did not allow it to stop their plans. There was so much on their doorstep that they had never realised.

It proved to be great fun and kept her mind occupied by day, but each night Lacey made deals with God to have her mother contact her. She would pray fervently on her knees, and even at times light a candle to her angels guiding her. Every morning when she woke, she reminded Him of their deal.

"I'm coming, take it easy," Lacey grumbled when she was wakened by someone pressing the doorbell incessantly for the fourth time. Whoever was outside meant business! She glanced at the clock, shocked to see how late she had slept.

Pulling on her fluffy dressing gown, she rushed downstairs and flung open the front door. Philip Sherman rushed by her without a word of greeting and Lacey could only close the door and follow him down the hallway.

"Philip," she called, when her voice found her.

"She replied, Lacey. It came in this morning's post." Excitement written all over his kind face, Philip waved an envelope in the air. He paced up and down in the kitchen.

"Sit down before you have another heart attack." Lacey pulled a chair out for him and quickly put on the kettle, before taking a seat on the other side of the kitchen table.

"Aren't you excited? Are you going to open it?" Eagerness shone from his eyes.

Lacey picked up the letter. She handled it with caution, afraid now that the answer may not be what she wanted to hear. She glanced at Philip.

"But, Philip, what if it's not good?"

"But, Lacey, what if it is?"

"I'm scared! Did she say anything to you? Did you get a letter, too?" Her pleading voice implored him for reassurance.

"She thanked me for handling the matter and asked if I would please forward the enclosed letter to you." He pointed at the life-changing cream envelope in her hand.

"Oh God, Philip, this is it." She slipped her finger under the flap on the envelope and, little by little, opened it. She squeezed her eyes shut, and then slowly opened them as she fixed her gaze over the letter she held.

Her eyes wandered over the page! It was handwritten. She drank all of it in, every detail, the curl of the y and g, the dark dot of the i; this was her mother's hand, her signature, the first real contact with Cora.

Philip sat in silence, unwilling to break the spell. He worked with letters, documents, and contracts all his life and, looking at Lacey now, he saw the true power of the pen.

She glanced up at him and a smile pulled at her mouth. She settled herself, planting her feet firmly under her on the chair and, getting ready to read aloud, she took a deep breath. Her eyes drank in the words as she read, without uttering a sound.

Lacey,

Thank you for your letter. I am still in shock that you decided to contact me. I don't know what you expect of me. Joe and Lillian are your parents, and I accepted a long time ago that it would remain so always. However, time moves on for us all and now that we have exchanged words I will consider a meeting sometime, but when I cannot say. I suggest we both think carefully before being involved with each other too deeply, if at all. Please continue to use Mr. Sherman's office as our mediator. Keep safe and well.

Cora Maguire

She handed the letter to Philip. Getting to her feet, she walked around the room, her mind filled with...with...nothing. The curt politeness of Cora's words was cold. It was nothing more than a business letter. There was no joy in it, no warmth, not even a hint of comfort. She heard Philip sigh. He, too, could see the emptiness emanating from the page. The excitement of holding her mother's written hand melted away in an instant within Lacey. She'd had more love from Lillian on a bad day than Cora had expressed on finding her lost daughter. She saw Philip turn to look at her.

"Please, don't say it. I know. I know you warned me, but Christ, Philip, a landlord evicting a family would show more emotion." She stood with her arms in the air in total disbelief.

"Listen, Lacey, you must remember that you knew you were sending the letter. You adjusted your thoughts, emotions, everything, but she wasn't to know this bolt of thunder was coming out of the blue."

"Clap."

"What?"

"It's a clap of thunder, a bolt of lightning."

"Whatever. You have had time to think, that's all I'm saying, she's probably still in complete turmoil." Philip stood up and went towards her.

"Do as she asks, think about the next move. Maybe consider cutting ties now before you get hurt any more." He drew her to him and held her in a fatherly hug, then walked silently down the hall leaving her with the warmth of his embrace. The joy and excitement of his arrival had disappeared, his leaving was quiet and subdued. Lacey remained standing while she heard the door close behind her friend. The letter lay on the table. She picked it up and looked over it again as she strolled to the sitting room, and then threw it back down on the coffee table. She needed fresh air. A walk would be good.

CHAPTER FORTY-SEVEN

The traffic crawled by her, people rushing to the next appointment of their day and yet getting nowhere. She overtook the same purple car, at least three times. It was like a race, who would reach the traffic lights first, the car or the pedestrians, and she seemed to be in pole position. The breeze was brisk and she shivered a little, yet welcomed the chill; it brought freshness to the air. Lacey refused to think about Cora. Instead, she filled her head with the sounds of life around her.

Engines purred as the cars continued to crawl, while other engines revved with impatience at roadworks blocking a lane further on. The drilling and shouting, along with the traffic, occupied her troubled mind. People on mobile phones talked aloud, while others had headphones in as they walked, snatches of their music drifting towards her as they passed. This was what she sought. Hustle and bustle, noise everywhere; she soaked it up as she strolled along. Allowing strangers' conversations to filter into her head, she watched their movements, how they stepped around each other without bumping, all in the dark sombre suits of business. Lacey had no idea how far she had walked. Spotting a café up ahead, she headed towards its friendly neon lights.

The strong aroma of hot coffee welcomed her as she stepped inside. A radio was tuned to a popular talk-show discussing the Government's latest cuts to the health system. She picked a table near the window and sipped at her drink, the world passing outside the sole occupant of her mind. She wiped the window down with a napkin, condensation from the November day gathering inside from the heat. A child's cry broke into her thoughts, interrupting the steady stream of strangers she was watching pass the window outside. She heard it again, and the strength of the wail forced her to look around the room.

Over in the corner of the café, a mother was battling with her toddler and a buggy. The child struggled without tiring against the woman, whose eyes showed weariness and despair. Shopping bags were stacked beneath the buggy on a tray. After more screams from the child, the mother finally got her strapped in. Lacey got up and held the door open and the mother smiled in grateful appreciation.

"Thank you, some days I feel like giving her away." The mother ruffled the child's hair playfully, her words a gentle joke.

Sitting back down at her table, Lacey watched the woman walk up the street.

"Some mothers actually do," she mumbled, to no-one in particular. Pushing the coffee cup away from her, Lacey paid and started the walk home.

* * *

"Lacey, is that you?" Sally shouted from upstairs.

"No, it's an axe-wielding murderer," she half-heartedly joked back.

Sally bounced down the stairs as her sister threw her jacket on a chair.

"What have you been up to? You look flushed, what's up?" Sally followed Lacey through to the sitting room.

"I went for a long walk, had a coffee, and realised how unfit I am, hence the red face," she groaned.

"Well, I have news. I went to a travel agent's and booked a ticket – one-way, to India." She flopped down onto the sofa and raised her hands in the air with joy. Sally's skin was glowing, her voice light, the happiness radiating from her filled the room.

"Oh, Sally, no! Really? When? Why?"

"Lacey, why not?" Sally sat upright, surprised at the questions.

Lacey couldn't answer. Who was she to rain on Sally's parade? She wasn't that surprised by the announcement, in truth; it was to be expected. She lifted Cora's letter where it still lay on the coffee table, folded it, and placed it in her bag.

"What's that?" Sally enquired.

"Nothing. So when do you leave? What about we get an Indian takeaway and have an early dinner, and get you in the mood for your new adventures?" She leaned down and hugged Sally.

"Great idea, Sis, and why not a bottle or two of vino?"

Lacey watched as Sally searched the kitchen drawers for the local takeaway's leaflet. She would miss her sister, but she had no right to dampen Sally's joy. They had all endured so much this year that Sally deserved – no, had the right – to seek happiness in her life again.

Having ordered their takeaway, Lacey popped out for a couple of bottles of wine at the nearby off-licence while Sally set the table and sorted the cutlery, humming quietly with pleasure.

The wind and rain that had been falling disappeared as the evening passed. "Hey, have you started on the drink without me?" Lacey heard her sister laughing as she approached the kitchen.

"Nope, just drunk on good thoughts and new adventures, my dear woman," Sally grinned.

Twenty minutes later their doorbell went, signalling the arrival of delicious spicy food. They ate with enthusiasm, sharing bites of the different dishes – a bit of chicken tikka and chicken jalfrezi, accompanied by poppadoms and naan bread – washed down with chilled white wine.

Sally's happy and relaxed mood had rubbed off on Lacey, and she found it easy to put thoughts of Cora's letter aside for the night.

"Why India, Sally?"

"There's so much to see there, Lacey. I love the colours, the spices, the off-the-beaten-track villages. It's a whole different world to explore."

"Are you not worried about travelling solo? I mean, there are dangers there, too. It's not all romance and roses."

"Well, I've done Australia, China, even the US, so why not India? If I don't like it, I'm free to move on. Nothing to stop me,

I'm a free woman." Sally poured the last of the wine and shook the bottle.

"You're so brave. Does anything faze you, Sal?" Lacey studied her sister. A sense of maturity oozed from her kind eyes. Her smile alone was calming, her laughter infectious.

"Yep, spiders or earwigs. Anything with more than four legs!" she chuckled.

"And you're heading to India!" Lacey shook her head in mock disbelief.

Both dissolved into laughter and Lacey took another cold bottle of wine from the fridge. If they were going to have a hangover, they may as well make it a worthy one!

"What about you, little sis? You're a pretty brave lady yourself. Anyone who has gone through such a huge personal upheaval and is still standing at the end of it, must be one tough cookie," Sally's voice was even, her tone serious, as she picked at the label of the wine bottle.

Lacey said nothing. Her thoughts turned to Cora's letter.

As if reading her mind, Sally asked gently, "So...what was in the letter? The one on the table. Anything you want to share?"

Lacey looked up, her face serious, and met Sally's gaze. "Nope, just another step in locating my mother. All good."

CHAPTER FORTY-EIGHT

Sally had all her vaccinations up-to-date and was well organised in what she would take with her; a seasoned traveller, this was what she did best. She had missed the dust of dirt-tracks, the heat and heavy rains of distant lands. She longed for new cultures and actually living the experience some people only dreamed of or watched on TV.

She and Lacey were at peace with each other about her departure. Sally didn't feel guilty about leaving her younger sister, and Lacey didn't appear to feel abandoned by Sally. They had both grown stronger, and were more contented with the directions in which their lives were going.

Robert and Aoife had been surprised when they heard that Sally was departing for pastures new. Aoife moving in with Rob had been the right move for both of them, and Sally could see that they were great together.

They promised to visit her for a holiday, perhaps join her for a few weeks in the New Year. Sally could sense he was a little disappointed she was leaving before Christmas – a time when families should be together, reuniting instead of parting ways, but he didn't voice his feelings. And, Sally assured herself, he had his new beginnings with Aoife, so he wouldn't be alone.

* * *

The evenings were short, dusk arriving earlier each week. Scarves, gloves and heavy winter jackets had been dusted off and brought out from the back recesses of wardrobes. For some reason, this unpredictable weather suited Lacey. It mirrored how she felt; one day was good, but the next day, just deciding what to have for breakfast was momentous.

When she thought of Cora's letter, the flame of hope in her heart dimmed a little each time. She also noticed that she now referred to the woman as Cora, and no longer as Mum or Mother. Cora's words had been so businesslike that they had put a different gloss on the whole situation now. The letter felt like a flat, cold dismissal.

Sally was leaving in a few days so Lacey would make her decision after that. One day at a time had become her motto. Sitting in front of her television, she flicked restlessly from channel to channel. Since her sister's announcement about going to India, Lacey had questioned her own path in life more. She had naively thought that with Cora in her life, her future would be sorted. How stupid and childish that was!

She needed to feel brave, to be in control, to feel like an adult again. This was the second time that a simple letter had knocked her down. She deserved better. She called Philip to give him Sally's news and to check if he would be free to meet someday soon. He told her to call around the following day.

* * *

"So have you made a decision, Lacey?" he asked, while pouring her some tea.

"Yes, only this morning actually. I made a decision and I've quit my job." Lacey waited for the backlash. Why? Are you crazy? Or something similar.

"I see, in a way I'm not that surprised. When people have endured major upheaval, they can rebel in many ways. You chose to quit your job. Yes, I'm not surprised." He nodded in a wise, knowing manner.

"Oh, right. I don't get any lectures then?"

"Lecture? Why, Lacey? What would that achieve? Plus, I'm not your parent." A faint smile played on his lips as he spoke. The ease with which he had taken her news had thrown her a little. She had been prepared to explain her actions, but now none of her speech was needed.

"I'm going to write to her again, Philip, and that will be it. No more waiting or wondering, I'm going to get on with my life, like Sally." Her bottom lip trembled a little, betraying the stern words she spoke.

"How do you feel about Sally leaving?" Philip watched her intently.

"Sad but happy. I must be more like her, I reckon. Be decisive, go out and greet the world rather than sit in the corner and watch it pass by."

They drank their tea and munched some ginger biscuits. The silence was easy between them.

"How are you so calm? I mean, I told you I've quit my job and you say nothing. You don't try to persuade me to think again or tell me I'll regret it. Why?" She couldn't let it go.

The old man looked at her. He put down his cup and sat back in the chair, his hands relaxed beside him on the armrests.

"Why would I?" he answered, raising his eyebrows. "Would it change anything? I think not. I've learned that life is full of change. In my line of work, I have seen people do what they think is right with their lives. Others do what they believe is expected of them by others. Often these people are sad and carry a veneer of bitterness for settling for what they know is not what truly lies in their hearts." He gave a little chuckle.

"What's so funny, Philip?"

"That sounded like a speech directed at a jury." He laughed properly this time.

Lacey smiled. She had an idea, but she would keep it to herself for now. Later, she would do a bit of research and maybe even take a little trip. Her mood brightened, the spark returned to her eyes as she schemed.

When she left Philip's office, she felt better. He seemed heartened to see her regain some enthusiasm, which pleased Lacey. He always made her feel grown-up and in control. His friendship was so special to her. I owe him so much, she thought.

* * *

The two sisters agreed there would be no long goodbyes or teary farewells. Sally wouldn't give Lacey her exact departure date but they agreed that when the day came for her to leave, they would go about their normal routine. It was not going to be a "goodbye" but a "see you later". After all, they had Skype and e-mails, so the distance between them would not be a great obstacle.

Lacey investigated her own travel arrangements. She looked up hotels, and compared fares for both ferry and aeroplane. There wasn't much difference in price, so she opted for flying. It would mean less time travelling, especially when she only had a weekend scheduled for the trip to Chester in England.

Sally's excitement of going to pastures new spilled over into the Taylor house. There was a gaiety and lightness that took the sting out of her leaving. Lacey loved how Sal always thought positively; everyone relaxed in her company. The darkness of Lillian's and Willow's deaths was no longer centre stage in Sally's life.

"What are you up to tomorrow?" she asked Lacey, as they climbed the stairs on what was to be her last night.

"I'm meeting a few friends from work for lunch, what about you?"

"Me? Nothing major, maybe go to India at some time during the day." She smiled, but Lacey stopped and held onto the banister.

"Is that tomorrow?" Lacey was surprised.

"So, take care of yourself and keep in touch." Sally put her arms around Lacey and held her tightly. Neither knew when they would see each other again, and both were trying hard to control tears as they turned to go into their bedrooms.

"Sleep well, Sally. I'll see you later, okay?" Lacey didn't dare look back.

At four am, a car pulled into the driveway. Lacey heard her sister tip-toeing down the stairs, then the click of the front door closing behind her.

She got out of bed and moved to the window. Lacey peered out and saw Sally getting into a taxi, with a quick glance up at the house. Lacey waved, and her sister waved back.

As the car pulled away, Lacey looked up at the stars in the blackness of the night and wished upon them. This was it, she sighed, slipping back into bed. It was now her time to make a difference in her life. Next weekend she would go to Chester and visit her mother. Whether or not she would tell Cora who she was, Lacey would decide when she got there.

"Travel safely, Sally," she whispered to the darkness, and pulled the duvet closely around her.

CHAPTER FORTY-NINE

The flight to Liverpool was uneventful. Lacey had travelled lightly, taking only one piece of hand luggage with her. She took a taxi to Lime Street railway station and, within 45 minutes of boarding the train, she was in Chester. She quickly checked into her hotel then went out to explore.

The city was buzzing. She wandered down the cobbled streets and marvelled at the black and white buildings which were one of the city's main tourist attractions. Dating from medieval times, they were called "the Rows" and consisted of covered walkways at the first floor level, with shops and other premises behind. Then beneath, at ground level, were more shops and businesses.

Further on, she could see the Eastgate Clock, claimed to be the most photographed clock in England after Big Ben. It was certainly impressive. The black Roman numerals with the bright red and gold colouring gave it a majestic feel. It had been erected to celebrate Queen Victoria's Diamond Jubilee and unveiled for her eightieth birthday.

This weekend might prove fruitful, Lacey thought; even the weather was working in her favour. No rain, just frosty cold days.

Feeling peckish, she went for some lunch. The choice of cafés was delightful. There were old-fashioned tearooms or the more modern internet types to choose from. She settled on a cosy, homely tearoom and ordered a toasted special. The surroundings were delightful – vintage buttercream walls with old sepia photos of Chester past, in slim black frames; green and white patterned tablecloths providing a cosy, informal feel; friendly and pleasant staff.

Outside, the street was full of young people, the men as groomed as the females. It seemed like an upper-class city, yet without any snobbishness. After lunch, she strolled further down the side streets enjoying the sense of history all around her. She discovered the Roman Walls and walked the outskirts of the city. Wandering along, she passed the racecourse and looked down on the splendid stadium where thousands of tourists visited for racing events.

As the evening closed in, Lacey went back to her hotel. She had purposely not searched for Cora's shop. She first wanted to soak in the atmosphere of where her birth mother had decided to settle. She ate her evening meal and settled in the hotel bar with a drink and a good book for company. Yet she couldn't concentrate; her mind was filled with thoughts of how different her life could have been if she had grown up with Cora.

Her name would be Maguire – Lacey Maguire, living in England, with different friends and very probably different expectations from life. She would, without doubt, be a whole different person. This would be home, not Ireland.

The morning came quickly. Showered and dressed, she stepped out again into the cobbled streets. The magnificent cathedral was first on her agenda for today – then Cora's shop. Following the tourist signs, she strolled up St. Werbrugh Street, catching sight of the dark brown stonework in the distance, the railings surrounding it, and the entrance way ahead of her.

She stepped through the cathedral's arched doorway. Inside, she was met with a welcoming craft shop, and the story of the splendid church displayed. The tranquillity and peace was comforting, especially in the hidden corners and altars tucked off the main aisle, while the beautiful carvings and windows almost demanded that visitors admire them.

Lacey sat in one of the pews and prayed silently. Not for herself, but for her siblings, and for Joe and Lillian. It was through their lives, their decisions, that she had now come to be here, in this city, on this day.

Moving on from the cathedral, Lacey spotted the town hall

with a tourist office nearby. She went into the office and bought some postcards and picked up some leaflets on the attractions available for the many tourists to enjoy while in Chester. There was a choice of walks, from haunted tours in the evenings to talks on the Roman highlights. She picked up some colourful fridge magnets as tokens for her brother and Philip. Of course, if she decided not to tell them of her visit, the gifts could remain in the white paper bag.

She stepped back out into the winter day. It was dry with a light breeze, but not too cold. She sat on one of the nearby benches and people-watched, gathering the courage to continue her quest. Pigeons and doves gathered at her feet. Looking for crumbs from lunch, they remained close, in competition with each other for the pickings.

Where would she start to seek out "Bridal Creations"? She could ask a passer-by, of course, but secretly she wanted to discover it herself. This, after all, was her adventure. Casting a look around, she spied a woman carrying a large bag with Cora's shop name on it. The bag was lilac with pink writing, the words *Bridal Creations* written in italic within a heart. What a lucky break! Maybe it was closer than she realised.

She jumped up and started to look around. She passed fashion shop after fashion shop, broken up by bookshops or jewellers. She crossed to the next street, and there, sandwiched between two hat shops, was "Bridal Creations".

Lacey stood still, feeling almost faint as it slowly sank in that her birth mother was quite possibly only a few hundred metres away. The shop boasted two large display windows, with the entrance in the centre. On the window to the left were two beautiful designs – a sleek cream dress on one mannequin, and a soft ivory on another. The other window held examples of bridesmaid dresses – some short with fur shrugs, suitable for winter weddings; others in cheerful colours for summer. Cora's name was not displayed on the shop front; there was no indication of who had designed the fabulous gowns on display.

People streamed by as she remained still and silent, trying to decide what to do next. She could peep in the window and see what lay inside. She had to at least look, after coming all this way.

But, a few steps later, Lacey found herself pushing the door open and stepping inside. This was so surreal; she was actually inside Cora's world! A little bell announced her entrance as the door eased shut behind her.

The mannequins were dressed in beautiful gowns. They displayed different designs, some long and flowing, some fitted and slender, others ball-gown style, all elegantly accessorised with costume jewellery. She saw shelves packed with different material, various colours and fabrics, silk and laces and satin. In another corner were veils and fascinators and tiaras, studded with pearls and precious stones. The walls were filled with photos of previous collections and some of celebrities who had worn Cora's designs on the red carpet.

"Can I help you?" a young blonde assistant, not much older than Lacey, asked politely.

"I'm only browsing, hopefully pick up some ideas," she mumbled in reply. She hadn't thought about being approached. She hadn't thought full stop! Lacey blushed at her own stupidity.

"Take your time. If there is anything you don't see, maybe we could make it for you." The assistant smiled, eager to help. "If you wish to try on any of the stock, please feel free to." The girl was full of encouragement.

"Thank you."

Lacey's heart was pounding. What if Cora appeared in the shop? This had been stupid, stupid, stupid. But she did not know if Cora was even on the premises. Breathe, Lacey, breathe, she silently chastised herself. Would she even recognise Cora?

"Are you getting married soon?" the blonde woman asked, keen to draw information from a potential customer as she sorted a nearby rail of garments.

"Um, yes, no. I mean, I'm planning on maybe next summer." Lacey knew she sounded so silly.

The assistant glanced at her left hand and saw no ring. She raised an eyebrow and stared at Lacey. They probably got lots of odd women coming into the shop; women who couldn't afford the designs, or didn't have boyfriends but dreamed of walking down the aisle in a designer dress.

Lacey noticed the woman's look of pity and realised the glance to her ring finger had given her away. She blushed again but with embarrassment this time.

"We plan on a short engagement," she stuttered.

"Is that an Irish accent? We get a lot of Irish customers, but then our designer Cora Maguire is Irish, of course." The woman remained professional and engaged her customer with conversation.

"Are you living here or over for a holiday?"

Lacey stuttered in her reply. "Dublin. I'm...I'm living in Dublin. I'm...over for the weekend."

Lacey kept a smile on her face and moved towards the door. She needed to escape. This was not turning out as she'd hoped, and she knew she was losing control of the situation. This assistant was getting too personal; it completely scared her. What if Lacey said something she didn't mean to from nerves? Time to escape.

"Cora is showing her new Spring Collection in Dublin next month. There might be something in the collection that may suit your taste when you decide on your wedding plans. It's her first showing there in a long time, so there is a lot of excitement about it." The girl had a sympathetic tone in her voice as she noted Lacey's scared look as she hurried towards the door.

"I'll check it out," Lacey replied, and shoved the glass door open, almost stumbling out into the fresh air.

* * *

A breeze greeted her and she ran to the cathedral railings. Lacey's hands were shaking, her pulse racing, and sweat breaking out across her forehead in drops. She was both angry and embarrassed with herself. She had acted like a complete fool in the shop, mumbling her words and behaving like a child caught with a hand in the cookie jar. She needed to focus, to get grounded and calm down. Pressing her head to the cold metal while she took control of her silly behaviour, Lacey wished with all her might that she had never come here. Philip had been right. Life went on around her; no-one was interested in the young girl clinging to the iron railings with clenched fists.

She gathered herself together and bought a coffee-to-go. After aimlessly wandering around the historic city, she found herself back sitting on a bench not far from the tourist office, watching Cora's shop. What had she been thinking of by going inside? What had she been hoping for? Finishing her coffee, she watched people pass by, unaware of the turmoil she was feeling. Did she think she would see Cora going in or out of the shop? Was she there now, hidden in the back sewing, or drawing new designs? Had the assistant told her about the strange Irish customer and they both got a laugh out of her odd behaviour? Or would it trigger warning signals for Cora, hearing about the Irish girl?

The ache in Lacey's heart grew stronger. She desperately wanted to meet her. She knew now more than ever that she needed it to happen, now that she was so close to the woman who had loved her father, the woman who – with Joe – had created her. Surely Cora felt this, too. How could she not be curious about her own daughter? Did she not want to see what they had in common, shared interests, how Lacey had turned out maybe? Did they look alike?

That night Lacey didn't sleep well. Her mind, ever restless, was in chaos. She listened to the strange sounds and noise of this city that was home to her mother. It wasn't so comfortable in the dark of night in the hotel, as she tossed and turned in the hostile bed; it felt lonely and she longed for her own familiar comforts. Was coming here a mistake?

CHAPTER FIFTY

The taxi dropped Lacey outside the house and she was relieved to put the key in her front door and step inside. On the plane journey home she had decided to contact Cora through the proper channels. Her visit had shown her how easily she could have destroyed everything between them if Cora had been present in the shop that day.

Realising she had acted selfishly; she decided that tomorrow she would pen another letter to her mother and give it to Philip to send. With such a fragile issue, it was dawning on her that she needed to accept the proper procedures.

Her home was welcoming; even Sally's absence was acceptable. The familiarity of the surroundings reassured Lacey and she was delighted to find a postcard from Sally along with other mail on the hall mat. It was a quick few lines, letting her know that she had arrived safely in Delhi. She would email Lacey and Rob every so often to keep in touch.

Lacey pinned the colourful postcard to her fridge, using a Chester magnet. Beside it, she placed a postcard of her own, depicting Roman Chester.

* * *

Cora Maguire re-read the letter she had received that morning from Ireland. Lacey was being persistent, a trait she possessed herself. It had stood Cora well as she progressed through her career, and now her daughter was showing the same characteristic. Would it be so harmful to meet the girl? She had ended all contact with that part of her life six weeks after her daughter was born. But that was then.

241

She had really loved Joe and had never found such sweet, tender love since. Being pregnant, unplanned in Ireland, was a black mark against women back then. Joe had been so strong and supportive though, willing to leave Lillian to be with Cora and their new baby. It all seemed so romantic now, as she thought back to her early days as a designer. He had been deeply hurt when Cora told him she didn't want a baby and three older children; she wasn't ready, not her time in life yet. So Joe had sorted it, like Joe always did with everything.

Now was it time? Was it the right moment to meet her daughter? She would be in Dublin next month and could meet her then. Cora admitted to being curious. This woman, no longer a little baby, wanted to meet her. Why? To heal the past and have closure maybe, to answer countless questions or questions that she felt had been unanswered by her father? What exactly had Joe told her? How was Lillian taking it? Would it mean awkward meetings between old foes?

Her decision to cut herself out of her daughter's life had come back to haunt her. Had it been the right decision? Yes, at the time. Over the years she had deliberately refused to acknowledge Lacey's existence, but there had been many times when she'd tried to picture how her own daughter would look as she designed her dresses. She wondered whether her daughter would approve of the decisions she had made when Lacey was a baby.

The latest communication through Sherman Solicitors was short but heartfelt. Lacey had not held back in her longing to meet Cora. She had kept her letter brief, but each word had been chosen for its clarity and meaning. Lacey's words were beginning to break through any barriers Cora tried to keep up.

The young girl had managed to sell her need, but not her dignity, and that was admirable. It was this which forced Cora to agree to meet while in Dublin, with no guarantees or promises. She sent her letter to Ireland and then waited. The forthcoming show would take up her time until the trip, and she was glad of it. Her energy and mind would be filled with dates, rotas, designs and bookings.

She would get her answer to her request in Dublin. The ball was now back in Lacey's court as to whether she would turn up. A part of Cora was secretly delighted and optimistic, which surprised her. But she also knew she would not enjoy a decent night's sleep again until she dealt with this issue.

* * *

Lacey danced around the kitchen the day Philip Sherman called over with Cora's second reply. She had not told him – or anyone – about her trip across the Irish Sea. She had learned from it, though. The letter she had written on her return was honest and clear. She had explained that her only intention was to meet Cora, and not to invade her life. She explained that she knew any mother-daughter bond was probably fruitless at this stage, but perhaps friendship and support were possible.

Philip laughed heartily at Lacey twirling and jumping with joy after reading Cora's letter. He insisted that he accompany her to meet her birth mother, and had looked a little taken aback when Lacey did not argue.

She felt like a different person now, more mature, more accepting of other's wisdom – and definitely more grounded. Her instincts growing up of not belonging, of not fitting in with Lillian, had been right. Her decision to quit her job and seek her true potential had been the right thing to do, too. The challenge of finding Cora had revealed her own inner strengths and offered a new world of possibilities.

She began reading up as much as she could find about the forthcoming fashion show, and about Cora Maguire designs. Tickets were selling fast, according to the many advertisements she came across. The Sunday papers carried interviews with background staff, but Cora Maguire herself avoided interviews as much as possible. The media had little to report on her; there had been rumours of a past affair with a married businessman, but nothing concrete, no evidence.

Lacey counted the days to the show. Cora had sent a special backstage pass, so that she and Philip would have no issues with security.

Bursting with excitement, Lacey had told Robert and Aoife what was happening, and they were delighted for her. They immediately offered to attend the fashion show with her to provide support, but she explained that Philip was going to be there in the background for her on the night.

She was so nervous, it took all her effort to sit and eat meals; most days she didn't feel hungry. But Aoife told her she must eat, or her skin would be spotty and grey and her hair wouldn't be shiny or glossy when the great reunion took place. She even insisted on taking Lacey for a manicure and a facial, to ensure she looked her best.

Christmas and the New Year were around the corner, and the new positive spirit around the remaining family members hinted at happier times ahead and the chance to find the peace and the closure they all desperately sought.

No-one mentioned what might happen if Cora did not want further contact or – Heaven forbid – she cancelled the meeting. Any dark thoughts were pushed aside with the fuss to make sure Lacey looked her best for the occasion. Robert was kept entertained by the girls' efforts to cover all beauty treatments and Aoife's delight at learning Cora Maguire was Lacey's mother. "If you both hit it off, there might be the chance of a discount for me when I come to choose my wedding dress," she had joked.

CHAPTER FIFTY-ONE

DECEMBER

The critics' reports of Cora's showcase were all favourable. There was an electric atmosphere within the fashion trade at having top designer Cora Maguire returning to Ireland for the first time in twenty years. All the glossy magazines carried previews and features, and all the models were clamouring to be photographed at the after-show parties. The event was a full weekend, with the rare appearance of Cora herself on the last night.

Philip picked up Lacey and they travelled together to the venue. There were bright spotlights everywhere, a red carpet entrance, and tables of champagne and orange juice inside the door, served by muscled, well groomed young men. Festive lights twinkled in the foyer, and a huge Christmas tree, tastefully decorated in creams and golds, stood proudly in a corner.

The previous week, Lacey and Aoife had gone shopping for the perfect dress to wear. They settled on a strapless, baby pink, satin, full-length gown. The soft material was layered and at the bust it was crossed over, leading the eye to her tiny nipped-in waist. She wore short drop diamond earrings and swept her silky hair into a bun. This showed her neck and shoulders off to perfection, and the understated elegance of the dress emphasised how stunning she was. Lacey, wrapped up in all the excitement of the night, was unaware of the attention she attracted, but Philip noticed the admiring glances cast in her direction as he led her to their seats.

They took their places for the show and studied the programmes left on each table. Lacey peeped into the goody bag and gasped at the wonderful items inside – vouchers for top spa treatments, discounts on fashion labels, free jewellery from Irish designers, and make-up from the latest range on offer. The wine coloured organza bag, with its delicate cream ribbon, was a real treasure trove. Lacey told Philip he must take one home to his wife, and she would give hers to Aoife.

The show was spectacular. The hostess for the evening – a presenter from RTE, the national television station – was both entertaining and professional. The garments themselves were spectacular, some so breathtaking that they attracted gasps and covetous sighs, followed by loud applause from the audience.

Lacey had not replied to Cora's last letter. She had simply left things as Cora had suggested: she would be in Dublin, if Lacey decided that it would be a good time to meet, or they could leave it until a time that may be more suitable, if Lacey preferred.

As the end of the show approached, she grew anxious. Tonight – if it was what she wanted – she would meet her birth mother; it was her decision. Her hands trembled and she reached out to Philip as the clapping and buzz of the room suddenly became claustrophobic. She felt weak and uncomfortable. It was all too much; she needed air. She needed to get out. She couldn't go through with the meeting after all, she was going to be ill.

Lacey rushed out of the room and straight to the ladies powder room, with Philip grabbing their belongings and following her out. People sitting nearby stared and whispered, unhappy at the rudeness of the young woman leaving as the show was in progress.

Hiding in the ladies' room, Lacey felt awful. It was all too much and she berated herself for being stupid enough to think it would be easy. Her make-up was patchy so she splashed some water on her face and, grabbing the tissues close by, wiped it off. Then she tidied her hair and replaced a hint of lipstick, before going out to the busy foyer, where Philip was waiting. His look of concern was so touching she had to blink away the tears stinging her eyes.

"You do realise the headlines tomorrow are going to scream

'Local Solicitor Exposes His Feminine Side'?" And he held up the two goodie bags he'd picked up before following Lacey out.

She gave him a feeble smile and hugged him close for support. "I'm sorry, I got cold feet." Philip nodded and clapped her back gently.

"How do I look?" she asked in an uneasy tone.

"Pretty as a picture," he reassured her.

Philip guided her to some nearby seats and they sat in silence. Waiters hurried in and out where the fashion show was being held, applause and music filtering out every time the double doors opened. Philip didn't speak. He had told her clearly that he would not influence her decision about leaving or meeting with Cora. Any decisions would be hers.

The cool air in the foyer calmed her a little, and the heady atmosphere began to fade. Twenty minutes went by before the doors were opened fully and the crowd emerged, chattering excitedly about what a success it had been, how outstanding the creations were, and what a talented designer Cora Maguire was. Photographers snapped away as wannabe socialites stood around sipping their champagne. The talk was all about Cora.

"Well?" Philip whispered.

"It's now or never, I suppose." She looked with anticipation towards the room from which she had fled.

"I'll wait here, or do you want me to go with you?" He spoke quietly, leaning a little closer to her.

"Whatever suits you, Philip." She smiled weakly.

"Then I'll stay," he said, and settled into a chair.

"Are you sure I look okay?" She had a pleading look in her eyes.

"You look beautiful. Now smile, and remember, confidence." He gestured towards the ballroom to signal she should go.

Lacey picked up her clutch bag and walked towards the doors. She opened her bag and slipped on the pass which had a strap to wear on her wrist. Already the backstage workers were taking the catwalk apart and stacking chairs. A satisfied air filled the room of a job well done.

She picked her steps carefully through the cables and equipment scattered around. Beyond the stage area were two brown timber doors. On the first, a sign in red lettering had the words HOTEL STAFF ONLY; the other door was free of any sign but was slightly ajar. She stepped through into a hallway.

This was crazy. She didn't even know where Cora was back here, or if she was even here at all. She needed to find out before she lost her courage. A noisy chattering led Lacey to another open door, and she pushed it slowly back to find a room crowded with models, stylists and make-up artists. Lacey stepped in and was amazed at how many people were packed into the room. There was constant chatter and laughter; a few turned and stared at her, their faces reflecting their curiosity of who the pretty young woman was.

She daren't speak – her nerves were beginning to stir again. She backed out into the corridor and spotted a man further down the hall.

"Excuse me, is Cora Maguire around?"

A young lad of twenty, with shocking green hair, glanced at her pass before answering her. The security bracelet to go backstage hung on her slim wrist. He nodded towards a door further up the corridor.

"Thanks," Lacey replied to the nodding, and walked on.

When she got further up the corridor, she noticed this door, too, was slightly open. The words CORA MAGUIRE – PRIVATE were stuck on it.

Lacey heard some shuffling of papers from inside, and hesitated. Should she knock or leave? Her heartbeat was pounding in her ears and her hands were sticky from anxiety. She had come this far, she couldn't go back now. She took a deep breath and gently tapped on the door, but there was no response.

Try again, she scolded herself. She swallowed and knocked harder, pushing the door slightly further open. A woman sat at a desk filled with flowers, writing furiously into a book. Congratulations banners and cards were scattered around the room.

She watched the woman work. She had done it. She had found her mother.

Lacey gave a gentle cough. Without raising her head or stopping the task she was concentrating on, Cora Maguire replied tersely, "I'll be out shortly to meet people, Tina. Just give me five more minutes, okay?"

Lacey didn't reply. She took a step closer; her voice had deserted her. This was her mother, here in front of her right now. The tingling in Lacey's body was electric and she felt a buzz as she stared at the woman seated by the desk.

* * *

Aware of someone staring at her, Cora turned to see who had entered the room.

"Oh my God!" she cried out. "You're not...not Tina, you're..."

Before her stood a mirror image of herself, of Cora in her early twenties. The dark chocolate eyes looking at her were her own, as was the silky auburn hair. This young version of Cora was smiling, a smile with echoes of Joe Taylor. The years melted away and Cora was stunned by this vision before her.

"Is it? I mean, is it really you?" Cora stood up, shaking. The resemblance was unbelievable.

"Lacey, my daughter," she whispered in shock.

For a few moments the two women remained still, then Cora slowly moved towards Lacey with her arms outstretched. She stopped briefly as fear of rejection fleetingly passed through her, but the feeling disappeared when the young woman stepped towards her. They both laughed as the awkwardness between them melted into the air. There was no clumsiness between them, only longing. Cora could not believe the impulsive way she had reacted. But holding her daughter in her arms, finally, after all these years, brought her warmth and contentment.

Through the gathering tears that now filled Lacey's eyes, she whispered in Cora's ear,

"Hello, Mum."

249

ABOUT MARY T. BRADFORD

Mary T Bradford has been writing mainly short stories for a number of years now and has enjoyed success with her fiction in many magazines, newspapers and anthologies both in Ireland and abroad. It was because of this success, Mary took the plunge and self published her first collection titled, A Baker's Dozen (2012) and is available in both print and e-book format from Amazon and other sites. She decided to tackle a novel when one of her stories kept getting longer and the word count continued to climb and so ended up with My Husbands Sin. She has also branched out into writing plays and has seen her work shortlisted and performed.

When taking a break from writing and reading Mary loves to crochet or cross-stitch, crafts in general interest her. Living in County Cork, Ireland, she is married and is a mother of four children. Having overcome open heart surgery in 2008, Mary made the decision to dedicate more time to her writing as her children were almost raised and were starting to spread their wings. Family is important to her and her writing often reflects the ups and downs of life that all families go through daily.

GET IN TOUCH WITH MARY

Connect with Mary through any of the links on this page and that is something else Mary enjoys, chatting with people!

Facebook
www.facebook.com/pages/Mary-T-Bradford-Author/464343040298924

Blog
marytbradford-author.blogspot.com

Twitter
www.twitter.com/marytbrad

Pinterest
www.pinterest.com/marytbradford

Tirgearr Publishing
www.tirgearrpublishing.com/authors/Bradford_MaryT

• • • • •

Thank you for reading My Husband's Sin.

If you liked this story, please log into Tirgearr Publishing and Mary's website and watch for other releases.

CPSIA information can be obtained
at www.ICGtesting.com
Printed in the USA
LVOW04s1610271015
459962LV00031B/1176/P